LAST COURTESIES
and Other Stories ❖

LAST COURTESIES

AND OTHER STORIES

BY ELLA LEFFLAND

GRAYWOLF PRESS

SAINT PAUL

"Vienna, City of My Dreams" and "Inside" originally appeared in *Quarterly Review of Literature*. "Last Courtesies" and "The House of Angels" originally appeared in *Harper's Magazine*. "Conclusion" originally appeared in *Mademoiselle*. "The Forest" originally appeared in *Epoch*. "The Famous Toboggan of Laughter" originally appeared in *Cosmopolitan*. "Water Music" originally appeared in the *University of California Graduate Student Journal*. "Gorm" originally appeared in *The Atlantic Monthly*. "The Linden Tree" originally appeared in the *Boston Review of the Arts*. "Eino" originally appeared in *The New Yorker*.

Published by arrangement with Harper & Row.
Published in hardcover by Harper & Row, 1980.
First Graywolf paperback edition, 1985.

ISBN 0-915308-71-1
Library of Congress Catalog Card Number 84-73374

Published by Graywolf Press
Post Office Box 75006
Saint Paul, Minnesota 55175

Contents

The Linden Tree

In the early years there had been passion, but now they were just a couple who had grown old together. The last twenty years they had owned a rooming house, where they lived contentedly on the ground floor with their cat, Baby.

Giulio was a great putterer. You could always see him sweeping the front steps or polishing the doorknobs, stopping to gossip with the neighbors. He was a slight, pruny man of sixty-eight, perfectly bald, dressed in heavy trousers, a bright sports shirt with a necktie, and an old man's sweater-jacket, liver-colored and hanging straight to the knees. He had a thick Italian accent and gesticulated wildly when he was excited.

George was quite different. Everything about him was slow and solid, touched by grandeur. Though he was a Negro from the Midwest, he spoke with an accent that sounded British, yet not exactly. He was seventy-four, but looked much younger, with a hard body and a hard face with only a few deep fissures in it. Giulio was a neat dresser, but George was attired. His perfectly creased trousers, his crisp white shirt, smoothly knotted tie, and gray sleeveless sweater seemed out of place in the stuffy little flat.

A home is usually the wife's creation, and so it was in their case. The doilies, the vases with their wax flowers, the prints of saints hanging among gaudy floral calendars—all these were Giulio's. George's contribution was less concrete but more important. He made their life possible, dealing with the rents and taxes, attending to the heavy chores, ousting tenants who drank or brawled. If Giulio were to run the building he would soon come to grief, for he had no real sense of work, and as for the rents, it was all he could do to add two digits together. In addition, he was fussy and fault-finding, so that he often took a dislike to perfectly good tenants, yet countenanced glib bullies.

They were a nicely balanced couple, and for years had been happy. When they were young they had had their troubles—living quarters had been hard to find not only because of George's color, but because of their relationship. In those days Giulio had had fetching ways, too obvious to be ignored. But gradually he passed into a fussy dotage, and now people thought of the pair merely as two lonely old men who lived together. George's color no longer presented problems now that he had proved what was not necessarily de-manded of those who asked for proof: that he was a responsible man, an asset to the neighborhood. His building was the best kept on the block, his rents reasonable, his tenants, for the most part, permanent. He would not rent to the fly-by-night element that was slowly invading the district.

The tenants consisted of a pair of raddled, gadabout sisters, a World War I veteran with one leg, and a few clerks and students. Giulio regaled George with facts about these people he gleaned by snooping through their rooms in their absence, and George put him down for this, even threatened him, but it did no good. And in any case, the tenants did not seem to care; there was something so simple about Giulio that his spying was like that of a mouse or a bird. They called him Aunty Nellie (his last name being Anto-nelli), and the younger ones sometimes invited him into their rooms so that his teeth might be enjoyed. These were ill-fitting, too large for his mouth, and clicked through his speech. When he grew excited, they slipped out of place, at which he would pause in a natural, businesslike way to jam them back in before going on.

Giulio was forever dragging the carpet sweeper up and down the halls, looking for an ear to gossip in. George, on the other hand, talked very little. Only tenants who had lived there a long time got to know him at all, when, once in a great while, he would invite them in for a glass of sherry when they came to pay the rent.

In his flat, the tenants found George to be a different man, less aloof and forbidding. Sitting there with Giulio and Baby, the cat, he had something patient, indulgent, altogether loving in his face. Giulio looked with pride at him, glancing now and then at the guest, as though to say: Isn't he wonderful? Sometimes he would go so far as to confess, "I no good at the paper work, but George, George, he *smart.*" Or, "We live together fifty years, never a yell, always happy." And George would give him a look to show him that he was saying too much, and then Giulio would sulk and refuse to rejoin the conversation. But the next day he would be the same as ever, whirling creakily around the steps with his broom, or around his garden with a green visor clamped to his head.

He had a shrine in the garden, with statues of the saints standing in sun-blanched profusion. He was an ardent Catholic, and there was no one with a greater collection of religious objects—rosaries and crosses and vestments, which he kept in his bureau drawer and brought out to enjoy their varied glass, wooden, and satin richness. But religious as he was, he would not divest his beloved garden of one fresh bloom for his saints. It was a skimpy garden, heavily bolstered with potted geraniums, and he was so proud of each green shoot that struggled through the hard ground, and attended its subsequent flowering with such worried care, that it was only when a flower had finally begun to wither on the stem that he would pluck it as an offering to his statues.

George understood this attitude and was properly grateful when once a year on his birthday he received a sacrifice of fresh daisies and marigolds. He was amused by Giulio's niggardliness toward the saints. He himself did not care about them. He, too, was a Catholic, but had become one only so that he and Giulio might be buried together. Two fully paid-for plots, side by side, awaited them under a linden tree in Our Lady of Mercy Cemetery just outside town. Whoever was the first to go, George because he was older, Giulio because he was frailer, the other would join him in due time. Giulio had vague visions of an afterlife. The older man did not.

He had had a good life, everything considered, and he would be content to die and be done with when the time came, and have his bones rest by his friend's forever. Sometimes he thought of the linden tree and gave a satisfied nod.

But lately George had noticed something strange about Giulio. His large red ears seemed to have grown less red.

"Giulio," he said one day, "your ears don't seem to be as red as they used to be."

Giulio touched his ear. When he was young he had been sensitive about their largeness. "Nothing wrong with my ears," he said defensively.

"I'm not criticizing you, Giulio. I think it's just strange." And now he realized that some definite change had been taking place in his friend, but he could not put his finger on it. It was as though he were a little smaller. The jacket seemed to hang lower than it had.

Ah, well, he thought, we're both getting old.

A few days later, as Giulio was raking the leaves in the garden, he complained to George of shortness of breath, and there was the faintest touch of blue in his lips.

"Why don't you go to the doctor for a checkup?" George asked as casually as he could.

Giulio shook his head and continued his raking.

That night, as Giulio was turning on the television set, he suddenly stepped back and dropped into a chair with his hand spread across his chest. "Help!" he shouted into the air. "Help!" and when his friend ran to his side, he gasped, "I gotta pain. Here! Here!" And his hand clutched at his heart so hard that the knuckles were white.

The next day George took him to the doctor, and sat by his side through all the tests. Giulio was terrified, but when it was all over and they came out of the doctor's office he seemed restored.

"See," he said, "I'm okay. The doctor he say no worry."

George's face did not reflect Giulio's good spirits. "I know he says not to worry, but . . ."

"He say no worry," Giulio repeated cheerfully.

But from then on Giulio was visited frequently by the paralyzing pains. He would stop what he was doing and crouch over, his eyes darting frenziedly in their sockets. If George was there he would hurry to his friend's side, but at these moments Giulio seemed totally alone even though his hand grasped George's arm. When it was over he would be stripped of his little ways; he would wander slowly around the room or stand for long moments looking at nothing. Patiently George would wait, and eventually the old Giulio returned. Uneasily, fretfully, he would say, "I no understand. Looka me, I never hurt a fly in all my life, and this pain, he come and scare me. It's not right."

"Well," George would venture soothingly, "if you'd just eat fewer starches and stop worrying, these pains would go away. You've got plenty of years ahead of you . . ."

"Plenty years?" Giulio would break in sharply. "I *know*, I *know* I got plenty years ahead. This pain, he no *important*, he just *scare* me."

In an effort to distract him, George broke a lifelong precedent and invited Myrna and Alice Heppleworth, the two aging sisters who lived on the third floor, down to the flat for the evening. He himself did not like women, but Giulio did, in a way that George could not understand. Giulio loved to gossip with them, and afterward delighted in describing their clothes and manners, which he usually found distressing. He was more interested in the Heppleworth sisters than in anyone else in the building, and always pursed his lips when he saw them going out with their rheumy escorts, and could never forget that he had once found a bottle of gin in a dresser drawer ostensibly given over to scarves and stockings.

The Heppleworth sisters came, drank all their wine, and turned the television set up as high as it would go. George grew rigid; Giulio went to bed. The sisters were not asked again.

It seemed to George that Giulio failed daily. His ears were as pale as his face, and this seemed particularly significant to George. He found himself suddenly looking at his friend to check his ears, and each time they looked whiter. He never discussed this with Giulio, because Giulio refused to speak about his fears, as though not daring to give them authority by acknowledging them.

And then one morning Giulio gave up this pretense. As he was getting out of bed he had an attack, and when he recovered this time he let out a piercing wail and began to weep, banging his head from side to side. The rest of the day he spent immobile, wrapped from head to foot in a patchwork quilt.

Toward evening George made him get up and walk in the garden with him. George pointed to the flowers, praising them, and gently turned his friend's face to the shrine. The white plaster faces looked peaceful. Even he, George, felt it, and he realized that for weeks he had been in need of some comfort, something outside himself.

"Look," he said, and that was all, fearing to sound presumptuous, because the statues belonged to Giulio and the Church—he himself understood nothing of them.

Giulio looked without interest, and then, forgetting them, he took George's arm and his eyes swam with tears. "What can I do?" he asked. "What will happen?"

As they walked slowly back to the house he drew his lips back from his big false teeth and whispered, "I'm gonna die."

"No, no, don't think that way," George soothed, but he felt help-less, and resentful that his friend must go through this terror. And now that Giulio had said the words, his terror would grow, just as the pain of a bad tooth grows when you finally acknowledge the decay and are plunged into a constant probing of it with your tongue.

When they came back inside Giulio went straight to bed. George stood in the kitchen and looked at his face in the little mirror that hung on the wall. He feared Giulio would die this very minute in the bedroom as he was removing his carpet slippers, and he wanted with every muscle to run to him. But it would not do to become as hysterical as Giulio, and he stood still. Presently the sound of the bedsprings released a sigh from his throat. The flat was silent. He looked again at his face in the mirror. It was as though he were one person and the reflection another, and he was uneasy and embar-rassed, and yet could not look away. He felt deeply aware of himself standing there, staring, and it seemed he was out of place, lost. He whirled around, catching his breath. He had felt entirely alone for the first time in fifty years.

The next day he decided to call for Father Salmon, the young priest from the neighborhood church Giulio attended. Father Salmon dropped in for friendly chats now and then, and Giulio liked him very much, so much, in fact, that the priest often had to silence him when he got carried away with intimate gossip.

A few days later the priest knocked on the door. He was horse-faced, with thinning hair and rimless glasses, and he was quiet and pleasant.

Giulio was wrapped up in his quilt in the armchair. He did not greet the priest with his usual beam of pleasure; he did not even smile.

"Well, Giulio," the priest said, "how are you feeling? I haven't seen you at church lately."

Giulio said at once, "Father, I'm dying."

"What is the trouble?" the priest asked gently.

"It's my heart," Giulio shot back, his hand scrounging around his shirtfront and fumbling with the buttons until it was clutching his bare chest. He looked as though he were prepared to pull the heart out for inspection. His eyes pleaded with the priest to set it right. The priest sat down next to him.

"What does your doctor say?" he asked.

"Oh, Father," Giulio moaned, "the doctor is a stupid. He never tell me one real thing. In and out and all around, around the bush. He no understand, but *I* understand—this heart, he gonna kill me. You think so, Father? What do you think? You think so?"

"Surely, Giulio," the priest replied, "you must accept the doctor's word. If he says there's no reason to fear . . ."

Giulio looked away, black with melancholy.

The priest sat silently for a moment, then began again. "Giulio, death is as natural as birth. Think of your flowers out there in the garden, how they grow from little seeds and then fade and fall—what could be more natural? God has been with you all your life, and He will not forsake you now . . ."

But Giulio, his eyes shutting tighter and tighter as the priest spoke, got up from his chair and crept into the bedroom, dragging his quilt behind him.

Afterward he said to George, "I no wanna see Father Salmon again."

"Father Salmon is trying to help," George told him.

Giulio shook his head, his fingers rubbing the area of his heart.

What a strange person he is, George thought, looking at him closely. All these years he has been immersed in the church, and now, suddenly, the church means nothing to him. He recalled a conversation he had overheard a few days ago as he was fixing a faulty burner in the second floor kitchen. Two of the students were going down the hall, talking. One had commented on Giulio's bad health. The other had replied, "Don't worry, Aunty Nellie could never do anything so profound as to die."

George had bristled, as he always did whenever anyone made fun of his friend—but it was true that Giulio was not profound. He liked pretty things, and the church gave him its rich symbols; he liked intimate conversation, and the church gave him patient Father Salmon; he liked the idea of an afterlife, and the church gave him that, too. He loved the church, but when you came right down to it, he believed only what he could see with his two eyes, and he could see only his blue lips and wasted face in the mirror. This oddly realistic attitude explained his stinginess toward the saints; they were, after all, only plaster. And yet when Baby had once jumped up on the shrine and relieved himself on St. Francis's foot, Giulio had screamed at the animal until the neighbors hung from the windows.

All these amiable contradictions in Giulio had been known to George for fifty years, and he had always believed that they would sustain his friend through everything. Now the contradictions were gone. All that was left in Giulio was the certainty of death. It made George feel forlorn, on the outside. He sensed that nothing could be set right, that Giulio would live consumed by fear until he died consumed by fear, and the linden tree would not mark two intertwined lives, but forever cast its shadow between two strangers.

They had met for the first time in front of the Minneapolis train station in the first decade of the century. George sat in the driver's seat of a Daimler, in his duster and goggles. His employer had gone inside to meet one Giulio Antonelli, just arrived from Calabria, nephew of the head gardener. When he emerged he had in tow a thin boy of eighteen dressed in a shabby suit and carrying a suitcase that looked like a wicker basket. He wore cherry-colored cigar bands on his fingers, and had a shoot of wilted wild flowers stuck through the buttonhole of his jacket. His eyes were red-rimmed; apparently he had been crying all the way from Calabria. Delicate and terrified, his cigar bands glittering hectically in the sunlight, he crawled into the Daimler and collapsed in a corner.

George had worked as a chauffeur and handyman on his employer's estate for five years, but was originally from an isolated Finnish farming community where God knows what fates had conspired to bring his parents, a bitter, quarreling, aloof, and extremely poor black couple. George became friends with only one thing native to that cold country, the stones that littered the fields. He could not say what attracted him to them, but he felt a great bond with them. When he was ten he built a wall of the stones. It was only a foot high and not very long, and there was nothing in the world for it to guard there in the middle of the empty field, but he knew he had discovered the proper use of the stones, and all his life he had the feeling he was that wall.

In Minneapolis, on the estate, he kept to himself. He liked the Daimler, which he drove with authority, and the appearance of which on the streets caused people to gawk with admiration. He picked up his employer's speech habits, and this, combined with the Finnish accent he had absorbed, gave a peculiar, unplaceable ring to his words, which he relished, because it was his alone.

The Calabrian boy turned out to be a poor gardener, not because he was listless with homesickness, for that soon passed, but because he made favorites of certain flowers and would have nothing to do with the others. The tulips, for instance, he apparently considered stout and silly-looking, and he made disparaging faces at them. He liked the wild flowers that cropped up in odd corners.

George was fascinated by Giulio, although he did not like him. He reminded him of a woman. Women had never respected George's wall, at least a certain type of woman had not—the bold Finnish farm girls, some of the hired women here on the estate. He was well favored, and maybe there was something in his coloring, too, that attracted women, something tawny, reminiscent of the sun, here, where everyone else looked like a peeled banana. In any case, they were always after him. He was not flattered. He felt they were not interested in him as he knew himself, proud and valuable, but in some small part of him that they wanted for their own use, quickly, in a dark corner.

But Giulio, though girlish, had no boldness in him. He would leave the garden and lean against the garage door where George was polishing the Daimler. *"Bella, bella,"* he would murmur, and his face shone with a kind of radiant simplemindedness. There was no calculation in him—sometimes you could see him cocking his head and singing before the wild flowers in the garden. Watching George, the boy spoke foreign words rich in their tones of admiration, and his quick, glittering fingers—he had bought flashy rings with his pay—seemed anxious to catch the sun and make a present of it to the tall, mute figure in the gloom of the garage.

Two months after his arrival Giulio was fired. George, filled with fear for himself, feeling a great chasm opening before him, quit his job, and the two of them, with hardly a word between them, took the train to San Francisco, where Giulio had another uncle. All during the trip George asked himself: "Why am I doing this? Why am I going with him? I don't even like him. He's a silly, ridiculous person; there's something the matter with him."

They got off at the San Francisco depot, and before George was even introduced to the uncle, who stood waiting, he picked up his baggage and, without a word of farewell to Giulio, walked quickly away from him.

First he found odd jobs, and finally he wound up on Rincon Hill with another Daimler. On his half day off each week he would wander around the city, looking at the sights. Whenever he saw a quick, thin figure that reminded him of Giulio his heart would pound, and he would say to himself, "Thank God it's not Giulio, I don't want to see him again." And then he found that what had begun as a casual walk around the city was turning into a passionate weekly search. The day he caught sight of Giulio sadly and ineffectively constructing a pyramid of cabbages in a vegetable market, he had to restrain himself from throwing his arms around him.

Giulio's face had blanched with surprise when he looked up, and then his eyes had filled with a dazzling welcome, and he had extended his hand to his returned friend with a tenderness George never forgot.

They were together from then on. In time they bought a vegetable stand, and as a result of George's frugality and common sense he was able to save in spite of Giulio's extravagances. They worked and invested, and in thirty years they were able to buy, for cash, the old apartment building they now lived in. Life had always been strangely easy for them. They had been incapable of acknowledging affronts, even when they were refused lodgings or openly stared at on the street, and the last twenty years in the security of their own flat had been free from problems, satisfying in all ways.

Now Giulio moaned, "Oh, I gotta pain, I gotta pain."

George would take his hand and say, "I'm here, Giulio, I'm here." But Giulio would look through him, as though he did not exist.

"Don't we *know* each other?" George finally exploded one day, causing Baby to speed under a table with his ears laid back. "Are we strangers after all these years?"

Giulio closed his eyes, involved with his fear.

George sighed, stroking his friend's hand, thin and waxy as a sliver of soap. "What are you thinking about now, this very minute, Giulio? You must tell me."

"I'm thinking of my dog," Giulio said, after a silence.

"What dog was that?" George asked softly.

"I had him in Nocera."

"And what about him?"

"He died, and my father he dug a hole and put him in." His lips turned down. "I dug him up later, I was lonely for him."

"What a foolish thing to do, my poor Giulio."

"His own mother wouldn'a wanted him. Bones and worms . . ."

"Hush, Giulio."

"Gonna happen to me."

"But your soul . . ."

"What's my soul look like?" Giulio asked quickly.

"Like you, Giulio . . . it's true . . ."

Giulio cast him a look of contempt George would not have thought him capable of.

"The little hole, the bones and worms," Giulio moaned.

"But you've *had* a life!" George suddenly cried with exasperation. "Do you want to live forever?"

"Yes," Giulio said simply.

From then on George felt a fury. In the past all Giulio's little fears had been bearable because he, George, could exorcise them, like a stevedore bearing a small load away. But this final cowardice excluded him. And there was nothing, no one he could turn to. He went halfheartedly to church, but got nothing from it. He began making small overtures to his tenants, but his sociability was stiff with rust. He looked with curiosity at the black people on the street, and thought there were more of them than there used to be. When a young black couple stopped him on a corner one day he listened attentively as they talked of civil rights. He accepted a pamphlet from them and read it thoroughly. But afterward he threw it out. He felt no connection with the problems it presented.

He cursed Giulio as he had cursed him fifty years ago when he had walked away from him at the train depot, and he wished for the oneness with himself that he had known in the empty fields of his youth.

In the daytime he was angrily helpful, like a disapproving orderly, but at night, as they sat in the small living room with Baby flicking his tail back and forth across the blank television screen, he went to Giulio and mutely pleaded with him. Giulio sighed abstractedly; he seemed far away, deep inside himself, listening to every heartbeat, counting every twinge, with a deep frown line between his eyes.

George moved the twin beds together, and Giulio allowed his hand to be held through the night. From then on they slept that way, hand in hand. George slept lightly, waking often. It was almost as if he wished to be awake, to enjoy the only hours of closeness he had with his friend as he held his hand. And also, in the back of his mind was the fear that if he drifted off, Giulio would be released into the arms of death. And so he lay quietly, listening to Giulio's breathing, to the wind in the trees.

Then gradually the bedroom window would turn from black to gray, and the breeze that ruffled the curtain carried in the scent of early morning. Dawn brought him sleep; the rising sun gave him a sense of security. Bad things never happened in the daytime—at least one felt that way. And so his fingers grew lax in Giulio's hand as he trusted his friend to the kindness of the dawning day.

But when he awoke later it would be with a sharp sense of foreboding. Quickly he would turn to look at Giulio, his eyes narrowed against the possible shock. But Giulio would be breathing evenly, his bluish lips parted over his gums, his teeth grinning from a water glass on the bureau. Giulio's clothes were neatly laid out, his liver-colored jacket hung over the back of a chair. How lifeless the jacket looked. George would shut his eyes, knowing that the sight of that empty jacket would be unbearable when Giulio was gone. He shook the thought from his head, wondering if life could be more painful than this. Then Giulio's eyes would open, George's face take on a formal nonchalance. And so another night had passed. Their hands parted.

"How do you feel?" George would ask shortly.

Giulio would sigh.

They took their breakfast. The sun shone through the kitchen window with a taunting golden light. George snapped at Giulio. Giulio was unmoved.

One summer morning George persuaded Giulio to sit outside in the backyard. He hoped that watching him work in the garden, Giulio might be persuaded to putter around again. He settled his friend into a chair and picked up the rake, but as the minutes wore on and he moved around the garden in the hot sun, raking the leaves together, Giulio showed no sign of interest. George stopped and put the rake down. Not knowing if he wished to please Giulio or anger him, he suddenly broke off the largest marigold in the garden and held it out.

Giulio shaded his watering eyes with his hand; then his eyes drifted away from the flower like two soap bubbles in the air. George flung the flower to the ground, staring at Giulio, then strode to the shrine and stood there with his hands in fists, blindly determined to do something that would shake his friend open, break him in two if need be. He grabbed the arm of the Virgin Mary and lifted the statue high, and heard Giulio's voice.

"George."

"That's right," George growled, replacing the statue and breathing threateningly through his nostrils, "I would have smashed it to bits!"

"Smash what?" Giulio asked indifferently, and George saw that under the awning of his thin hand his eyes were closed.

"Were your eyes closed?" George thundered. "Didn't you *see* me?"

"You no care that I can't open my eyes—this sun, he hurt them. You *mean*, George, make me sit out here. Too hot. Make me feel sick. I wanna go inside."

"I was going to smash your Virgin Mary!" George cried.

Giulio shrugged. "I wanna go inside."

And then George's shoulders hunched, his face twisted up, and he broke into a storm of tears. Turning his head aside with shame, he made for the back door; then he turned around and hurried back, glancing up at the windows, where he hoped no one stood watching him cry. He put his arm around Giulio and helped him up from his chair, and the two old men haltingly crossed the garden out of the sun.

"Humiliating," George whispered when they were inside, shaking his head and pressing his eyes with a handkerchief. He slowly folded the handkerchief into a square and replaced it in his pocket. He gave a loud sniff and squared his shoulders, and looked with resignation at his distant friend.

Giulio was settling himself into the armchair, plucking the patchwork quilt around him. "Time for pills," he muttered, reaching next to him, and he poured a glass of water from a decanter and took two capsules, smacking his lips mechanically, like a goldfish. Sitting back, he looked around the room in his usual blank, uninterested way. Then a puzzled expression came into his eyes.

"Why you cry then, George?"

George shook his head silently.

"I do something you no like?"

"You never talk. It's as though we're strangers." And he broke off with a sigh. "I've told you all that before—what's the use?"

"I got big worry, George. No time to talk."

"It would be better than to think and think. What do you think about all day?"

Giulio slowly raised his eyebrows, as though gazing down upon a scene. "Bones and worms."

"Giulio, Giulio."

"Big worry, George."

"You'll drive yourself mad that way."

"I no mad at you. Just him." He lay one thin finger on his heart, lightly, as though afraid of rousing it.

"I don't mean angry . . ."

But Giulio was already tired of talking, and was plucking at the quilt again, ill, annoyed, retreating into sleep.

"Giulio, please, you've talked a little. Talk a little more—stay."

With an effort, his eyes sick and distant, Giulio stayed.

But now that he had his attention, George did not know where to begin, what to say. His mind spun; his tongue formed a few tentative words; then, clubbed by an immense fatigue, he sank into a chair with his head in his hands.

"I'm sick man," Giulio explained tonelessly, closing his eyes. After a silence he opened them and looked over at George, painfully, as though from under a crushing weight. "Tonight I hold your hand in bed again, like always. Hold your hand every night, you know that."

"You hold *my* hand?" George asked softly, lifting his head.

"In daytime," Giulio said slowly, his eyes laboriously fixed on George's attentive face, "in daytime only the bones and worms. But in the night . . . in the night, I see other things, too . . ." He was silent for a moment until a twinge had passed, then spoke again. "See you, George. And I hold your hand. Make you feel better . . ." His eyes still fixed on George's face, he gave an apologetic twitch of the lip as his lids closed, and slowly he nodded off to sleep.

Vienna, City of My Dreams

. . . the Opera, the Rathaus, the Votivkirche, Schönbrunn Palace
. . . Schönbrunn, where Napoleon once slept with Madame Wal-
ewska, and L'Aiglon languished . . . *and* where the prolific and prognathous Habsburgs overate and bumbled through the centuries.
Keep that in mind. What you are leaving wasn't worth seeing in
the first place. Don't doubt it.

"Ich kann nicht verstehen." That is almost all the German I know.
And it takes care of everything. I should have it carved on my
tombstone.

It has been over a month; everything piles up around me. Or
rather, nothing piles up around me, no letters, no duties, only days—
a stack of greasy solitaire cards. SHE comes in at seven in the morning. She holds me in the greatest contempt. Once, it is true, she
inquired (with the help of sign language) if I were ill. But there
was no care in her tone; a sick boarder is a complication. HE I see
later, at mealtime; he pays no heed to me at all. HE and SHE . . .
they are so enormous in my poor head. They are too big to be
Neusses or Schwartzes or Müllers or anything else; they stand alone.
As for me, no one has called me by name since I came. I don't
know anyone. THEY don't bother with the courtesy of names. Some
of the old, permanent boarders they address properly, the names
like numbers in their mouths, but for the main part, no; everyone
is treated uniformly and democratically, as anonymities: students,
tourists, salesmen, truck drivers, poor families on holiday. It is called
a Workman's Hotel, or some such thing, cheap, but not half so

cheap as it should be, the rooms disheartening, the food worse. Here I have been for this very long while, thirty days or more, without being addressed by name; when I say my name to myself, it no longer fits. I have become simply I, or rather i, or to be absolutely accurate, a flicked-over i, a small, shriveled dash, as at the end of a futile paragraph . . .

Sorting fingernail parings from sacks of wheat. That is my most common nightly occupation. Another is adding up columns of Chinese characters. Though I pursue sleep with the most shameless, groveling desire, going so far as to make begging faces, I am thrown only half an inch beneath the surface of oblivion, nose and feet sticking out, like a badly buried corpse . . . and then some small noise will like a sudden wind scrape away the thin layer, leaving my mind meticulously working through those endless sacks of wheat and tortured columns, my eyelids fluttering, my hands burrowing to the crumpled warmth of my nightclothes as though the good sleep lay concrete in the folds.

All the capsules I've collected over the years! Filled (I mused hopefully at the beginning) with multicolored grains picked from the beaches of Impressionist paintings. I took them until I could not stand up to their fee: dizziness, nausea, depression. Tit for tat. I still have them, bottles and bottles crowded together in the suitcase. To fall back on at very bad times. But I have not fallen back on them this time. And God in heaven, I look like the Duke of Windsor . . . which is acceptable for an elderly man, but tragic for a girl of twenty-three.

SHE can be no older, it came as a great surprise, for when I first saw her in the foyer (whose tile floor echoed with the massive door's rattling and sliding of bolts, and whose dimness was such that I had to blink several times to ascertain that the lumps scattered throughout were small children) she appeared a middle-aged wardeness; heavy medieval-looking keys dangled from her coarse hand; the face was a lump of suet in the gloom. *"Kinder,"* I said hopefully (how often on this summer holiday had I not discovered that a timid, heavily accented random word drew an indulgence, a sense of responsibility from the listener, regardless of age or sex? I was not often exploited. It was something in my face, a face to be found on the ceilings of chapels, not among the self-sufficient saints but the cavorting cherubs, sweet, marginal, harmless. At Dachau I was aware of appearing badly out of place). *"Kinder,"* again, quite uselessly, for she was walking away with an impersonal scowl. HE then appeared, with a little English, his eyes—as hers—dipping down to the leather suitcase and alligator shoes and trim ankles and sheer stockings, swinging up to the face with its platinum (natural) curls (natural), his lips ejecting something whitish onto the floor—phlegm, gum, a leftover from breakfast?—and told me the price. Higher than I had expected. Raised on the spur of the moment, no doubt. It could come down with a little bargaining, but I never bargained, never felt I had the right. I paid a week's rent and was repelled by the room, not that it was dirty—far from it—but that it was barren, threadbare, and sorrowful and gave off a smell of sweat, urine, canned food, and cheap cigarettes. I was not accustomed to that.

Noise. I suffered from the first minute. Trams, cafés, radios, gangs of boys playing in the street. And so I sat down and asked myself why I had wished to come here. The selection had been quite arbitrary. I had asked someone on the street (one of those mellow, multilingual, elderly gentlemen with soft, intelligent eyes, the sort with whom I had always associated Europe) where I might find an extremely cheap hotel. (Not that I lacked money. No.) Hesitantly, he directed me to the Neuss establishment. And I was now here, settled in (having unpacked quickly for fear of changing my mind), and realizing that one was often more strange to himself than he was to others.

In the evening I went down to supper. It was there, in the electric light, that I realized how young they were. She marched back and forth with the food, her arms bare and red in the chill, sweat standing out on her brow, the very picture of solid, unconcerned strength. Early multiple motherhood had broadened her bosom so that her gray sweater could be buttoned only at the waist and gaped in woolen surprise at the breasts which shrugged heavily against the material of her dress, a liverish brown. On her feet were square, cleated shoes, laced to the ankles and worn over a pair of striped worsted stockings. She was pasty, gross-featured, coarse-haired, the hair a brown rope twisted tightly—painfully, I should think—into a peculiarly geometric knot just above her forehead. And yet, for all that, quite young. And he, poor thing, a premature ruin choked by a weed or mildew of black hair growing solidly up his scrawny neck. Bony wrists black as the neck, a blue, debased chin, and a big bone of a nose from whose dank nostrils sprouted more hair, eyebrows growing into each other and into his sideburns, ears like hairy grottoes. There was something about this rampant hair that implied a lack of control, and I was not surprised to see that he was startled by sudden noises and that he swiped his bone of a nose nervously. And yet, for all their difference in type, the two of them worked together beautifully, a real team, unsmiling, solidly preoccupied, superbly efficient, keeping both service and quality down to the finest minimum. Profoundly serious people. So seemed the others in the room, but differently, with the long, patient faces of the eternally short-changed. All of them, served and servers, had grown up.

It was with my usual naïveté that I left a tip under the plate, imagining those two plate-hard faces creasing with gratitude, indulgence, and shame. ("See here, husband [wife]. Observe what that peculiar child has done. Thanked us for nothing. I cringe for our long defection of duty.") I continued for a week to secrete coins (prepolished in my room) under the heavy, large-pored plate, a coin more a day, until I suddenly grew embarrassed and stopped. They had not responded in any way.

At the beginning I was intrigued by their children, sorry for them; I wished to rejuvenate them, to bless them. I could not read them stories, for I knew no German; I could not play with them, for they had no sense of playfulness. So I bought them candy at the store around the corner. Then, one day, in the space of a minute, I was through with them. To be rejected by a dog or a child is the worst cut of all, and they had been implacably thankless once too often. There were four of them altogether and already. Stout, moonfaced, immaculately clothed, they looked curiously prosperous, but not quite human. Too small to help with the work, too lethargic to play with abandon, they were, I saw, very close to some thriving vegetable matter. Their parents' attitude confirmed this. Frau Neuss would interrupt her work to blow noses in a row, straighten a dress, pull up a sock. Then exit Mama. Herr Neuss gazed at them with a dull reflectiveness that exploded in a nervous bark, and he would bear down on the toadstool patch to slap a finger from a nostril or clap the oldest boy's shoulder, as though to test its incipient masculinity. I saw so clearly, so clearly, that they had been too doglike or too oxlike to sense the flower of youth within themselves, and without a second thought had pumped up progeny which they now served and observed as a poor farmer tends his crops, tired, cross, but unquestioning. Early marriage and early parenthood were gestures of defeat . . . I saw the cells of my body and personality dividing to accommodate someone else only after the triumph of youth had been squeezed dry . . .

And so I was finally able to return their contempt. There! I will move out next week. I told them, my thumbnail gouging the open page of my English-German dictionary which trembled in my hand. Why, if it had been a comment on the weather they could not have been less moved. It was then that my insomnia slipped into high gear. The skin of my face began to sag; black circles formed under my eyes; my hair grew lank, my breath tasted foul; even my fingernails grew dirty. Lying under this film of personal neglect, I did not touch them with compassion; instead, I offended their lust-hate for dirt, which I deemed Teutonic, unseemly so far south . . . and I asked her if she had not migrated from some northern city, say Hamburg? She responded to this, as to everything I say, with simulated deafness. Oh, God, she is so busy. I see her old and dead, buried with the implements of her trade, as were the Egyptians (or was it the Chinese? My mind parts like a rotten fabric), stuffed into her casket among buckets of suds, gray rags, twig brooms, poor Frau Sisyphus, for the place is eternally dirty, and she eternally scrubbing. No wonder she despised me when she saw me, slipped from my chapel ceiling onto her streaked tile floor. An incongruous sight. For the unimaginative person, the incongruous

is vastly troubling. In her and in him this uneasiness probably mani-
fests itself in indigestion. I am sure that all their thinking processes
take place within a swollen inch of intestine. And I with the divine
gift of observation and articulation, I lie here in this tangle of gray
sheets which she no longer bothers to change and am possessed
by these two sodden, elementary existences.

The noise comes from the outside, not from within the building.
In the evenings it is very quiet inside; the building rolls into a tight
ball for the night like a sow bug. Sometimes the sound of footsteps
can be heard . . . at the beginning they were my own, for I would
wander through the halls when the sun went down. And I would
pause by the door of their apartment which leads off the foyer,
and I would hear them. Oh! they talk then, when they are inside
their four walls (and I can imagine the decor: all prickly khaki-
colored plants in pots of cracked earth; and naked floorboards still
wet from her scrubbing; and lace curtains—I've seen them from
the outside—snarled, lank, and phlegm-colored with age, old heir-
looms no better than the broken venetian blinds in the rest of the
building and yet affording her, I know, a solid, offhand pride; and
on the walls no pictures, but gray, mildewing wallpaper from ceiling
to wet floor, and reflected in the chilled shine of the floor, the thick
legs of tables and chairs all crowded together so no one can breathe;
and in their bedroom a high, thick, uncomfortable bed, where every
night, her coarse hair slung like an unbraided rope across the pillow,
and his bone of a nose sticking up into the close air, they sleep,
oh, they sleep, their rich, wet snores intertwined like the notes of
a *Konzertstück,* starting in their very entrails, rising up through the
lungs, the throat, gathering vibrato in the palate, finally expelled
through the loose lips, which smack now and then, or smile, or
form some hazy night word which the other answers . . . I can
picture their private life down to the last detail, never having to
lay my eyes on it, that's how well I know them and the four toadstools). You would never believe they had so much to say. No doubt
it has to do with the kitchen sink, whose drains are failing, or Herr
P., who cannot pay his rent, or with the broken window on the
third floor. And the toadstools pipe up one at a time; they never

22

clamor or giggle; already life is a serious business. I hear him gulping something down, beer probably; he belches; he sets the mug down with a thud. The toadstools' piping diminishes until they have all, apparently, been stuffed into bed. Then I hear the lights being clicked off, and he and she are talking again, in the dark, softly. Can you talk about drains and broken windows forever? The bedroom door is closed, and I am left standing in the silence of the foyer. It is only nine o'clock. Why don't they go out into the city, to the Ferris wheel in the Volksprater, or to a café where Strauss is played? But their eyes, I know, bear the responsibilities of the ages; we are a million light years apart; I look away. My pity floods out to the boarders. What do they do in the evenings? The student pores over his books; the salesman writes home to his wife; the family on holiday washes out their underwear in the sink; the truck driver falls asleep early. I never see them do anything frivolous or at their leisure; they are grown up and full of care; time is their master. I am sorry for them; how did they get that way? I want terribly to know how they got that way.

I wait for sleep to take me, but it takes me too late, early in the morning, and she is already here with her twig broom, sweeping out my shred of repose. The door shuts. I look to the new day. My breath quickens; I envision crowns, crests, gardens, clock towers, orchestras, crowds, laughter . . . If all my life I have been a painted cherub with immovable limbs, the light from the rose window has, nevertheless, instead of fusing me more perfectly with the pink plaster, plucked at me as though it wished to draw me through its eye into the great world. When I reached my majority I decided all at once, quite unlike myself, that I must travel to some country very far away, rich in love, war, and art. But "ready-made significance," my father suggested when once—and only once—I described this desire; and I acquiesced and did not go. It was fully two years later (two years full of nothing, of trips to the library and afternoon tea with the aunts and an occasional evening at the movies with Gerald, who was thirty-nine and a second cousin and full of a pale admiration for me that tightened his lips when the boys at the movie made casual, flattering overtures to me; afterward he would deliver me back to my old father and older aunts, all of whom looked just like Gerald, only older, and who shared with him his pale admiration, as though I were a holy relic. My room was the only room in the house that was still beautiful—bright and pink as the day I was born, scarcely a thing changed in twenty years, dolls still reclining against the little pillows, Alcott and Andersen leaning against Schopenhauer—which one tutor had thrust into my hands the day he left—the curtains frilly and white, everything meticulously clean, for the housekeeper loved me too, and nothing was too much work for her) . . . it was fully two years later, the summer already waning, that I finally moved my limbs, shook off my father and aunts and Gerald, who all insisted I would come to grief alone (but I was over twenty-one and had my own money) and flew here, literally, where I wandered without seeming direction from one guided tour to another, nursing a cold one day, a blister the next, until I saw that it was Vienna I was approaching, unquestionably the other side of the rose window . . . but when I finally arrived on the tailfeathers of September and tumbled from train into tram and saw vibrating on either side the flags and spires and crowds, I only knew: not yet.

And so every morning I say to myself I have now rested sufficiently, and the city, like a dream, creeps toward me on the bed; I rise to meet it, standing like a drunk, dazed with exhaustion, my fingers holding the swollen lids of my eyes apart, and I say again: not yet. What is all that noise and music and color and history to me? It would not clutch me; it would not detain me; I would float through as I floated through the guided tours, weightless. I lie down again, thinking of nothing, of mealtime.

They began at some point—I don't remember when—to deny me even the smallest courtesies that they extended to the others. If they dropped food over the side of the plate they did not bother to wipe it up; if they saw me in the hallway they would not give that slight, peremptory nod so uniquely theirs, no, no sign of recognition at all, and to make matters worse would brush against me as they passed, as though I were not there. She, when she cleans the room (and she does not clean it for me, she cleans it because it belongs to her), clatters the broom under the bed with such preoccupied vigor that I must believe I am no more than part of the bedclothes. "Please stop, for heaven's sake," I cried out one morning, and I realized that my voice was unmistakably a whine. When she was gone I repeated the sentence several times but could not rid it of this new quality. It was as though the lightness and purity (I have always been told that I should have been a singer) had grown puckered and blotched, as the skin of a suddenly aged peach. From then on it has been out of my control, and in the dining room I discover impatience on the faces of my fellow boarders, who have heretofore been courteous.

I amazed myself one day by taking my empty dish and glass into the kitchen. As amazed as I, he and she pointed back to the dining room. "Go back to your table. We don't serve in the kitchen."

"I only wished to save you the trouble of clearing up," I said in English, every word of my small stock of German locked in the confusion of my brain. They swept me out of the kitchen like a ball of dust, and I crept past the curious eyes of the boarders and up to my room with tears standing in my eyes.

I began leaving tips under the plate again. I developed a passion for small change, and, my eyes narrowed against the sun, I took the tram down to Cook's, where I broke all my bills into coins. Then in my room I polished them and arranged them in stacks according to their size. Sometimes, when it was dark, I would open the window and drop a few to the pavement below, imagining some poor girl or boy pouncing on them and looking up to marvel aloud: "There is an angel of mercy up there."

"Yes," I would whisper back. "Her name is Margaret Henshaw." Margaret Henshaw. Sometimes I can remember it, but usually I can't.

One afternoon there was a knock on my door. "Now, certainly, something will happen," I told myself; no one had ever knocked on my door before. Hastily I covered my money with a newspaper and opened the door. He stood there uneasily.

"Come in," I said quietly, motioning.

He shook his head.

I was aware that the harsh afternoon light shining through the broken blinds threw my haggard face into the cruelest relief, and I lowered my eyes, seeing my crumpled dress soiled with long use, my slippered feet gray to the ankles, my dirty fingernails, my hair hanging like a split awning across my eyes. I reddened with shame.

He ignored everything. "You must move," he said loudly. "It is too dirty, too much work for my wife."

"You've worked on your English. In order to speak with me." My tongue was charged with gratitude.

He did not understand. "If not, we must charge twice the rent." His eyes moved around the room and came back to my face, where they remained steadfast and honest with contempt. "Three times more the rent," he ventured, and I flicked the newspaper from my silver castle. If I had laid that castle flat it would have taken twenty plates to cover it, a hundred movements of my timid hand, a hundred covert glances at the kitchen. A hundred, all rolled into one, soaring like Schönbrunn from the spindly table.

I gestured for him to take it.

"Bah," he said, wrinkling his nose nervously, and he walked away, only to return a moment later, angry, shaken, as though sorely offended.

"But take it," I breathed, and he grabbed the wastebasket and swept the castle into it with one resounding clap as from a giant bell, and backed away.

"And I can stay?" I whispered. "There's more." I picked up my traveler's checks and held them before his taut nostrils. "Call me by my name," I urged, ". . . bei meinem Namen," but I could not remember it at that moment, and he was turning, anyway, closing the door behind him with unbelievable softness.

In order not to go back to Cook's (Father, Gerald, the aunts, in pieces from my silence—could they trace me there?) I cashed my checks at stores, each time buying some small useless article which I threw away outside. Then I went to as many different banks as I could find and had the bills broken into coins. It was an exhausting day; I hated the turmoil of the streets and stores, the waiting in the banks, the curious looks, the arm-breaking suitcase. But when I came back I had a much greater castle than the first. It stood in

lonely beauty for five full days before a knock again sounded on
my door. They had both come. The newspaper was over the castle;
I threw it off, looking at their faces, which were frightening. They
shut the door quickly behind them and spoke to each other in bitter
undertones, their hard gray eyes striking first the castle, then me.

"You must leave," he cried angrily, trying to keep his voice down,
and she gave a powerful, supporting nod.

"But I can pay," I whispered. "You can see as well as I . . . it's
all for you."

"Nein"—grabbing my arm and thrusting his face close to mine—
"you must move." I pointed at the money, and he stuck out his
underlip with disdain, and she marched to the table with her hands
on her hips and looked as though she saw garbage. Pulling myself
from his grasp, I leaned over the castle, touching it eagerly with
my fingers, and he picked off a coin and threw it to the floor, where
it rolled silverly under the bed. I, too, picked off a coin and held
it out in my palm. She pushed it away. Their mouths looked as if
they could bleed. With profound unity they turned heavily from
the table, which, touched by a thigh, jogged so that the left wing
of the castle cascaded to the floor; then we were all on our knees,
and something had broken in the Neusses: they were still angry
but they were putting the money in their pockets, in perfect silence.
I got to my feet. They were working very hard, just as when she
mopped the floor or he mended a broken step.

"I want to know how you became so serious. Everything you
do is heavy, full of weight." They did not answer; they stood up,
the floor beneath them picked clean, and without looking at each
other they turned to the table, where they swept the right wing
into the newspaper. Hurrying, he reached toward the rest of the
money, but suddenly he stopped, letting his hand fall heavily, and
I saw their eyes meet sideways, shamed.

"Talk to me," I said, though they looked too weary to speak.
"Call me by my name." They were moving to the door; they were
not even listening.

"Fräulein Henshaw," he said with his head bent, "you must
move."

That was not the name I wanted, I realized as the door closed in my face. I turned back to the remains of the castle and looked at it for a long while. Eventually I took the coins to the window and dropped them out, after which I lay down.

What did I want them to call me? Neuss? Fräulein Neuss? Yes! Breathe yourselves into my bones, give me a bucket, let me scrub, let me walk heavily. But how can I say such things? I who hate them so deeply?

Time passes slowly. It has been three days since they were here in my room, but it seems much longer. In the dining room I have noticed that the other boarders draw away from me because I am so unkempt, but other than that everything is the same as always. He and she treat me as though nothing had happened; they slap the food down under my nose, looking over my head at other things. But in time they will see me; I have faith. I have faith, and I have time, and I have money. I have enough traveler's checks for many, many more castles. Even if they quadruple the rent, I will have enough.

Last Courtesies

"Lillian, you're too polite," Vladimir kept telling her.

She did not think so. Perhaps she was not one to return shoves in the bus line, but she did fire off censorious glares; and true, she never yelled at the paper boy who daily flung her *Chronicle* to a rain-soaked fate, but she did beckon him to her door and remind him of his responsibilities. If she was always the last to board the bus, if she continued to dry out the paper on the stove, that was the price she must pay for observing the minimal courtesy the world owed itself if it was not to go under. Civilized she was. Excessively polite, no.

In any case, even if she had wanted to, she could not change at this stage of life. Nor had Aunt Bedelia ever changed in any manner. Not that she really compared herself to her phenomenal aunt, who, when she had died four months ago at the age of ninety-one, was still a captivating woman; no faded great beauty (the family ran to horse faces), but elegant, serenely vivid. Any other old lady who dressed herself in long gowns *circa* 1910 would have appeared a mere oddity; but under Bedelia's antiquated hairdo sat a brain; in her gnarled, almond-scented fingers lay direction. She spoke of Bach, of the Russian novelists, of her garden and the consolations of nature; never of her arthritis, the fallen ranks of her friends, or the metamorphosis of the neighborhood, which now featured motorcycles roaring alongside tin cans and blackened banana peels. At rare moments a sigh escaped her lips, but who knew if it was for her crippled fingers (she had been a consummate pianist) or a repercussion from the street? It was bad form, ungallant, to put too fine a point on life's discomfitures.

Since Bedelia's death the flat was lonely; lonely, yet no longer private since a supremely kinetic young woman, herself a music lover, had moved in upstairs. With no one to talk to, with thuds and acid rock resounding from above, Lillian drifted (too often, she knew) into the past, fingering its high points. The day, for instance, that Vladimir had entered their lives by way of the Steinway grand (great gleaming relic of better times), which he came to tune. He had burst in, dressed not in a customary suit but in garage mechanic's coveralls and rubber thong sandals, a short, square man with the large disheveled head of a furious gnome, who embellished his labors with glorious run-throughs of Bach and Scarlatti, but whose speech, though a dark bog of Slavic intonations, was distinctly, undeniably obscene. Aunt Bedelia promptly invited him to dinner the following week. Lillian stood astonished, but reminded herself that her aunt was a sheltered soul unfamiliar with scabrous language, whereas she, Lillian, lived more in the great world, riding the bus every day to the Opera House, where she held the position of switchboard operator (Italian and German required). The following morning at work, in fact, she inquired about Vladimir.

Several people there knew of him. A White Russian, he had fled to Prague with his parents in 1917, then fled again twenty years later at the outbreak of the war, eventually settling in San Francisco, where he quickly earned the reputation of an excellent craftsman and a violent crackpot. He abused clients who had no knowledge of their pianos' intestines, and had once been taken to court by an acquaintance whom he had knocked down during a conversation about Wagner. He wrote scorching letters of general advice to the newspapers; with arms like a windmill he confronted mothers who allowed their children to drop potato chips on the sidewalk; he kept a bucket of accumulated urine to throw on dog walkers who were unwary enough to linger with their squatting beasts beneath his window. He had been institutionalized several times.

That night Lillian informed her aunt that Vladimir was brilliant but unsound.

The old woman raised an eyebrow at this.

"For instance," Lillian pursued, "he is actually known to have struck someone down."

"Why?" Her aunt's voice was clear and melodious, with a faint ring of iron.

"It was during a conversation about Wagner. Apparently he disapproves of Wagner."

Her aunt gave a nod of endorsement.

"The man has even had himself committed, Aunt. Several times, when he felt he was getting out of hand."

The old woman pondered this. "It shows foresight," she said at length, "and a sense of social responsibility."

Lillian was silent for a moment. Then she pointed out: "He said unspeakable things here."

"They are mutually exclusive terms."

"Let us call them obscenities, then. You may not have caught them."

The old woman rose from her chair and arranged the long skirt of her dove gray ensemble. "Lillian, one must know when to turn a deaf ear."

"I am apparently not in the know," Lillian said dryly.

"Perhaps it is an instinct." And suddenly she gave her unique smile, which was quite yellow (for she retained her own ancient teeth) but completely beguiling, and added: "In any case, he is of my own generation, Lillian. That counts for a great deal."

"He can't be more than sixty, Aunt."

"It is close enough. Anyway, he is quite wrinkled. Also, he is a man of integrity."

"How can you possibly know that?"

"It is my instinct." And gently touching her niece's cheek, she said good night and went to her room, which peacefully overlooked the back garden, away from the street noises.

Undressing in her own smaller room, Lillian reflected, not for the first time, that though it was Bedelia who had remained unwed— Lillian herself having been married and widowed during the war— it was she, Lillian, who felt more the old maid, who seemed more dated, in a stale, fusty way, with her tight 1950s hairdo, her plain wool suits and practical support stockings . . . but then, she led a practical life . . . it was she who was trampled in the bus queue and who sat down to a hectic switchboard, who swept the increasingly filthy sidewalk and dealt with the sullen butcher and careless paper boy—or tried to . . . it seemed she was a middlewoman, a hybrid, too worldly to partake of Aunt's immense calm, too seclusive to sharpen herself on the changing ways . . . Aunt had sealed herself off in a lofty, gracious world; she lived for it, and would have died for it if it came to that . . . but what could she, Lillian, die for? . . . she fitted in nowhere, she thought, climbing into bed, and thirty years from now she would not have aged into the rare creature Aunt was—last survivor of a fair, legendary breed, her own crimped hairdo as original as the Edwardian pouf, her boxy suits as awesome as the floor-sweeping gowns—no, she would just be a peculiar old leftover in a room somewhere. For Aunt was *grande dame,* bluestocking, and virgin in one, and they didn't make that kind anymore; they didn't make those eyes anymore, large, hooded, a deep, glowing violet. It was a hue that had passed . . . And she closed her own eyes, of candid, serviceable gray, said the Lord's Prayer, and prepared to act as buffer between her elite relative and the foulmouthed old refugee.

Aunt Bedelia prepared the dinner herself, taking great pains; then she creaked into her wet garden with an umbrella and picked her finest blooms for a centerpiece; and finally, over the knobbed, arthritic joint of her ring finger, she twisted a magnificent amethyst usually reserved for Christmas, Easter, and Bach's birthday. These touches Lillian expected to be lost on their wild-eyed guest, but Vladimir kissed the festive hand with a cavalier click of his sandals, acknowledged the flowers with a noisy inhalation of his large hairy nostrils, and ate his food with admirable, if strained, refinement. During coffee he capsized his cup, but this was only because he and Bedelia were flying from Bavarian spas and Italian sea resorts to music theory, Turgenev, and God knew what else—Lillian could hardly follow—and then, urged by Aunt, he jumped from the table, rolled up the sleeves of his coveralls, and flung himself into Bach, while

Aunt, her fingers stiffly moving up and down on her knee, threw back her head and entered some region of flawless joy. At eleven o'clock Vladimir wrestled into his red lumber jacket, expressed his delight with the evening, and slapped down the steps to his infirm 1938 Buick. Not one vulgar word had escaped his lips all evening.

Nor in the seven following years of his friendship with Bedelia was this precedent ever broken. Even the night when some drunk sent an empty pint of muscatel crashing through the window, Vladimir's respect for his hostess was so great that all scurrility was plucked from his wrath. However, when he and Lillian happened to be alone together he slipped right back into the belching, offensive mannerisms for which he was known. She did not mention this to her aunt, who cherished the idea that he was very fond of Lillian.

"You know how he detests opera," the old lady would assure her, "and yet he has never alluded to the fact that you work at the Opera House and hold the form in esteem."

"A magnanimous gesture," Lillian smiled.

"For Vladimir, yes."

And after a moment's thought, Lillian had to agree. Her aunt apparently understood Vladimir perfectly, and he her. She wondered if this insight was due to their shared social origins, their bond of elevated interests, or their more baroque twinhood of eccentricity. Whatever it was, the couple thrived, sometimes sitting up till midnight with their sherry and sheet music, sometimes, when the Buick was well, motoring (Bedelia's term) into the countryside and then winding homeward along the darkening sea, in a union of perfect silence, as the old lady put it.

Bedelia died suddenly, with aplomb, under Toscanini's direction. Beethoven's Ninth was on the phonograph; the chorus had just scaled the great peak before its heart-bursting cascade into the finale; Aunt threw her head back to savor the moment, and was gone.

The next morning Lillian called Vladimir. He shrieked, he wept, he banged the receiver on the table; and for ten days, helpless and broken, he spent every evening at the home of his departed love while Lillian, herself desolated, tried to soothe him. She felt certain he would never regain the strength to insult his clients again, much less strike anyone to the ground, but gradually he mended, and the coarseness, the irascibility flooded back, much worse than in the past.

For Bedelia's sake—of that Lillian was sure—he forced himself to take an interest in her welfare, which he would express in eruptions of advice whenever he telephoned. "You want to lead a decent life, Lillian, you give them hell! They sell you a bad cut of meat, throw it in the butcher's face! You get short-changed, make a stink! You're too soft! Give them the finger, Lillian!"

"Yes, of course," she would murmur.

"For your aunt I was a gentleman, but now she's gone, who appreciates? A gentleman is a fool, a gentleman's balls are cut off! I know how to take care of myself, I am in an armored tank! And you should be, too. Or find a protector. Get married!"

"Pardon?" she asked.

"Marry!"

"I have no desire to marry, Vladimir."

"Desire! Desire! It's a world for your desires? Think of your scalp! You need a protector, now Bedelia's gone!"

"Aunt was not my protector," she said patiently.

"Of course she was! And mine too!"

Lillian shifted her weight from one foot to the other and hoped he would soon run down.

"You want to get off the phone, don't you? Why don't you say, 'Vladimir, get the shit off the phone, I'm busy!'? Don't be a doormat! Practice on me or you'll come to grief! What about that sow upstairs, have you given her hell yet? No, no, of course not! Jesus bleeding Christ, I give up!" And he slammed the receiver down.

Lillian had in fact complained. Allowing her new neighbor time to settle in, she had at first endured—through apparently rugless floorboards—the girl's music, her doorslams, her crashing footfall which was a strange combination of scurry and thud, her deep hollow brays of laughter and shrieks of "You're *kid*ding!" and "Fan*tas*tic!"— all this usually accompanied by a masculine voice and tread (varying from night to night, Lillian could not help but notice)—until finally, in the small hours, directly above Bedelia's room where Lillian now slept, ears stuffed with cotton, the night was crowned by a wild creaking of bedsprings and the racketing of the headboard against the wall. At last, chancing to meet her tormentor on the front steps (she was not the Amazon her noise indicated, but a small, thin creature nervously chewing gum with staccato snaps), Lillian decided to speak; but before she could, the girl cried, "Hi! I'm Jody—from upstairs?" with a quick, radiant smile that heartened the older woman in a way that the hair and hemline did not. Clad in a tiny childish dress that barely reached her hip sockets, she might have been a prematurely worn twenty or an adolescent thirty—dark circles hung beneath the eyes and a deep line was etched between them, but the mouth was babyish, sweet, and the cheeks a glowing pink against the unfortunate mane of brassy hair, dark along its uneven part.

Having responded with her own name (the formal first *and* last), Lillian paused a courteous moment, then began: "I'm glad to have this opportunity of meeting you; I've lived in this flat for twenty-four years, you see . . ." But the eyes opposite, heavily outlined with blue pencil, were already wandering under this gratuitous information. Brevity was clearly the password. "The point is—" restoring attention, "I would appreciate it if you turned down your music after ten P.M. There is a ruling."

"It bugs you?" the girl asked, beginning to dig turbulently through a fringed bag, her gum snaps accelerating with the search.

"Well, it's an old building, and of course, if you don't have carpets . . ." She waited to be corroborated in this assumption, but now the girl pulled out her house key with fingers whose nails, bitten to the quick, were painted jet black. Fascinated, Lillian tried not to stare.

"Not to worry," the girl assured her with the brief, brilliant smile, plunging the key into the door and bounding inside, "I'll cool it."

"There's something else, I'm afraid. When that door is slammed—"

But the finely arched brows rose with preoccupation; the phone was ringing down from the top of the stairs. "I dig, I dig. Look, hon, my phone's ringing." And closing the door softly, she thundered up the stairs.

After that the phonograph was lowered a little before midnight, but nothing else changed. Lillian finally called the landlord, a paunchy, sweating man whom she rarely saw, and though she subsequently observed him disappearing into his unruly tenant's flat several evenings a week, the visits were apparently useless. And every time she met the girl she was greeted with an insufferable "Hi! Have a nice day!"

Unfortunately Lillian had shared some of her vexation with Vladimir, and whenever he dropped by—less to see her, she knew, than to replenish his memories of Bedelia—his wrath grew terrible under the commotion. On his last visit his behavior had frightened her. "Shut up!" he had screamed, shaking his fist at the ceiling. "Shut up, bitch! Whore!"

"Vladimir, please—this language, just because Bedelia's not here."

"Ah, Bedelia, Bedelia," he groaned.

"She wouldn't have tolerated it."

"She wouldn't have tolerated *that!* Hear the laugh—hee-haw, hee-haw! Braying ass! Bedelia would have pulverized her with a glance! None of this farting around you go in for!" His large head had suffused with red; his hands were shaking at his sides. "Your aunt was a genius at judging people—they should have lined up the whole fucking rotten city for her to judge!"

"It seems to me that you have always appointed yourself as judge," Lillian said, forcing a smile.

"Yah, but Vladimir is demented, you don't forget? He has it down in black and white! Ah, you think I'm unique, Lillian, but I am one of the many! I am in the swim!" He came over to her side and put his flushed head close, his small, intense eyes piercing hers. "You read yesterday about the girl they found in an alley not far from here, cut to small bits? Slash! Rip! *Finito!* And you ask why? Because the world, it is demented! A murder of such blood not even in the headlines and you ask why? Because it is commonplace! Who walks safe on his own street? It is why you need a husband!"

Lillian dropped her eyes, wondering for an embarrassed moment if Vladimir of all people could possibly be hinting at a marital alliance. Suddenly silent, he pulled a wadded handkerchief from his pocket with trembling fingers and wiped his brow. He flicked her a suspicious glance. "Don't look so coy. I'm not in the running. I loathe women—sticky! Full of rubbishy talk!" And once more he threw his head back and began bellowing obscenities at the ceiling.

"It's too much, Vladimir—please! You're not yourself!"

"I *am* myself!"

"Well then, I'm not. I'm tired. I have a splitting headache—"

"You want me to go! Be rude, good! I have better things to do, anyway!" And his face still aflame, he struggled into his lumber jacket and flung out the door.

That night her sleep was disturbed not only by the noise, but by her worry over the violence of Vladimir's emotions. At work the next day she reluctantly inquired about her friend, whose antics were usually circulated around the staff but seldom reached her cubicle. For the first time in years, she learned, the weird little Russian had gone right over the edge, flapping newspapers in strangers' faces and ranting about the end of civilization; storming out on tuning jobs and leaving his tools behind, then furiously accusing his clients of stealing them. The opinion was that if he did not commit himself soon, someone else would do it for him.

On the clamorous bus home that night, shoved as usual into the rear, Lillian felt an overwhelming need for Bedelia, for the sound of that clear, well-modulated voice that had always set the world to rights. But she opened her door on silence. She removed her raincoat and sat down in the living room with the damp newspaper. People at work told her she should buy a television set, such a good companion when you lived alone, but she had too long scorned that philistine invention to change now. For that matter, she seldom turned on the radio, and even the newspaper—she ran her eyes over the soggy turmoil of the front page—even the newspaper distressed her. Vladimir was extreme, but he was right: everything was coming apart. Sitting there, she thought she could hear the world's madness—its rudeness, its litter, its murders—beat against the house with the rain. And suddenly she closed her eyes under an intolerable longing for the past: for the peaceful years she had spent in these rooms with Bedelia; and before that, for the face of her young husband, thirty years gone now; and for even earlier days . . . odd, but it never seemed to rain in her youth, the green campus filled the air with dizzying sweetness, she remembered running across the lawns for no reason but that she was twenty and the sun would shine forever . . .

She gave way to two large tears. Shaken, yet somehow consoled, and at the same time ashamed of her self-indulgence, she went into the kitchen to make dinner. But as she cooked her chop she knew that even this small measure of comfort would be destroyed as soon as her neighbor came banging through the door. Already her neck was tightening against the sound.

But there was no noise at all that night, not until 1:00 A.M., when the steady ring of the telephone pulled her groggily from bed.

"Listen, you'll kill me—it's Jody; I'm across the bay, and I just flashed on maybe I left the stove burners going."

"Who?" Lillian said, rubbing her eyes. "Jody? How did you get my number?"

"The phone book, why? Listen, the whole dump could catch fire, be a doll and check it out? The back door's unlocked."

Lillian felt a strange little rush of gratitude—that her name, given to such seemingly indifferent ears on the steps that day, had been remembered. Then the feeling was replaced by anger; but before she could speak, the girl said, "Listen, hon, thanks a million," and hung up.

Clutching her raincoat around her shoulders, beaming a flashlight before her, Lillian nervously climbed the dark back stairs to her neighbor's door and let herself into the kitchen. Turning on the light, she stood aghast at what she saw: not flames licking the wall, for the burners were off, but grimed linoleum, spilled garbage, a sink of stagnant water. On the puddled table, decorated with a jar of blackened, long-dead daisies, sat a greasy portable television set and a pile of dirty laundry in a litter of cigarette butts, sodden pieces of paper, and the congealed remains of spareribs. Hesitating, ashamed of her snoopiness, she peered down at the pieces of paper: bills from department stores, including Saks and Magnin's; scattered food stamps; handwritten notes on binder paper, one of which read

"Jamie hony theres a piza in the frezzer I love U"—then several big hearts—"Jody." A long brown bug—a cockroach?—was crawling across the note, and now she noticed another one climbing over a sparerib. As she stood cringing, she heard rain blowing through an open window somewhere, lashing a shade into frenzies. Going to the bedroom door, which stood ajar, she beamed her flashlight in and switched on the light. Under the window a large puddle was forming on the floor, which was rugless, as she had suspected, though half carpeted by strewn clothes. The room was furnished only with a bed whose convulsed gray sheets put her in mind of a pesthouse, and a deluxe television set in a rosewood cabinet; but the built-in bookcase was well stocked, and having shut the window, she ran her eyes over the spines, curious. Many were cheap paperback thrillers, but there was an abundance of great authors: Dostoevsky, Dickens, Balzac, Melville. It was odd, she puzzled, that the girl had this taste in literature, yet could not spell the simplest word and had never heard of a comma. As she turned away, her eardrums were shattered by her own scream. A man stood in the doorway.

A boy, actually, she realized through her fright; one of Jody's more outstanding visitors, always dressed in one of those Mexican shawl affairs and a battered derby hat, from under which butter-yellow locks flowed in profusion, everything at the moment dripping with rain. More embarrassed now than frightened—she had never screamed in her life, or stood before a stranger in her nightgown, and neither had Bedelia—she began pulsating with dignity. "I didn't hear anyone come up the stairs," she indicted him.

"Little cat feet, man," he said with a cavernous yawn. "Where's Jody? Who're you?"

She explained her presence, pulling the raincoat more firmly together across her bosom, but unable to do anything about the expanse of flowered flannel below.

"Jody, she'd forget her ass if it wasn't screwed on," the boy said with a second yawn. His eyes were watery and red, and his nose ran.

"If you'll excuse me," she said, going past him.

He followed her back into the kitchen, and suddenly, with a host-like warmth that greatly surprised her, he asked, "You want some coffee?"

She declined, saying that she must be going.

At this he heaved a deep, disappointed sigh, which again surprised her, and sank like an invalid into a chair. He was a slight youth with neat little features crowded into the center of his face, giving him, despite his woebegone expression, a pert, fledgling look. In Lillian's day he would have been called a "pretty boy." He would not have been her type at all; she had always preferred the lean profile.

"My name's Jamie," he announced suddenly, with a childlike spontaneity beneath the film of languor; and he proffered his hand.

Gingerly she shook the cold small fingers.

"Hey really," he entreated, "stay and rap awhile."

"Rap?"

"Talk, man. Talk to me." And he looked, all at once, so lonely, so forlorn, that even though she was very tired, she felt she must stay a moment longer. Pulling out a chair, she took a temporary, edge-of-the-seat position across the hideous table from him.

He seemed to be gathering his thoughts together. "So what's your bag?" he asked.

She looked at him hopelessly. "My bag?"

"You a housewife? You work?"

"Oh—yes, I work," she said, offended by his bold curiosity, yet grateful against her will to have inspired it.

"What's your name?" he asked.

He was speaking to her as a contemporary; and again, she was both pleased by this and offended by his lack of deference. "Lillian Cronin," she said uncertainly.

"I'm Jamie," he sighed.

"So you mentioned." And she thought—Jamie, Jody, the kinds of names you would give pet rabbits. Where were the solid, straightforward names of yesteryear—the Georges and Harolds, the Dorothys and Margarets? What did she have to say to a Jamie in a Mexican shawl and threadbare derby who was now scratching himself all over with little fidgety movements? But she said, breaking the long silence, which he seemed not to notice: "And what is *your* bag, if I may ask?"

He took several moments to answer. "I don't know, man . . . I'm a student of human nature."

"Oh? And where do you study?"

"Not me, man, that's Jody's scene . . . into yoga, alpha waves, the whole bit . . . even studies macramé and world lit. at jay cee . . ."

"Indeed? How interesting. I noticed her books."

"She's a towering intellect," he yawned, his eyes glassy with fatigue. He was scratching himself more slowly now.

"And does she work, as well?" Lillian asked, once more ashamed of her nosiness.

"Work?" he smiled. "Maybe you could call it that . . ." But his attention was drifting away like smoke. Fumbling with a breadknife, he picked it up and languidly speared a cockroach with the point. Then, with the side of the knife, he slowly, methodically, squashed the other one.

Averting her eyes from the massacre, Lillian leaned forward. "I don't mean to sound familiar, but you seem a quiet person. Do you think you might ask Jody to be a little less noisy up here? I've spoken to the landlord, but—" She saw the boy smile again, an odd, rueful smile that made her feel, for some reason, much younger than he. "You see—" she continued, but he was fading from her presence, slowly mashing his bugs to pulp and now dropping the knife to reach over and click on the food-spattered television set. Slouched, his eyes bored by what the screen offered, he nevertheless began following an old movie. The conversation appeared to be over.

Lillian rose. She was not accustomed, nor would Bedelia have been, to a chat ending without some mutual amenity. She felt awkward, dismissed. With a cool nod she left him and descended the splashing stairs to her own flat. Such a contrast the youth was of warmth and rudeness . . . and Jody, an illiterate studying Dostoevsky at college . . . food stamps lying hugger-mugger with bills from Saks . . . it was impossible to bring it all into focus; she felt rudder-

less, malfunctioning . . . how peculiar life had become . . . everything mixed up . . . a generation of fragments . . .

Climbing heavily back into bed, she wondered what Bedelia's
reaction would have been to Jody and Jamie. And she remembered
how unkempt and disconcerting Vladimir had been, yet how her
aunt had quickly penetrated to the valuable core while she, Lillian,
fussed on about his bad language. No doubt Bedelia would have
been scandalized by the filth upstairs, but she would not have been
so narrow-souled as to find fault with spelling mistakes, first names,
taste in clothing . . . Bedelia might not have pulverized Jody with
a glance, as Vladimir suggested, but instead seen some delicate trag-
edy in the worn cherubic features, or been charmed by the girl's
invincible buoyancy . . . it was hard to tell with Bedelia which
facet she might consider the significant one . . . she often surprised
you . . . it had to do with largeness of spirit . . .

Whereas she, Lillian, had always to guard against stuffiness . . .
Still, she tried to hold high the torch of goodwill . . . too pompous
a simile, of course, but she knew clearly and deeply what she meant
. . . so *let* Vladimir rave on at her for refusing to shrink into a
knot of hostility; what was Vladimir, after all? Insane. Her eyes
opened in the dark as she faced what she had tried to avoid all
day: that Vladimir had been wrenched off the tracks by Bedelia's
death, and that this time he felt no need to commit himself. Without
question it was Lillian's duty to enlighten him. But she winced at
the thought . . . such a terrible thing to have to tell someone . . .
if only she could turn to Bedelia . . . how sorely she missed her
. . . how sorely she missed George's lean young face under his
army cap . . . youth . . . sunlight . . . outside the rain still fell
. . . she had only herself, and the dark, unending rain . . .

"Stop this brooding," she said aloud; if she had only herself,
she had better be decent company. And closing her eyes, she tried
to sleep. But not until a gray, watery dawn was breaking did she
drop off.

The Opera House telephoned at three minutes past nine. Leaden,
taut-nerved, sourly questioning the rewards of her long, exquisite
punctuality, she pulled on her clothes and, with burning eyes and

empty stomach, hurried out of the house. At work, though the board was busy, the hours moved with monumental torpor. She felt increasingly unlike herself, hotly brimming over with impatience for all this switchboard blather: calls from New York, Milan; Sutherland with her sore throat, Pavarotti with his tight schedule—did they really think if another *Rigoletto* were never given that anyone would notice? She felt an urge to slur this fact into the headphone, as befitted a truant traipsing in at a quarter to ten, as befitted someone with minimally combed hair and crooked seams and, even worse, with the same underwear on that she had worn the day before. As if a slatternly, cynical Lillian whom she didn't recognize had squeezed slyly into prominence, a Lillian who half considered walking out on the whole tiresome business and indulging in a lavish two-hour lunch downtown—let someone else serve, let someone else be polite.

Sandwiched into the bus aisle that night, she almost smacked an old gentleman who crunched her right instep under his groping heel; and as she creaked into the house with her wet newspaper and saw that a motorcyclist had been picked off on the freeway by a sniper, she had to fight down a lipcurl of satisfaction. Then, reflectively, still in her raincoat, she walked to the end of the hall where an oval mirror hung, and studied her face. It was haggard, flinty, stripped of faith, scraped down to the cold, atavistic bones of retaliation. She had almost walked off her job, almost struck an old man, almost smiled at murder. A feeling of panic shot through her; what were values if they could collapse at the touch of a sleepless night? And she sank the terrible face into her hands, but a ray of rational thought lifted it again. "Almost." Never mind the querulous inner tremble; at each decisive moment her principles had stood fast. Wasn't a person entitled to an occasional fit of petulance? There is such a thing as perspective, she told herself, and in the meantime a great lust for steam and soap had spread through her. She would scrub out the day in a hot bath and in perfect silence, for apparently Jody had not yet returned from across the bay. God willing, the creature would remain away a week.

Afterward, boiled pink, wrapped in her quilted robe, she felt restored to grace. A fine appetite raced through her, along with visions of a tuna casserole, which she hurried into the kitchen to prepare, hurrying out again at the summons of the telephone. It was Vladimir, very excited, wanting to drop by. Her first response was one of blushing discomfort: entertain Vladimir in her quilted bathrobe? Her second she articulated: she was bone-tired; she was going to bed right after dinner. But even as she spoke she heard the remorseless doorslam of Jody's return, and a violent spasm twisted her features. "Please—next week," she told Vladimir, and hung up, clutching her head as tears of rage and exhaustion burst from her eyes. Weeping, she made a tuna sandwich, chewed it without heart, and sank onto her unmade bed. The next morning, still exhausted, she made an emergency appointment with her doctor, and came home that night with a bottle of sleeping pills.

By the end of the week she was sick with artificial sleep, there was an ugly rubber taste in her mouth, her eye sockets felt caked with rust. And it was not only the noise and pills that plagued her: a second neighborhood woman had been slashed to death by the rainman (the newspapers, in their cozy fashion, had thus baptized the slayer). She had taken to beaming her flashlight under the bed before saying the Lord's Prayer; her medicinal sleep crackled with surreal visions; at the sullen butcher's her eyes were morbidly drawn to the meat cleaver; and at work not only had she upset coffee all over her lap, but she had disconnected Rudolf Bing himself in the middle of a sentence.

And never any respite from above. She had called the landlord again, without audible results, and informed the Board of Health about the cockroaches, its reply being that it had no jurisdiction over cockroaches. She had stuck several notes under Jody's door pleading with her to quiet down, and had stopped her twice on the steps, receiving the first time some capricious remark, and the second a sigh of "Christ, Lilly, I'm trying. What d'you want?" Lilly! The gall! But she was gratified to see that the gum-snapping face was almost as sallow as her own, the circles under the eyes darker than ever, new lines around the mouth. So youth could crumble, too. Good! Perhaps the girl's insanely late hours were boomeranging,

44

and would soon smash her down in a heap of deathlike stillness (would that Lillian could implement this vision). Or perhaps it was her affair with Jamie that was running her ragged. Ah, the costly trauma of love! Jealousy, misunderstanding—so damaging to the poor nervous system! Or so she had heard . . . she and George had been blessed with rapport . . . but try not to dwell on the past . . . yes, possibly it was Jamie who was lining the girl's face . . . Lillian had seen him a few times since their first meeting, once on the steps—he smiled, was pleasant, remembered her, but had not remembered to zip his fly, and she had hurried on, embarrassed— and twice in the back garden, where on the less drenching days she tended Bedelia's flowers, but without her aunt's emerald green thumb . . . a rare sunny afternoon, she had been breaking off gerani- ums; Jody and Jamie lay on the grass in skimpy bathing suits, their thin bodies white, somehow poignant in their delicacy . . . she felt like a great stuffed mattress in her sleeveless dress, soiled hands masculine with age, a stevedore's drop of sweat hanging from her nose . . . could they imagine her once young and tender on her own bed of love? Or now, with a man friend? As if everything closed down at fifty-seven, like a bankrupt hotel!—tearing off the head of a geranium—brash presumption of youth! But she saw that they weren't even aware of her, no, they were kissing and rolling about . . . in Bedelia's garden! "Here, what are you doing!" she cried, but in the space of a moment a hostile little flurry had taken place, and now they broke away and lay separately in charged si- lence, still taking no notice of her as she stood there, heart thumping, fist clenched. She might have been air. Suddenly, sick from the heat, she had plodded inside.

The next time she saw Jamie in the garden was this afternoon, when, arriving home from work and changing into a fresh dress for Vladimir's visit, she happened to glance out her bedroom win- dow. Rain sifted down, but the boy was standing still, a melancholy sight, wrapped in a theatrical black cloak, the derby and Mexican shawl apparently having outlived their effectiveness as eye-catchers . . . youth's eternal and imbecile need to shock . . . Jody with her ebony fingernails and silly prepubescent hemlines; and this little would-be Dracula with his golden sausage curls, tragically posed in the fragile mist, though she noticed his hands were untragically busy under the cloak, scratching as usual . . . or . . . the thought was so monstrous that she clutched the curtain . . . he could not be standing in the garden abusing himself; she must be deranged, suffering prurient delusions—she, Lillian Cronin, a decent, clean-minded woman . . . ah, God, what was happening, what was happening? It was her raw nerves, her drugged and hanging head, the perpetual din . . . even as she stood there her persecutor was trying on clothes, dropping shoes, pounding from closet to mirror (for Lillian could by now divine the activity behind each noise) while simultaneously braying into the telephone receiver stuck between chin and shoulder, and sketchily attending the deluxe television set, which blared an hysterical melodrama . . .

Outside, she saw the youth sink onto a tree stump, from which he cast the upstairs window a long, bleak look . . . they must have had a lovers' quarrel, and the girl had shut him out; now he brooded in the rain, an exile; or rather a kicked puppy, shivering and staring up with ponderous woe . . . then, eyes dropping, he caught sight of Lillian, and a broad, sunny, candid smile flashed from the dismal countenance . . . odd, jarring, she thought, giving a polite nod and dropping the curtain, especially after his rude imperviousness that hot day on the grass . . . a generation of fragments, she had said so before, though God knew she never objected to a smile (with the exception of Jody's grimace) . . . and walking down the hall away from the noise, she was stopped woodenly by the sound of the girl's doorbell. It was one of the gentlemen callers, who tore up the stairs booming felicitations which were returned with the inevitable shrieks, this commingled din moving into the front room and turning Lillian around in her tracks. With the door closed, the kitchen was comparatively bearable, and it was time to eat anyway. She bought television dinners now, lacking the vigor to cook. She had lost seven pounds, but was not growing svelte, only drawn. Even to turn on the waiting oven was a chore. But slowly she got herself into motion, and at length, pouring out a glass of burgundy to brace herself for Vladimir's visit, she sat down to the steaming, neatly sectioned pap. Afterward, dutifully washing her glass and fork at the sink, she glanced out the window into the rain, falling in sheets now; the garden was dark, and she could not be sure, but she thought she saw the youth still sitting on the stump. It was beyond her, why anyone would sit still in a downpour . . . but everything was beyond her, insurmountable . . . and soon Vladimir would arrive . . . the thought was more than she could bear, but she could not defer him again, it would be too rude . . .

He burst in like a cannonball, tearing off his wet lumber jacket, an acrid smell of sweat blooming from his armpits; his jaws were stubbled with white, great bushes sprouted from his nostrils.

"You look terrible!" he roared.

Even though she had at the last moment rubbed lipstick into her pallid cheeks. She gave a deflated nod and gestured toward the relatively quiet kitchen, but he wanted the Bedelia-redolent front room, where he rushed over to the Steinway and lovingly dashed off an arpeggio, only to stagger back with his finger knifed up at the ceiling. "Still the chaos!" he cried.

"Please—" she said raggedly. "No advice, I beg of you."

"No advice? Into your grave they'll drive you, Lillian!" And she watched his finger drop, compassionately it seemed, to point at her poor slumped bosom with its heart beating so wearily inside. It was a small hand, yet blunt, virile, its back covered with coarse dark hair . . . what if it reached farther, touched her? . . . But, spittle already flying, Vladimir was plunging into a maelstrom of words, obviously saved up for a week. "I wanted to come sooner, why didn't you let me? Look at you, a wreck! Vladimir knew a second one would be cut—he smells blood on the wind! He wants to come and pound on your door, to be with you, but no, he respects your wish for privacy, so he sits every night out front in his auto, watching!" Here he broke off to wipe his lips, while Lillian, pressing hard the swollen, rusty lids of her eyes, accepted the immense duty of guiding him to confinement. "And every night," he roared on, "while Vladimir sits, Bedelia plays *Komm, Jesu, Komm*, it floats into the street, it is beautiful, beautiful—"

47

"Ah, Vladimir," broke pityingly from her lips.

Silence. With a clap of restored lucidity his fist struck his forehead. It remained tightly glued there for some time. When it fell away he seemed quite composed.

"I have always regretted," he said crisply, "that you resemble the wrong side of your family. All you have of Bedelia is a most vague hint of her cheekbones." Which he was scrutinizing with his small, glittering eyes. Again, nervously, she sensed that he would touch her; but instead, a look of revulsion passed over his features as he stared first at one cheek, then the other. "You've got fucking gunk on! Rouge!"

With effort, she produced a neutral tone. "I'm not used to being stared at, Vladimir."

"Hah, I should think not," he snapped abstractedly, eyes still riveted.

Beast! Vile wretch! But at once she was shamed by her viciousness. From where inside her did it come? And she remembered that terrible day at work when a malign and foreign Lillian had pressed into ascendancy, almost as frightening a character change as the one she was seeing before her now, for Vladimir's peering eyes seemed actually black with hatred. "Stinking whore-rouge," he breathed; then with real pain, he cried, "Have you no thought for Bedelia? You have the blessing of her cheekbones! Respect them! Don't drag them through the gutter! My God, Lillian! My God!"

She said nothing. It seemed the only thing to do.

But now he burst forth again, cheerfully, rubbing his hands together. "Listen to Vladimir. You want a husband, forget the war paint, use what you have. Some intelligence. A good bearing— straighten the shoulders—and cooking talent. Not like Bedelia's, but not bad. Now, Vladimir has been looking around for you—"

"Vladimir," she said through her teeth.

"—and he has found a strong, healthy widower of fifty-two years, a great enjoyer of the opera. He has been advised of your virtues—"

"Vladimir!"

"Of course, you understand Vladimir himself is out, Vladimir is

48

a monolith—" A particularly loud thump shuddered the ceiling, and he jumped back, yelling, "Shove it, you swine! Lice!"

"Vladimir, I do not want a man!" Lillian snapped.

"Not so! I sense sex boiling around in you!"

Her lips parted; blood rushed into her cheeks to darken the artificial blush. For certain, with that short potent word, "sex," his hands would leap on her.

"But you look a thousand years old," he went on. "It hangs in folds, your face. You must get rid of this madhouse upstairs! What have you done so far—not even told the landlord!"

"I *have!*" she cried; and suddenly the thought of confiding in someone loosened a stinging flood of tears from her eyes, and she sank into a chair. "He has come to speak to her . . . time and time again . . . he seems always to be there . . . but nothing changes . . ."

"Ah, so," said Vladimir, pulling out his gray handkerchief and handing it to her, "the sow screws him."

She grimaced both at the words and the reprehensible cloth, with which she nevertheless dabbed her eyes. "I don't believe that," she said nasally.

"Why not? She's a prostitute. Only to look at her."

"You've seen her?" she asked, slowly raising her eyes. But of course, if he sat outside in his car every night . . .

"I have seen her," he said, revulsion hardening his eyes. "I have seen much. Even a batman with the face of a sorrowful Kewpie doll. He pines this minute on the front steps."

"That's her boyfriend," Lillian murmured, increasingly chilled by the thought of Vladimir sitting outside all night, spying.

"Boyfriend! A hundred boyfriends she has, each with a roll of bills in his pocket!"

Tensely she smoothed the hair at her temples. "Forgive me, Vladimir," she said gently, "but you exaggerate. You exaggerate everything, I'm afraid. I must point this out to you, because I think it does you no good. I really—"

"Don't change the subject! We're talking about her, upstairs!"

She was silent for a moment. "The girl is—too free, I suppose, in our eyes. But I'm certain that she isn't what you call her."

"And how do you come to this idiot conclusion?" he asked scornfully.

She lifted her hands in explanation, but they hung helplessly suspended. "Well," she said at last, "I know she reads Dostoevsky . . . she takes courses . . . and she cares for that boy in the cape, even if they do have their quarrels . . . and there's a quality of anguish in her face . . ."

"Anguish! I call it the knocked-out look of a female cretin who uses her ass every night to pay the rent. And that pea-brain boyfriend outside, in his secondhand ghoul costume to show how interesting he is! Probably he pops pills and lives off his washerwoman mother if he hasn't slit her throat in a fit of irritation! It's the type, Lillian! Weak, no vision, no guts! The sewers are vomiting them up by the thousands to mix with us! They surround us! Slop! Shit! Chaos! Listen to that up there! Hee-haw! Call that anguish? Even pleasure? No, I tell you what it is! Empty, hollow noise—like a wheel spun into motion and never stopped again! It's madness! The madness of our times!"

But as he whipped himself on, Lillian felt herself growing diametrically clear and calm, as if the outburst were guiding her blurred character back into focus. When he stopped, she said firmly, "Yes, I understand what you mean about the wheel spinning. There is something pointless about them, something pitiful. But they're not from a sewer. They're people, Vladimir, human beings like ourselves . . ."

"Ah, blanket democracy! What else would you practice but that piss-fart abomination?"

"I practice what Bedelia herself practiced," she replied tartly.

"Ah," he sighed. "The difference between instinct and application. Between a state of grace and a condition of effort. Dear friend Lillian, tolerance is dangerous without insight. And the last generation with insight has passed, with the things it understood. Like the last generation of cobblers and glass stainers. It is fatal to try to carry on a dead art—the world has no use for it! The world will trample you down! Don't think of the past, think of your scalp!"

"No," she stated, rising and swaying with the light-headedness that so frequently visited her now. "To live each moment as if you were in danger—it's demeaning. I will not creep around snarling like some four-legged beast. I am a civilized human being. Your attitude shows a lack of proportion, Vladimir; I feel that you really—"

A flash of sinewy hands; her wrists were seized and crushed together with a stab of pain through whose shock she felt a marginal heat of embarrassment, a tingling dismay of abrupt intimacy. Then the very center of her skull was pierced by his shriek. "You *are* in danger! Can't you *see!*" and he thrust his face at hers, disclosing the red veins of his eyes, bits of sleep matted in the lashes, and the immobile, overwhelmed look of someone who has seen the abyss and is seeing it again. Her heart gave the chop of an ax; with a wail she strained back.

His fixed look broke; his eyes grew flaring, kinetic. "One minute the blood is nice and cozy in its veins—the next, slice! And slice! And slice! Red fountains go up—a festival! Worthy of Handel! Oh, marvelous, marvelous! The rainman—" Here he broke off to renew his grip as she struggled frantically to pull away. "The rainman, he's in ecstasies! Such founts and spouts, such excitement! Then at last it's all played out, nothing but puddles, and off he trots, he's big success! And it's big city—many many fountains to be had, all red as—as—red as—"

Her laboring wrists were flung aside; his hands slammed against her face and pressed fiercely into the cheeks.

"Vladimir!" she screamed. "It's Lillian—Lillian!"

The flared eyes contracted. He stepped back and stood immobile. Then a self-admonishing hand rose shakily to his face, which had gone the color of pewter. After a long moment he turned and walked out of the house.

She blundered to the door and locked it behind him, then ran heavily back into the front room, where she came to a blank stop, both hands pressed to her chest. Hearing the sound of an engine starting, she wheeled around to the window and pinched back the edge of the shade. Through the rain she saw the big square car jerk and shudder while its motor rose in a crescendo of whines and abruptly stopped. Vladimir climbed out and started back across the pavement. Her brain finally clicked: the telephone, the police.

With long strides she gained the hall where the telephone stood, and where she now heard the anticipated knock—but mild, rueful, a diminished sound that soon fell away. She moved on haltingly; she would call the police, yes—or a friend from work—or her doctor—someone, anyone, she must talk to someone, and suddenly she stumbled with a cry: it was Vladimir's lumber jacket she had tripped over, still lying on the floor where he had dropped it, his wallet sticking out from the pocket. Outside, the Buick began coughing once more; then it fell silent. A few moments later the shallow, timid knock began again. Without his wallet he could not call a garage, a taxi. It was a fifteen-block walk to his house in the rain. If only she could feel Bedelia's presence beside her, look to the expression in the intelligent eyes. Gradually, concentrating on those eyes, she felt an unclenching inside her. She gazed at the door. Behind it Vladimir was Vladimir still. He had spoken with horrifying morbidity and had even hurt her wrists and face, but he was not the rainman, Bedelia would have seen such seeds. He had been trying to warn her tonight of the world's dangers, and in his passion had set off one of his numerous obsessions—with her fingertip she touched the rouged and aching oval of her cheek. Strange, tortured soul who had stationed himself out in the cold, night after night, to keep her from harm. Bending down, she gathered up the rough, homely jacket; but the knocking had stopped. She went back into the front room and again tweaked aside the shade. He was going away, a small, decelerated figure, already drenched. Now he turned the corner and was lost from sight. Depleted, she leaned against the wall.

It might have been a long while that she stood there, that the noise from above masked the sound, but by degrees she became aware of knocking. He must have turned around in the deluge and was now, with what small hope, tapping on the door again. She hesitated, once more summoning the fine violet eyes, the tall brow under its archaic coiffure, which dipped in an affirmative nod. The jacket under her arm, Lillian went into the hall, turned on the porch light, and unlocked the door.

It was not Vladimir who stood there, but Jamie, as wet as if he had crawled from the ocean, his long curls limply clinging to the foolish cape, his neat little features stamped with despair, yet warmed, saved, by the light of greeting in his eyes. Weary, unequal to any visit, she shook her head.

"Jody?" she thought she heard him say, or more likely it was something else—the rain muffled his voice, though she caught an eerie, unnatural tone that she now sensed was reflected in the luminous stare. With a sudden feeling of panic she started to slam the door in his face. But she braked herself, knowing that she was overwrought; it was unseemly to use such brusqueness on this lost creature because of her jangled nerves.

So she paused for one haggard, courteous moment to say, "I'm sorry, Jamie, it's late—some other time." And in that moment the shrouded figure crouched, and instantaneously, spasmlike, rushed up against her. She felt a huge but painless blow, followed by a dullness, a stillness deep inside her, and staggering back as he kicked the door shut behind them, she clung to the jamb of the front room entrance and slowly sank to her knees.

She dimly comprehended the wet cloak brushing her side, but it was the room that held her attention, that filled her whole being. It had grown immense, lofty, and was suffused with violet, overwhelmingly beautiful. But even as she watched, it underwent a rapid wasting, paled to the faint, dead-leaf hue of an old tintype; and now it vanished behind a sheet of black as the knife was wrenched from her body.

Eino

It was an afternoon in early November of 1951. I was walking through France on my way to Copenhagen, and I was being rained upon viciously. Never before on the trip had I been defenseless in the lashing wrath of a rainstorm, and every time I took a step along the road my toes squeezed out a froth of bubbles through the worn blue of my tennis shoes. I had no hat, and my hair hung like a congestion of rats' tails studded with the slipping jewels of water. My coat and my blouse and pedal pushers were soaked through, and I was cold and wet to the skin. There was something humiliating in this assault by the elements, and I continued to walk because it was the only gesture of pride I could manage. In the past when it rained I had always found shelter in a doorway or under a tree, where I could set down my medicine kit, which served as my rucksack, and enjoy the smell of wet dirt or pavement and the noise of the rain until it withdrew haltingly, leaving only a handful of drops to be shaken loose from leaves and telephone-pole wires. Here there were only flat fields, some dented by old shell craters, stretching in every direction into the fluid horizon.

In the youth hostel at Verdun that morning, I had only eaten three rolls and drunk two cups of instant coffee, and now I was hungry. The medicine kit was breaking my back, and despite the cold I was sleepy, for I had been the only occupant at the hostel and had lain open-eyed most of the night in an upper bunk, my penknife in hand, imagining some fiend creeping toward me, his footsteps covered by the thunder that sounded intermittently. Now

I was walking at as rapid a pace as the kit would allow, like an office girl hurrying to Macy's for a bargain during her lunch hour, but gradually the kit, ponderous with the water it had absorbed, bent my right shoulder toward the ground and finally settled itself in the mud, puddles instantly forming on its flat, creased top. I looked at it for a moment, poured off the puddles, and sat down on it. In actual fact, it bore no resemblance to rucksack, haversack, suitcase, or overnight bag. It was a large, cumbersome, square khaki canvas affair with black numbers stenciled across the back and a canvas shoulder strap with big rusty buckles. It was clearly some sort of medical-supply kit from the war—possibly the First World War. I had found it in a dark shop at the open market in Rome, and in my greenness had paid the equivalent of seven and a half dollars for it. At that time I had a bicycle, which I intended to ride to Copenhagen, where I had relatives, and I wanted something that would fit on the back of my bike.

"It certainly smells," I had told the shopkeeper.

"Put it in the sun for one day," he said, pointing out the door at the brilliant sunshine.

So I had brought it back to the hostel in Rome where I was staying, thrown open the lid, and set it on a balcony. There was nothing inside but an aged wad of cotton, which I tossed over the railing. I left it in the sun for a day, but the smell remained. It was the smell of damp, crumbling earth, of victorious mold. I took it into the washroom and scrubbed its dark insides with a Roman cleanser and set it outside again. The next day I put my stick perfume to it in great loops until the stick was whittled down to a stump, and the following day I sprinkled it heavily with face powder. Still, it smelled of earth—of the trenches, I imagined—and from that day on my clothes gave off the aura of an ancient battlefield.

After six weeks my bicycle, which I had bought secondhand, had fallen apart in most of its departments; no one would buy it as a bicycle, so I had received a few francs for it as junk, and was left with some pleasant memories and my hateful medicine kit. I had decided then—I was at a hostel in Cannes—to continue by foot. At this, the other hostelers shook their heads and raised their eyebrows.

"It's affected and pointless," a Swedish boy said. He was traveling by motorcycle.

"You'll give up inside two days," another boy said, one of an Australian hitchhiking couple.

I felt I might have argued with eloquence if only I hadn't been burdened with that peculiar medicine kit; it ruined my morale. How readily would I have thrown it out and bought a rucksack had I the money for it. I envied the others their beflagged, bepinned sacks and thought of myself as a strange creature far removed from hostel decorum.

"When it rains you'll be sorry," the Swede said.

"No. No, I'll enjoy it," I said, and suddenly believed, since the idea was perverse, that I would. I had set out for Paris, but my resolve to walk broke down almost immediately—five miles out of Cannes—when three English girls in an old car stopped for me. We drove all the way to Paris and had a glorious time; however, during three weeks in Paris I repented, and when I left for Copenhagen it was with the firm intention of not setting foot in a vehicle before I got there.

You may well wonder why I was so determined to walk to my destination. The reason dated back almost fifteen years, when as a child I saw a movie in which there was a memorable (to me) cocktail-party scene. The camera cruised among the guests and recorded snatches of their conversation. One pretty and animated girl was saying, "Oh, yes! We had a delightful time . . . walked across France, Switzerland, Germany . . ." She had a cigarette in a holder, a brilliant smile, and was holding her cocktail glass rather unsteadily. The camera moved on, never again to rest upon her bright enthusiasm, but her words were the only ones in the picture I remembered. Thinking back, I believe she was meant to represent a tasteless frivolity dancing in the jaws of approaching war, but as a child I merely savored the names of the countries, her wonderful gaiety, a vision of flower-covered fields and glittering trees, and I realized I must one day follow suit. I had at first acceded to the idea of a bicycle, but when it came apart I was certain Fate was telling me to go by foot.

But things were not what I had envisioned. I now had a clumsy medicine kit on my back, too little money, blisters that bled. I was alone—even if I had felt gay there was no one with whom to share my gaiety—and it was, and had been for days, raining in huge, wind-billowed sheets. I sat there on my kit, feeling more ridiculous every minute. Finally, I decided that if a car approached I would make no effort to stop it, but if it stopped of its own accord I would get in. I got up stiffly and began to walk again; the storm had ceased for a while, and the rain fell evenly.

About an hour later a Volkswagen stopped a few yards ahead of me and a middle-aged man slid his head out the window. I walked up to him and he helped me put the kit in the back seat, at the same time saying a few words to me in German. I told him, in English, that I understood no German and got into the front seat, where a puddle instantly formed around my feet.

"What are you doing?" he asked in excellent English.

"Oh, I seem to be dripping all over your car."

He waved that away. "No, why are you walking here, so far from everything, in the rain?"

"Well, just walking, you know. That should be a common sight to you. Aren't the Germans great walkers?"

"Not girls, my dear."

"Times have changed," I said.

"American?" he asked, and I nodded. "And you are going where?" he continued.

"Copenhagen."

"Copenhagen!" He laughed again. "You *are* silly. But why do you not ride with me as far as Hamburg? Hamburg, the great white Phoenix of the North!"

The invitation was appealing. It had taken eight days just to walk this far from Paris, and there wasn't really much point in walking when the weather turned all the colors a uniform gray. "Today?" I asked.

"No, I am stopping over at Saarbrücken tonight. Saarbrücken, the no-man's-land between two eternal enemies!"

I consulted my hostel map. "Yes, there's a hostel in Saarbrücken where I could stay."

"Hostel?"

"Jugendherberge."

"Ah." He had just started the car along the road, but now he slowed down and looked at me with hooded, ice-cube eyes. "You must stay at my hotel."

"Oh, no, I wouldn't think of it."

"I insist. You will be my guest."

We rode in silence for a few minutes, still slowly, as though he were waiting for an answer. At last, I managed to utter the embarrassing but necessary clarification. "I hope you won't think me rude for saying this, but I hope you haven't anything like an escapade in mind."

He stopped the car. "What do you mean by 'escapade'?"

I looked at the puddle on the floor and tried to think of some casual means of explaining. At the same time my right hand crept into my coat pocket and through a great rent therein to my pedal pushers' pocket, where I carried my penknife.

"I have taken you in out of the rain," he stated professorially. "You are drenching my new upholstery. So is your pack in the back seat. Do you not think you owe me a little something?"

I shook my head worriedly.

He leaned slowly across me and flicked open my door, then sat back and lit a cigar. I got out, pulled out my kit, and, leaving the door wide open, walked away a few paces and stopped, my coat wrapped wetly around me. He slammed the door shut and drove off. I watched the car disappear, and then began walking once more in the rain.

In the next couple of hours, two cars passed me, and one slowed down, but I waved it on. It was almost dark before I decided to accept a ride. I was so cold by that time I would have ridden with anybody. And I was overcome by a loneliness of the sort that, if you have a room and a lamp, makes you unable to turn out the light and go to sleep. I had felt this loneliness a little more each day since leaving Paris. I walked on and waited. Every few minutes I felt a sudden slash of rain between my limp collar and my neck. In time, a car, black in the grayness, slowed down and stopped. It was a junk heap. The driver was a dark young man with a humorless, long, almost postlike face, dressed in a shiny suit with a crooked, stained tie. He said nothing as I put the kit on the back seat and climbed in beside him, and nothing as we drove along. With my right hand I took hold of my penknife.

At length, I asked, "How far are you going?"

He shook his head, not taking his eyes from the road.

"Français?" I asked.

"Nein."

"Deutscher."

He nodded, turning on the headlights.

I knew only a few words of German. "Saarbrücken? Kaiserslautern? Frankfurt?"

"Saarbrücken." He lit a cigarette and, rather grudgingly, offered me one. I took the cigarette with my left hand, not for a second releasing the hidden knife with my right. We drove for miles through the rain and darkness, and he said nothing. Rain seeped through the top. When we approached Saarbrücken he spoke in German, asking me, I assumed, which area I wished to be left off at.

"Jugendherberge," I said. I wanted to explain that I wasn't asking him to drive me there, that he could simply set me off near there and I would walk or take a streetcar. *"Parlez-vous Français?"* I asked.

"Nein!" Then he asked me something in German again. I caught the word *"Strasse."*

"Oh, no," I insisted. I let go of the penknife and waved my hands in a gesture of refusal, meaning that he needn't take me to the exact street. Then I made the fingers of my right hand walk along the dashboard. He grunted and pointed with his chin to the rain. At last I took my hostel book from a pocket and looked up the street address. "Kohlweg Two," I said, holding up two fingers.

The hostel was about three miles from the center of town, in a reconstructed area, a large brick building sleeping a hundred and twelve and standing in the middle of a black lawn. We drove up to the front door, and the young man jumped out, grabbed my medicine kit, and led me, running through the rain, to the shelter of the doorway. I pushed open the door, and we walked in. He

put down the kit. It was cold inside, but the lights were burning
fiercely. The warden, an elderly, bald man, sat behind a counter
in his office, and beside him was a little girl who sucked on a piece
of hard candy.

"*Guten Abend,*" he said, pushing forward a ledger and pencil on
the counter and glancing absently at us.

I signed in: name, age, nationality, card number, last stop, destination. The young man leaned against a wall and watched the words
form under the pencil.

"American," the warden murmured as he turned the ledger
around. The child sucked her candy audibly, and another girl, older,
poked her head out from a door. I could hear the rattle of dishes
and a faucet being turned on and off.

"One hundred francs, please," the warden said. "You have a sleeping sheet?"

I nodded.

"You have missed dinner. We serve only until seven. But you
may use the community kitchen to cook your own food until nine."

"I'm afraid I didn't have a chance to buy anything today," I said.
"I don't have any food."

"We do not serve after seven," he said.

On the counter there were things for sale—candy bars, gum, dried
fruit. I looked at them and then turned to the young man and held
out my hand. "*Danke schön* very much," I said.

He touched my hand and started to leave, but stopped and put
his hand to his mouth, as though eating, and lifted his eyebrows
questioningly.

"*Nein,*" I answered in mock despair.

"*Nein?*"

"*Nein,*" the warden stated flatly.

The young man motioned for me to follow him. Happily, I did.

"A moment!" the warden called. "Take that thing away." He
pointed to the medicine kit, which had formed a small puddle on
the floor. "Dormitory Two-A. You are the only one here; it is late
in the season. And we lock at eleven. Tell that boy to have you
back by eleven. You know the hostel rules. Eleven."

I reached for the glistening kit, but the young man picked it up and slung it over his shoulder. We went out, and he put the kit in the back seat, and we climbed into the car and drove back toward the center of town, through streets of old buildings, untouched by the war, with lighted windows twinkling in the rain, and through bare patches where the ruins had been cleared away. He passed a number of restaurants, and I supposed he was driving to a place that was particularly reasonable. Back at the hostel, in the bright light, I had noticed the frayed cuffs of his shirt, his scuffed shoes, and his neglected hair, which curled around his ears like ebony ferns. His face was sallow, as though he had always eaten soggy cream puffs. At college, my face had turned sallow when I ate too many cream puffs, drank too much coffee, or smoked too many cigarettes. My fingernails had then accumulated ten black half wreaths as his had now, but my clothes had never been frayed. As we drove along, the water worked its way through the top in sporadic spurts. I was cold—as cold as I had been on the road. My socks were wet, and my toes numb.

"Zengerstrasse," he announced suddenly, in a low voice. It was a bare, dimly lit street lined with tall brick apartment buildings. He stopped the car before one of them and, going around to the trunk, took out two black, battered suitcases. I assumed he was a salesman of some kind. He led the way to a door of the building and opened it, motioning me ahead. Suspicion told me to object, to get my kit and fly down the street. Instead, I smiled politely and went in. It was dark, but I could make out a staircase. We walked up seven flights. Then he stopped, took out a key, and opened a door. We entered a dim hall. He led me down the hall to another door, opened it, and took me inside. He motioned toward a radiator, gestured for me to take my coat off, and disappeared.

Hungrily I laid my hands on the radiator, but it was only luke-warm. I felt the iciness of my hands dousing its little warmth and took them away guiltily. I unbuttoned my coat and laid it, lining out so it wouldn't drip, across a chair and looked around the room. It was a living-dining room, bathed in the sickliest of lights—a kind of water-barrel brown—that left the corners in darkness. A dark brown rug with worn spots covered the floor. A round table, centered exactly, took up most of the room. On it was an apple green velvet cloth, scarred by cigarette embers, and in the center stood a glass vase with three wax lilies. A blue kitchen stool, a straight chair, a sagging magenta rocker, and a leather sofa chair that had grown dull with age circled the table. Someone had left a newspaper on the rocker. There was a buffet, too, and a desk with two framed photographs on it. One showed the young man as a boy, rosy-tinted and smiling. The other was of an older boy. At first I thought it was the young man, but the nose was fleshier and the chin more prominent. The walls were covered with pictures, mostly original watercolors of thatched-roof cottages in meadows full of stiff cows and grinning pigs. There was not a speck of dust anywhere, but instead a gray patina.

I sat down on the edge of the leather chair and waited, shivering. From the hall I heard the young man's voice, muffled, and then a female voice, farther off. He came in, shutting the door behind him, and pointed again to the radiator. I got up obligingly and walked over to it again, and spread my hands out on it. Behind it, where the pipes entered the wall, bare boards and fresh plaster showed, marking the radiator's newness. I turned around and curled my toes, trying to put some life into them; not succeeding, I stared at my feet. The young man stared, too, and left the room. He returned in a minute with a pair of carpet slippers. Gratefully I took off my shoes and socks, put them under the radiator, and slipped my feet, which were curiously worm white, into the slippers.

The young man removed the vase from the table and took three plates from the buffet and set them carefully on the green velvet. He pointed to the door, then to his mouth, and nodded his head, as though to say "Soon." Sitting down, he looked at the newspaper, only to let it slip from his hand to the floor. For a moment, I thought he had fallen asleep, but he stood up and stretched, and then pointed to the watercolors on the wall.

"*Mein Vater,*" he said.

I looked with courteous appreciation at his father's cows and pigs.

"*Schön,*" I said.

He smiled at my pronunciation, and turned to leave the room again. I started to follow him, thinking I could help, but he shook his head. He stepped out and was back in a moment with two bowls of food, which he put on the table. He went out again and returned with another bowl in one hand and three bottles of beer tucked between an arm and his chest. "Franz!" he shouted, nodding at me to sit down. In a moment he began dishing out the food.

A seedy man of about thirty shuffled in. He wore a long gray-and-yellow striped robe, the sash of which was loosely knotted somewhere around his thighs. "Good evening," he said to me, in English, sitting down in the rocker and ignoring the young man. "My brother said he had a visitor, but I insisted I eat, too. Please excuse my appearance. In the winter I have bronchitis."

"It's very kind of your brother to ask me to eat here. Would you tell him that?"

Franz waved his hand. "He knows that."

I began to eat. There were three colors on the plate: green, white, rust. String beans, boiled potatoes, frankfurters. But they were warped by the sickly light into khaki, gray, and brown. I gazed inadvertently at the frankfurters. They were withered and wrinkled, like the skin of a mummy, but I couldn't wait to cut them up and eat them. Suddenly I felt embarrassed, and said stupidly, "This is wonderful!"

"My brother tells me you are an American," Franz said. "I am surprised: he hates Americans. I teach English at the *Gymnasium.*"

"No wonder you speak so well," I said.

"I suppose I speak like an Englishman."

"More than like an American."

"You Americans speak flatly. You whine."

"I suppose that's true."

The young man said something irritably to Franz, with his mouth full.

"My brother says to eat more and talk less. He does not speak English. He does not speak French, although our mother is French. I am surprised he speaks German. I am surprised he speaks at all."

"What's your brother's name?"

"Eino."

Eino wrinkled his forehead but looked at neither of us. I tried to eat slowly, but I was so hungry that I was finished before either of them. Eino looked at my plate and dished me up another potato and frankfurter. *"Danke schön,"* I said, and tried to eat more slowly. But bit by bit, the pathetic frankfurter disappeared, until I was once again finished. When I arrived in Copenhagen, I was sure my relatives would feed me to the bursting point. I had thought of this often as I was nibbling my rolls on the road. Now, although the edge of my hunger was pleasantly blunted, I indulged in thoughts of yellow mayonnaise, pickled herring, pink salmon, pastries. Then, catching the flicker of a pleased smile from Eino, I guiltily shoved the thoughts away.

When the brothers had finished, Eino sat back and folded his arms, obviously wishing Franz would go back to his bed or couch or wherever he had risen from for his meal. But Franz stayed. He pulled a pipe from his robe pocket and lit it. "What are you doing in Europe?" he asked, leaning back. Eino lit a cigarette and gave it to me, then lit one for himself and stared at his empty plate.

"I'm on a walking tour," I said.

"Alone?"

"Yes."

"And in November?"

I shrugged.

"It cannot be pleasant."

"Sometimes it isn't."

"Then why do it?"

I knew that the cocktail girl had faded days ago in the rain, and slowly the thought had come to me, and today it had blossomed, that my tour was to prove something—exactly what, I could not have said. But I tried to explain. "I think that people should sometimes do things that are difficult and unpleasant," I said.

"How stupid!" he said with profound contempt, looking with vague restlessness around the room.

"Isn't that rather a lightweight attitude?" I asked, hurt.

"Lightweight!" he repeated sarcastically, leaning forward and taking the pipe from his mouth. "A little American student tramps through the mud for a few weeks and tells herself she has accomplished something. Do it for a year. Do it for five years. Then you may say that you have been uncomfortable. I think you are a silly person."

"It's my own affair. I don't harm anyone."

"You ask favors of strangers."

My face colored, and my neck muscles tightened. "Just give me your name and address," I said with as much scorn as I could muster. "I'll send you the money for the meal I ate."

Eino grabbed Franz's arm and apparently asked what had been said. Franz brushed him away. "No, you will not do that," he said to me.

"Oh, yes, I will!" I said. "In fact, as soon as Eino leaves the room I'll give you the money."

"Oh, do as you please. I think you are stupid and silly. It is the ultimate in childishness to suffer when you don't have to. No one will be impressed."

"I wish you'd tell Eino I have to get back," I said sharply.

But Franz said nothing. He picked up the newspaper from the floor and went out of the room. Eino looked hatefully at the retreating figure of his brother.

We smoked our cigarettes in silence, and I could feel the crimson gradually fade from my face. After a while I made a gesture to clear the table. Again Eino shook his head. Later, when I went to the door with some dishes, he took them from me and carried them out. I sat down again. I was still cold, and the room was depressing. Eino returned, sat down, and jiggled one foot. Then he took a photograph album from the desk and, moving his chair next to mine, laid the album across our laps. He flipped past brown, faded photographs of women in brow-obscuring hats and men in tight-waisted suits with narrow trousers and stopped at a page of snapshots of him and an older woman I assumed was his mother. In these pictures, he wore his solemnity with a lightness; he was a young owl that had some of the lark in it. His hair was swept straight back from a thin but soft face. The mother resembled Eino greatly; she had the same dark, fine eyes, the same grave watchfulness.

He gave only a few seconds to this and to each succeeding page, flipping them soberly, without comment. One picture caught my eye. It was of a man sitting on a chair in a backyard, with one hand holding a puppy tightly by the scruff of the neck and with the palm of his other hand supporting the puppy so that it looked as if it were sitting up like a human being. The man had a toothy smile and lively, empty eyes.

"Your *Vater?*" I asked.

"*Ja.*" He smiled. Then he explained that his father was dead. At first I didn't understand, so he grudgingly, fleetingly drew his finger across his neck. "*Der Krieg.*"

The last picture in the book was of the whole family—the father, the mother, Franz, and Eino. The father wore the Nazi uniform: the long coat similar to the kind movie doormen wear, the tall boots, the ski-slide hat. He looked powerful and content. The mother seemed to be edging off the border of the snapshot, her face turned to the side and down, as though she were ashamed. The next page was blank. Eino closed the album and put it back on the desk. He took my coat from the chair and helped me on with it, and I got my shoes from under the radiator and eased my feet into their clammy insides; the soggy socks I stuffed into my pockets. We went out into the hall and came to a door, which was open. I saw a woman standing by a kitchen sink, washing the dishes we had used. The room was small and dark, crowded with a wooden icebox, two gas burners, and a wooden drain holding the sink, which was made of tin. There was a smell of gas and frankfurters. I recognized the woman from the pictures and touched Eino's sleeve, intimating that I wanted to thank her. He said something vaguely negative, but I poked my head in the door and said, "*Danke schön.*"

The mother's face had aged more than one would normally expect since the last photographs were taken. She looked as flattened as a penny that has been put on the tracks and run over by a train. But a gleam flickered from her dark, ringed eyes, and she looked at Eino with love. "*Bitte, bitte,*" she said, turning to me and drying her hands on her apron.

"It was very good," I said, patting my stomach.

She smiled, amused at my sign language, and glanced uncertainly at Eino to share the joke with him. He smiled perfunctorily. She wiped her hands once more on her apron. *"Kaffee?"* she asked him suddenly, and clasped the handle of a chipped yellow coffeepot.

Eino shook his head.

She then asked me with a nod of her head, and patted the coffeepot, smiling. Although it was late, I turned to Eino to ask if we might stay for coffee, but he had turned and was walking to the hall door. She looked at his back with resignation, touched, it seemed, by wonder. *"Leben Sie wohl,"* she said to me quietly, and held out her hand.

I remembered that Franz had said she was French, and I pressed her hand with all the urgency of articulation that suddenly filled me, but it found little voice. *"Auf Wiedersehen,"* I said.

At the hall door I joined Eino, and we descended the seven flights to his car without speaking and got in. The car was not much colder than the apartment had been, but the rain, which had not stopped, seeped through the top onto our shoulders. My feet were again numb. The gloom of the rooms in which Eino lived did not leave us now that we were out of them. His profile, outlined by the dim light of the streetlamps, was harsh.

Suddenly angered, I said, "Your *Mutter bist gut!*"

"Hah!" he laughed at my German.

"Yes, but your *Mutter bist gut!*"

He turned on me bitterly. *"Aber mein Vater . . . mein Vater . . ."*

He started the car, and we drove to the hostel in silence. He parked near the door. It was not quite eleven, but I could see no lights at all in the building. A small waterfall splashed from its roof and burst like glass on the paved walk below. Eino heaved himself back in his seat and sat crumpled and long-faced. We sat in silence a few minutes, at opposite ends of the seat, twitching under the drops that now trickled through the top, our hands lying in our laps. Finally, he took my medicine kit from the back seat, and we ran through the rain to the door. Then he put down the kit, and we shook hands. I then tried the door, but it was locked, so I rang the bell. Light filled the ground-floor windows, and the old man, dressed, but in slippers and with his shirt unbuttoned, opened the door with some irritation. I was about to go in when Eino stepped forward, mindless of the old man in the brilliant doorway, and, raising his arms as though he were going to fly away, threw them heavily around me in a quick, suffocating embrace. Then, without a word, he ran back to the car.

I picked up my kit and stepped inside. The old man closed the door and began at once to admonish me for being late, but I excused myself and hastened up the stairs to the dormitory. Ten empty bunks stood on a cement floor. I chose one by the windows. Early the next day, after sleeping poorly, I resumed the journey on foot to Copenhagen.

Conclusion

The Burkes' housekeeper comes walking home from the grocery store in her coat with the fur collar. A woman of forty, she holds her head low in suspicion and defense. Her face is the sallow hue of aged linen. The nose veers one way, the mouth another, as if at birth they had been given a wrench along with her mind. What exactly this mind contains, no one knows.

It was with coolness that the young couple welcomed the silent, unkempt, head-hanging Helene thirteen years ago, bequeathed to them by Mrs. Burke's mother, and they saw an eventual change of address for her. They did not bargain on growing interested in her. She was apparently feebleminded, but seemed to wage an inner war with her dimness, and this fascinated them. Here was no half-hearted struggle, but one that gave her the look of a tormented insect whose wings refuse to lift. She was just keen enough to sense the world's complexities without grasping them, and somehow her mind had grown a few sensitive shoots that rued the paltriness of their soil. She became the Burkes' project. They observed, they asked gentle questions, they read Adler and Wembridge. But after a few months they regretfully agreed that Helene was a closed case; and taking with them the image of a creature standing before a tapestry forever beheld as a maddening blur, they retired from their explorations.

By the time they dropped her as a project they had accepted her as an employee. She was a dogged worker, she kept to herself, and she was perfectly harmless. They grew fond of her, and hoped their fondness was reciprocated. But Helene's attitude, like her face, went in all directions: sometimes she expressed an undemonstrative, faintly doglike warmth in their presence; but at other times she brought off an obscure remark whose tone left no doubt that it was meant as a scathing sarcasm; and on still other occasions she was overcome by awe of them, and would stand wringing her hands and blushing to her ears.

They asked if she was happy working for them, and she replied that she was, that this was now her home. It was more her home than theirs; she never left it unless forced. Stores, strangers, noise— all terrified her. When the Burkes threw a party they were obliged to hire someone from the outside to serve, because Helene flatly refused, escaping to her room a full hour before the first guest was likely to appear.

During the thirteen years she has been with the Burkes, only two important things have happened to her. One came about when it was discovered that she could read the newspaper, laboriously forming each word with her lips, eyebrows severely knotted. The Burkes were elated. Why hadn't she ever mentioned this accomplishment to them? Helene shook her head; she didn't know. Obviously she hadn't the haziest idea of what a tool she held. With a burst of hope they bought her some children's primers, which she looked over carefully and put down with a tactless grunt. But the next day Mrs. Burke found her standing in the study, gazing at the bookshelves with mingled fear and resolution. "Go ahead, Helene," she urged. Gingerly the housekeeper extracted a novel, studied it for a while, and then replaced it, glancing sharply over her shoulder at her mistress; she did not like to be spied on. When Mrs. Burke was gone she continued her search, turning the pages of biographies, essays, travel books, none of which pleased her. She returned to her chores. Then a week later, dusting the shelves, she withdrew a thick black volume with a gold cross embossed on its cover. After examining it, she stuck it tightly under her arm and took it to her room. The Burkes never laid eyes on it again.

It was soon evident that she had a remarkable ability, amounting to that of an idiot savant, to recognize and quote the most impressive passages from her filched Bible. And she has quoted and quoted over the years, with unflagging intensity, as if the mouthing of a sonorous phrase might unlock one of the thousand doors closed to her.

The second thing that happened to Helene had to do with Carl Maria Lutzow, the great German silent screen star. One evening, as the Burkes were leaving to see an old Lutzow film at an art theater, they caught sight of Helene standing in the doorway of the kitchen, looking at them. On an impulse they whisked her off between them. She slunk into the crowded theater with her head bitterly lowered, but as the picture got under way they noticed that she was engrossed in the magnificent Lutzow's adventures.

When they came home Helene was excited, her sallow face was flushed, and the Burkes indulgently capped her evening by giving her their *Pictorial History of the Cinema* to look through. A few days later they found that a page had been ripped from the book. Helene was called in. Yes, she had torn the page out. Why? Because there was a picture of Lutzow on it. Well, wasn't she sorry? Yes, of course, but could she keep the picture? Mr. Burke nodded with a sigh, and when she was gone he exchanged a look with his wife. The lonely housekeeper was enamored of the fierce, monocled Prussian with his tight uniform and high black boots. "Maybe we should have taken her to a cartoon festival instead," he said.

After that, Helene wanted to be taken to the theater whenever her idol was featured. Her wish was not often fulfilled, partly because of the scarcity of old Lutzow films, and partly because the Burkes were reluctant to be seen with their peculiar-looking housekeeper; and it was just as well, for when she did see Lutzow on the screen she seemed to experience an inner upheaval that left her more lost and morose than usual. About five years ago the Burkes informed her that all Lutzow's films had been recalled to Germany (an idiotic lie, but one she did not question), and they have never heard her mention the actor's name since.

The other developments in Helene's life have been of lesser moment. She achieved a minimal neatness of person under Mrs. Burke's supervision. She began borrowing words from her employers' vocabulary, embellishing her rare statements with "fantastic" and "insufferable." She took up smoking cigarettes with an ivory holder, and made a fur collar for her coat. She also conceived a dislike for timepieces: refused to wear her wristwatch, put her alarm clock in the garbage can (where Mrs. Burke found it), and dusted the grandfather clock with averted eyes. When asked what she had against clocks, she replied only that they "kept after her," but would not or could not say more.

When Helene comes home from the store she sets the grocery bags down and removes her coat, looking closely at the collar. Several years ago she felt a desire for a coat with a fur collar, but fearing that if she mentioned this, she would be taken to a department store, she cut up a discarded fur muff of Mrs. Burke's and painstakingly sewed it around the collar of her old gabardine coat. She had been proud of the smart decoration and brushed it every day, but for a long time now she has disliked it and feels inclined to rip it off.

"How was your walk?" Mrs. Burke asks, coming into the kitchen.

"Insufferable."

"Well. You've got to have a breath of air once in a while."

Helene begins to pull out little tufts of fur.

"Don't ruin your nice collar, Helene."

Helene takes the coat up to her room, where she continues to pull the fur out, grimacing with every tug, as though plucking the skin from her own face. Finally, she throws the mutilated thing aside and looks out the window.

Across the street are big brown-shingled old houses like the Burkes'. Above hangs a white afternoon sky. The street is empty. She looks around her room. It is large, with comfortable furniture. From a knickknack shelf smiles down a crowd of little china dogs, presented en masse to Helene by Mrs. Burke, along with the small television set in the corner. (The Burkes do not like television, but they hoped Helene might; she has never mentioned to them that the set went dead long ago, a matter of indifference to her since the screen was never enriched by Lutzow.) A red cellophane fire sits in the fireplace, its mantel graced with potted plants that Helene forgets to water. Everything in the room is covered with dust; clothes lie strewn about.

Now the afternoon suddenly livens with the sound of schoolchildren passing by. Helene watches them sharply until the last one disappears around the corner and the street falls silent again. She listens to the clock ticking on the night table. It is as if nothing exists. Even though she knows Mrs. Burke is cooking in the kitchen downstairs, and Mr. Burke is busy in an office uptown, and somewhere speeches are being given, and somewhere else ships are colliding.

She goes over to her dresser, hesitates, then opens a drawer and rummages through some clothes until she finds a ball of tightly crushed paper. Taking it out, she slowly, nervously begins to uncrumple it; but abruptly she balls it up again and throws it back into the drawer, slamming it shut.

She goes down to the kitchen. Mrs. Burke is bustling around, a frilly apron over her velvet slacks.

"Can I help?" Helene asks.

"Not really, thanks."

Helene leans against the wall with her arms crossed, watching. Mrs. Burke never uses a cookbook; she knows everything. She pours something into a bowl, adds a dash of something else; within an hour she will have created an unusual and attractive dish from the clutter of jars and cartons on the table. "Fantastic," the housekeeper thinks. Sometimes when she serves the Burkes dinner she forgets that she is only capable of making a tolerable pot of coffee, and feeling herself the author of the succulent meal she sets before them, she swells with pride. But in the kitchen, watching her mistress at work, she enjoys no such fancy.

Mrs. Burke lights the oven and straightens up. "Can't you try to look a little happier, Helene?"

Helene takes her pool of darkness into the dining room and sets the table for two. When Mr. Burke comes home she tucks the loose strands of her hair behind her large ears, puts on a clean white apron, and serves the couple.

"How's Madame Malheureuse this evening?" Mr. Burke asks.

She does not respond to the title, whose foreign flavor used to please her. Mute, she returns to the kitchen and sits listening to their voices, rising at intervals to bring in the other courses, and finally to clear up after them. Then she sits down at the kitchen table to eat. The only sound she can hear is her own chewing and swallowing. "He smote them hip and thigh!" she says loudly. "A little leaven leaveneth the whole lump!" With a sigh, she resumes her chewing and swallowing. When she is finished she does all the dishes with rote care. She pulls out the plug and watches the gray dishwater inch down the sides of the sink; with a muffled burp it is gone, leaving the sink empty, somehow vast.

"Helene, Helene," she murmurs.

She makes a pot of coffee and brings it into the living room, where the Burkes are sitting before the fire. "Have a cup with us," says Mrs. Burke, who never knows if Helene will refuse with a curt shake of her head, or overwhelm them with her haste in accepting. Tonight she responds eagerly, hurries back to the buffet for an extra cup, and sinks into a chair as Mrs. Burke pours. Friends are expected later on, but Helene knows the room is safe for a good while yet.

"Well, how's everything?" Mr. Burke asks her, putting his newspaper aside.

"Insufferable."

"Anything in particular?"

"The sink. The sink is empty."

"Something wrong with the sink?" he asks his wife. She shakes her head.

"Don't worry about the sink," he reassures Helene.

"Helene took a nice walk to the grocery store today," Mrs. Burke says.

"That's nice," he says, nodding.

Helene is squinting into her coffee cup. "The hart panteth after the water brooks," she quotes suddenly, looking up at their faces.

"That's a fine one," Mr. Burke tells her.

But Helene feels that more should grow from the words. The

hart (she thinks it means heart) hangs before her eyes shriveled with thirst. She casts into her mind for other hearts and comes up with broken hearts and bleeding hearts. "There are the broken ones, the bleeding ones, and the thirsty ones." That is all she can think of to say, though the Burkes are waiting receptively. She heaves forward in her chair. "Strain at a gnat and swallow a camel! New wine into old bottles! Bring forth the fatted calf!"

The Burkes, who often regret having brought the printed word to Helene's attention, nevertheless look appreciative. At one time they would have tried to draw her out as to the meaning these words had for her; but she has too often sat pondering and self-conscious, darting miserable glances at them, unable to say. And so they nod, and ask for more. She obliges them. "God said let there be light, and there was light!" She sips her coffee, looking at their faces over the rim of her cup. But Mrs. Burke gets up to answer the telephone, and Mr. Burke returns to his newspaper. She puts her cup down and goes to her room, where she turns the lamp on and pulls down the shade. Outside it has begun to rain.

"Two things happened today," she announces. "I took a walk and I ruined my fur collar." She is struck by the childishness of the words, and clasping her hands angrily together, she cries out: "Would God I had died for thee, O Absalom!" The powerful sound of the words fills her with a kind of light, a beauty, but the feeling does not last; it never does. She unlocks her hands and wanders around the room, glancing from the corner of her eye at the dresser. Circuitously she arrives there, pauses, then quickly opens the drawer. Out comes the ball of paper; she sits down with it and smooths it flat against her knee with trembling fingers.

It is the picture of a man in the flower of his arrogance. The cheekbones and nose are massive, but the lips are very fine, curved in a knowing smile. In one eye a monocle is screwed. Above it a black-billed military hat is cocked. The glossy paper is a network of frayed wrinkles. It has been crushed and rescued and crushed again too many times to count.

"What are you staring at?" she mutters to the face. "I could tear you to pieces." But her eyes are widening, filling with an intense glow; his roles cascade through her mind. He is dancing with a lovely woman in a ballroom; the chandelier quakes in his monocle; his hand is spread hard against her back. He is standing before a group of cowed prisoners, dangerously flicking a riding whip against his high black boot. He is astride a rearing mount, his sword unsheathed and raised high to the heavens. "Fearfully and wondrously made," she whispers, holding her head between her two hands. And looking apprehensively around the room, she crumples the picture and thrusts it back in the drawer.

She looks at her bed. She undresses and puts her flannel pajamas on, pausing irritably as she hears a bloom of greetings from the front door downstairs. Leaving the lamp on, for she does not like darkness, she climbs beneath the covers and says her falling-asleep quote: "The wild beasts shall cry in their desolate houses, and her time is near to come, and her days will not be prolonged."

Then, closing her eyes, she waits for sleep.

Hours later her eyes flick open. Her heart hammers through her body. It is not that she is shocked—she has seen him too often for that—but her terror each time remains excruciatingly fresh. He is as gray and transparent as a piece of celluloid; the yellow flowers of the wallpaper show through him. He stands there, his hand tapping his riding whip against his boot, making a faint noise. This delicate sound tears a moan from Helene's throat. Over the years he has grown more real, developing from a vague, shapeless presence, no more than a feeling, really, that made her look over her shoulder, into a clear-cut, motionless figure; then gradually his statuelike stance was abandoned for a living being's mobility, though soundless. And now he is losing his silence, too; when he strikes the whip against his boot a noise is produced.

She wants to cry out and rouse the Burkes, but she has never been able to do this; she cannot even pull the blankets over her eyes. His gaze is depthless, shot through with the yellow flowers, but she is transfixed by it, impaled. How long she lies staring at him, her nails digging into her palms, she does not know.

Abruptly she is alone. Gray morning light fills the room. Shivering, she sits up on the edge of the bed and lowers her head to her hands. The palms are still mottled from the pressure of her nails. She looks at her nails. They are long and tapered like Mrs. Burke's, but the skin around them is bitten, and the hands are red. The alarm clock goes off, and with haggard fury she bangs its stem down. Then, slowly nudging her feet into her carpet slippers, she shuffles over to the window and raises the shade on the new day. It is still raining.

She feels better after her cup of steaming coffee in the kitchen. Mrs. Burke comes in and makes herself some toast, glancing out the window. She likes rain. After eating, she says, "If anyone calls I'm just going out for a walk."

A fantastic thing, Helene thinks, how a simple little walk seems so meaningful when taken by Mrs. Burke. Her mistress's face is calm with an instinctive belief in what she is doing as she slips on her raincoat, ties a plastic hood around her smooth hairdo, and opens the door. Helene pictures her with that look on her face even when fast asleep. Mr. Burke has the look, too, and all their friends, and the people on the street and in the grocery store. She plods into the living room, disarranged from the night before, and collects glasses and dirty ashtrays and places them on a tray. She brushes the crumbs off the sofa, and running her hand down between the cushions, she finds, as she often does, a couple of forgotten items: a silver cigarette lighter and a dime. Musingly she lays them on the tray, touches them with a forefinger. She loves the departed guests achingly for their careless, skillful approach to life, for their smooth communication with each other. Grabbing one of their half-full glasses, she raises it to her lips, but notices a scum of ashes on the liquor's surface and sets the glass down reproachfully. Taking the tray into the kitchen, she drops it on the table with a harsh clatter, and returns to the living room to dust.

When she comes to the grandfather clock with her dustrag, she looks away from the big face as she gingerly swipes the cloth here and there. The slow, hollow ticking fills her ears until she steps back. All the days that have been ticked off in her lifetime! They lie in a huge pile, but a pile so hollow that it weighs no more than a minute, a second. "My days are swifter than a weaver's shuttle," she says, and feels a grief so intolerable that her pulse seems crushed in her veins.

The front door slams, and Mrs. Burke can be heard hanging up her coat in the hall closet. She comes into the living room, wiping the rain from her pink cheeks. "Don't bother too much in here," she says. "We'll just mess it up again tonight when the Wilsons come."

Tonight, Helene thinks. Tonight Lutzow will come again, a shade more real and terrible, perhaps in possession of a voice. She looks over at Mrs. Burke. If she could tell her mistress about his visits, and hear from her lips that a piece of film cannot turn into a human being, it would help, it might even tear him from her life. Tightening her lips, she goes on with her work.

The morning unfolds to the roar of the vacuum cleaner as she goes from room to room with it. In the afternoon she does the week's ironing with tense efficiency, trying to keep her fears at bay, and finishes just before dark. She sits down at the kitchen table and picks at her food while Mrs. Burke works around her, preparing the meal for the guests. The housekeeper's eyes do not follow her mistress's hands as they so enviably measure and stir but, instead, fix themselves on the calm, pink face.

An egg, about to be cracked, is held suspended. "What is it, Helene?"

The housekeeper's eyes burn anxiously into her own.

"What's wrong? You've hardly touched your food."

Helene glances abstractly at her plate, then fastens her eyes again on the concerned face.

"What is it?" Mrs. Burke repeats gently. She watches the housekeeper's lips try to move, but it is as if they were glued together.

Suddenly they wrench apart. "Her time is near to come, and her days will not be prolonged!"

Mrs. Burke has not heard this particular quotation before, but she has heard many others just as ominous. At the beginning the dark hints of death worried her enough to take Helene to the doctor for a thorough physical examination, from which the poor soul, reeling with shame and terror, was a month in recovering. The housekeeper's body, at any rate, was pronounced healthy. As for the troubled psyche—outsiders would be useless; Mrs. Burke can depend only on herself, on reassuring words and pats. But she has never seen Helene look as anxious as she does tonight.

"Dear, try to tell me, and try to speak plainly."

Silence, though a struggle is clearly going on behind Helene's eyes.

Mrs. Burke scours her mind. "Is it the sink?" she asks.

Helene's eyes flick to the sink. She nods.

"Just the sink? Or something more?"

"More," Helene whispers.

"Was it your trip to the grocery store yesterday?"

Helene nods again.

"Is it the grocery store, then? Or is there more?"

"More," she whispers.

"Your fur collar? You were picking it—you don't like it anymore? Or is it that we're having people over two nights in a row?"

Helene nods again, to both questions.

"Is there more?"

"Yes. Yes."

"Then tell me. Please."

But suddenly the lips clamp tightly shut. A loud sigh comes trembling through the nostrils. She sits staring at her plate.

The egg is cracked; the whir of the beater fills the air. "I tell you what," Mrs. Burke says a little later, sliding the dish into the oven. "Let's make a fire in the other room and bring some coffee in. We'll just sit."

Helene looks at her gratefully.

The fire blazes, the coffee is good; Mrs. Burke has made it. Mrs. Burke sits with her on the sofa and talks of soothing things—of the new curtains she plans to buy for Helene's room; of the weather, the garden. Helene would like to sit there all night, but she knows the Wilsons will be along, and she begins to check the hateful grandfather clock every few minutes. Suddenly, without a glance at her mistress, who is asking what kind of material she would like for her curtains, she rises and flees to her room. She stands leaning against the door. She hears Mr. Burke go past, whistling, and descend the stairs. After a while the doorbell rings and the air throbs with voices. Then silence creeps in.

She leaves the door and lowers herself into a chair. She is persecuted by the vision of an insect whose dim existence begins and ends in the smallest corner of time, a corner so monstrously unimportant that the human eye is hardly aware of it. If someone stepped on an insect it bled a yellow juice.

Let her put a cigarette in her long holder and smoke, gracefully, turning the prettily carved ivory in her fingers. Surely these hands are human, real blood courses beneath their skin. There is no doubt about that, she thinks, exhaling, and looking at her hands, which are slender. They are red, but the nails are long and tapered. They are nice hands. Yet they disgust her. Has it always been this way, she wonders? Has it only been a few weeks, or has it been years, or has she always felt this horror of herself and the corner she occupies? What an emptiness fills the room; how the clock accuses her, ticking off waste, waste, waste.

She stubs the cigarette out and makes an effort to read the Bible, mumbling aloud. It is no good tonight; nothing is. And she is afraid to go to bed. She lights another cigarette, putting the burned match in the ashtray that Mrs. Burke gave her along with the gentle admonition to be careful. She knows she does not inspire confidence; it is why she has red cellophane in the hearth instead of real flames. It is why she is allowed to make only coffee; they are afraid she will waste their flour and eggs. It is why she is not invited to join them for an entire evening in the living room; they are afraid she will waste their time.

With precision, she moves the cigarette ember toward the back of her left hand. She feels a stab of pain. She wets her fingertip, dips it in the ashes, and rubs the wound with black. Somehow gratified, yet appalled, she stares before her.

The clock ticks. Nine o'clock. Nine-thirty. Ten. It is past her bedtime, yet she dares not move to her place of rest, where she has suffered so often. She will stay in the chair tonight. She closes her eyes, the knuckles of her hands white.

She starts at the creak of boot leather. He is crossing the room toward her. He stops before the chair, riding whip in hand, and his fine lips part. She crushes her hands to her ears but she can hear him clearly: the voice is like a cannon blast.

"So, you have been thinking of getting rid of me?"

"No!"

"No. You want me."

But to this she shakes her head passionately.

"You want me. To finish you off, Helene! To lash you to shreds!"

The words reverberate through the room. The Burkes must hear it downstairs; they will be running up to pound on her door. "They'll come!" she cries. "The Burkes!"

"No one ever comes in here," Lutzow says calmly. He steps closer. "Look at me, Helene." Her eyes move, horrified, from the fine wrinkles around the eyes to the individual threads in the tunic. Yet he is still flat, shiny, transparent. He, in his turn, is studying her. "You wrong thing," he says. "You hopelessly wrong thing."

All at once she feels her eyes brimming with tears. "I know that's said about me . . . but I can't help how I am . . ." She hates the self-pity in her voice; it is something new, dredged up from some part of her she did not know existed. And now a craven tear burns down her cheek. She turns her face away.

"I want weight, Helene. And blood under my skin. Color. Give them to me."

He paces back and forth, and she hears his footfall growing into a thunder. The ashtray trembles on the arm of the chair; the knick-knack shelf clinks. Surely the Burkes will come bursting in now. Her neck is stretched wildly toward the door. But the noise ceases. He stands before her. She feels something give way in her head, like the side of a cliff.

The eyes are pale blue, the skin ruddy. The uniform is crimson and black, adorned with bright gold braid. He stands swatting the whip against his boot. The smell of leather is strong in her nostrils.

"Do you understand?" he asks. "To be lashed into nothing? Do you understand? And afterward?"

"Afterward?" she whispers.

"Afterward, when Helene is no more A new Helene will rise, a clean, fine Helene. I will take her with me."

She stares up at his face, rigid. Then, slowly, her head still lifted, she closes her eyes.

"This is what you have always longed for, Helene." So saying, he brings the whip down across her face. The pain sears through her, sends her lunging up from the chair, but she sinks down under the slashes, and as the flesh begins to fall from her bones she feels a fierce light bursting behind her eyes, like the sun.

She is aware of the stillness of early morning. Her face throbs and stings. She is sitting on her knees on the floor, the toppled ashtray beside her. Lutzow is nearby, leaning against the wall, watching her. Slowly she climbs to her feet and moves across to the dresser mirror, where she gazes bitterly at herself. Her face is lacerated; the sight sets her chin quivering, and she bursts into unrestrained weeping. Then her wet eyes flash to Lutzow. "You never meant to take me with you!" she cries. She wrenches open the drawer and with her blood-caked nails claws out the ball of paper, ripping it in two with a grimace that shudders her face. "Good, Helene!" she cries, ripping the halves in two. "This is good!" She throws the pieces to the floor and turns around, breathing unevenly. "Good," she says again, in a triumphant whisper, looking at the empty space where Lutzow had been.

Then with a wail she flies to a shelf of odds and ends and frantically searches for something. Wheeling, she runs from the room and pounds down the stairs into the study, where she tears through the desk until her hand closes around the Scotch tape. Gripping it, she runs back up the stairs. Mrs. Burke is coming down the hall in her bathrobe; she stops dead. "Your *face*, Helene!" Helene runs past her into her room and slams the door shut. Falling to her knees, she swiftly tapes the pieces together and looks wildly around. Nothing. She waves the restored picture back and forth like a flag. Nothing. The door opens, but it is only the Burkes, filling the air with their voices. Then with a painful intake of breath she sees him. He stands a few feet away, his pale blue eyes fixed on her, his hand rapidly tapping the whip against his boot.

The Forest

Jeppe's first memory was of a little alcove with tumbled bedclothes where he leaned against the boxes his mother stacked against his intrusion and, sucking his fist, watched her. She lay on her bed, sleeping, her clothes flung around the dim room in vivid splashes. His eyes wandered from one bright article to another and then back to her face, pale and secret as the moon. Having learned not to howl, he would move away from the boxes and poke around the cold alcove, his diapers hanging wet and heavy below his naked belly. When the room was filled with noon light his mother would wake and have a cup of coffee and a cigarette; then, dropping the butt into the cup where it went out with a hiss, she changed Jeppe and gave him something to eat. Dry and no longer hungry, he forgot all but the present moment and gazed at her with gratitude. She dressed, then, and went off, and a woman from the building took him to her room where he played under the table with some old spoons. Often when he was brought back in the evening and put to bed in the alcove, his mother had not yet returned, and he would lie there waiting for her until sleep took him.

His mother was no longer in his life. He was with her sister, Tante Klara, a widow with plenty of children. He was older now, with real shoes on his feet, even though they had come apart at the toes so that when he walked they opened and closed like two mouths. In the mornings he stood nervously in the middle of the crowded room while his oldest cousin buttoned him into his clothes, grunting as the difficult top button was secured. At first his eyes followed everything worriedly, but in time he could be seen racing around the alleys with the others, his shoes flapping and his cap askew. Then he was given a new pair of shoes, buttoned into his coat, and taken to the train station. There Tante Klara fastened to his coat a piece of paper with his name and destination on it, and gave him a brown bag and a ticket.

"You'll come back to Copenhagen for visits," she told him, "but you won't even want to, you'll be so wild about the country. I've got too many others, otherwise you could stay. Hurry now. Kiss me good-bye." She pressed her sharp-nosed face next to him, and he boarded the train.

It was too long a journey. At one point, in the evening, the train still hurtling north, he murmured aloud: "We'll be driving into the sea soon."

"Nonsense," replied the passenger sitting next to him, a lady who wore a hat like a barrel lid, "the train will stop at Hjørring, that's as far north as one can go."

Then, he reflected, Hjørring was at the end of the earth, frozen.

Earlier, the lady had taken the liberty of opening his brown bag and had withdrawn the bread and cold meatballs that Tante Klara had packed. She had made him eat. He felt she must be a relative, like Tante, and now he suddenly asked, "Where is Mama?"

"Heavens, I have no idea," she replied in a kind voice, adding, "I myself am just returning from Paris."

He remembered the splashes of color in the dim room, and his mother's fleeting touch; then he thought of her no more; the train had stopped.

He was met by a strange woman, another aunt, Tante Rosa. "Didn't Klara send a suitcase along?" were her first words, and he shook his head. She sighed and led him to her car. It was a pretty light blue thing, and he timidly asked if he might touch the steering wheel. Without replying she started the motor, and they drove out of Hjørring into a flat dark landscape of heaths and marshes. Once she reached over abruptly and ruffled his hair. Her eyes were hard and narrowed. Her hair was dark red, coming out from under its hairpins, and she was always brushing it roughly from her eyes. Eventually she stopped before a small cottage and took him inside.

She made a bed for him on a couch and stripped him to his under-pants. He crawled under the blankets, and she turned the lamp out.

In the morning after he had dressed he looked around the room he had slept in. The little windows, set in deep recesses, were hung with white lace curtains, and through them the sun fell, lying in broken strips along the wooden floor and up the rough yellow walls, striking glints from the edges of the furniture. In one corner was a black wood stove, and in another a black upright piano. He went over to the piano and very softly struck a note. Framed photographs looked down at him from the top of the piano. He saw Tante Klara's sharp nose. It was odd, her being both here and in Copenhagen. He struck another note and took his hand away, the surrounding silence was so great.

Tante Rosa came up behind him and put her hands on his shoulders. "Now you must be happy, Jeppe. Give us a smile." He turned and smiled, as asked. She patted his head. "Uncle Anton wants to meet you."

He did not know anyone else lived in the house. He looked around and saw emerging from the bedroom a man with a quilt around his waist. To Jeppe his uncle, as his aunt, seemed very old, although they were only in their late thirties. Uncle Anton seemed, in fact, extraordinarily old, with sunken eyes and drawn skin. The hand he offered Jeppe was as light as a leaf.

"So it's Jeppe, is it?" the man asked with a thin smile.

Jeppe said nothing. No one had taught him manners. He stared at the quilt and the big plaid carpet slippers from which the man's bony ankles protruded. A strong, unpleasant odor drifted in through the open bedroom door. The boy wrinkled his nose.

"That's my medicine you smell," his uncle said.

Jeppe opened his mouth to ask what was the matter with him, but Tante Rosa spoke first. "Uncle Anton has a bad back," she said, looking at her husband with those hard eyes of hers. Then she helped settle him at the piano bench and went into the bedroom to change the bedclothes.

Uncle Anton looked from the piano to Jeppe. "Do you like music?"

he asked. Jeppe nodded uncertainly, and his uncle began to play, pausing to say, "This is an old foreign song called 'A Bicycle Built for Two.'" The piano was old, and echoed and vibrated like a mass of plucked harpstrings so that you could hardly distinguish one note from another. Uncle Anton sang "Dai . . . sy, Dai . . . sy . . ." Suddenly he stopped and crept to a sofa chair by one of the windows. He seemed to doze, his veined, yellowy hands crossed in his lap. Jeppe sat down on a footstool and looked at him, his own hands crossed in his lap.

"And how old are you, Jeppe?" he was asked at length.

"Four." But he was not sure. "Five."

His uncle's eyes were still closed. "And what do you think of this part of the country?"

No one had ever asked him such a deep thing before. He looked around nervously, unable to answer.

"Well, I hope you'll like it here. There are no children nearby, but we have a few chickens, and then there's the sea. You can go outside and explore, if you like, but don't go far." The last sentence was so faint that Jeppe had to lean forward to catch it.

He crossed the room. Through the bedroom door he could see Tante Rosa rattling a table of bottles as she shook a pillow into its slip. It was a tiny room like the living room. He hoped he would never have to sleep in there with them, in the smell.

Outside there was a little windswept road with two or three cottages on it, that was all. Here and there a black hen pecked at the dirt, which was damp from a shower the night before. Stretching in every direction were the heaths, pink under the August sun, and in the distance stood a forest whose branches shook in the wind. He struck off toward it. It grew in sand, and inside it was wild or still according to the wind, which quickened and died, and quickened again. A small building had once stood there, but it had burned and now only its foundation remained, covered with lichen and small, hardy wild roses, dark red, almost black. Near the ruins were wooden crosses aslant in the sand, some hung round with decaying life preservers. He poked at these with a stick, wondering what they were. Then his stick hung poised in midair as a sound like one deep sigh after another came to his ears. He moved toward the sound and saw that it came from the sea which lay beneath him, green at the edge, and dark, almost black, farther out. Long ropes of kelp moved up and down in the water, as though breathing, glistening brown and red. He plunged down the sand slope and across the beach into the water, shoes and all, stomping and splashing. Gradually he stopped, looking all around, stunned by the bigness in which he stood. The beach continued forever on both sides of him, guarded by towering white cliffs, and the sea was greater yet, though not so great as the sky, which was suddenly filled with shrieking gulls. He stepped back out of the water, frightened, and noticing his shoes, he flung himself down on the sand trying to undo his shoelaces; failing, he began to weep, stabbing his stick hopelessly in the sand. Tante Klara would have given him a sharp slap for soaking such fine shoes, but Tante Rosa was sure to do much worse. For a moment he considered walking back down the beach to Copenhagen, but coming had been so long that going was bound to be just as long. He rubbed the shoes with his shirt sleeve and squished back toward the cottage.

An old man was walking along the road in wooden clogs. His face lit up with interest when he saw Jeppe, and he turned all the way around as the boy passed, and then called after him, "You there, who is it you belong to?"

"Tante and Uncle," Jeppe murmured.

"Aye, so you've come. And a bad time, too."

Jeppe was working again at the shoes. The old man bent down and under his thick, fumbling fingers the laces were finally undone. He straightened up, wiping his ugly face. Jeppe poured the water from his shoes. "What will Tante do to me for ruining my shoes?" he asked.

"Hang you from a tree for the crows to peck at, that's what," the old man said, as the crows overhead cried Caw! He was a tall, heavy ancient in faded castoff clothes. He had a toothbrush mustache stained brown and yellow, and sparse, sharp-worn teeth like slivers of rock. "Give me your hand and we'll walk together," he said.

"You were going the other way," Jeppe said faintly.

"Aye, and now I'm going this way." He grabbed the boy's hand and dragged him along. "You've been to Hjørring, have you not? My own grandfather, he was the mayor, that's right, he was the mayor, it isn't a lie. And did you go down the big street by the park? Have you a notion of what it's called? Why it's called Hans Norden Street. Nay, it's not a lie, the street sign says it clear as day, Hans Norden Street, named after my own grandfather." He looked at the boy, whose fingers hurt. "Well, what have you to say to that?"

"I don't know," Jeppe replied, sick with fear for the punishment in store for him.

"You don't know. Well, well." He proceeded in silence for a while; then his face brightened again. "It's the youngest one's boy you are, aren't you? Ha, the troubles she brought her family, a roll in the hay here, and a roll in the hay there. Aye, I can still see her walking down this road, too fine to speak, it was enough to make a cat laugh. Your mum, she was a fine lady all right. Where is she these days?"

"Paris," Jeppe replied, staring up at the crows.

"Nay?" the old man marveled. "That's a distance, to be sure."

"Do the crows peck your eyes when you hang there?" Jeppe asked gingerly.

"Do they peck your eyes!" He clucked his tongue. "But it's not as bad as when they hang you by the neck at the crossroads. You're right dead then. They done that in Hans Norden's day, my boy. He led the ceremonies, he did. He was a great man in these parts, and they named a whole street after him."

They had come to the boy's cottage, and the old man released his hand. The boy put his fingers in his mouth. "Tell Anton I asked for him," the old man said. "He used to sit out here in the sun between his hospitals, but I don't see him no more. There'll be crepe on that door soon enough." He walked away with a wave. Jeppe crept inside with his wet shoes in his hand and stood silently by the door. Rosa and Anton were sitting in the living room with coffee and buttered bread. Rosa looked at his shoes.

"I ran into the water," he whispered.

"Oh, for heaven's sake!" She snatched them from him and put them outside on the steps to dry in the sun.

"Is that all?" he asked as she sat down again. "Won't you be hanging me from a tree?"

"He's been talking with Per," she said to Anton, who nodded. He was chewing his bread slowly, his hand at his jaw as though to aid him in getting it down. "Don't listen to Per," she told Jeppe. "His brain has gone soft."

"He said his grandfather was mayor of Hjørring," Jeppe said enthusiastically, full of relief at having escaped the crows. "What's a mayor?"

"The head of a town. That's true enough."

"And he said my mother was a fine lady."

Rosa gave an imperceptible shrug.

"And that crepe would be hanging on your door."

"Sit down and have your coffee." She poured a great quantity of milk into his coffee and gave him a thick slice of buttered bread. He snuggled into his chair, smacking his lips loudly.

When they were finished Uncle Anton went back to the bedroom. Tante Rosa followed him and helped him into bed. When she came back she motioned to Jeppe. She took him outside behind a shed and pushed him roughly against it. "Never another thing like that out of you! I tell you, if you speak like that again I'll beat you, oh I'll beat you!" and by way of making her point she pushed him against the wall once more. He looked up at her too frightened to move, burning with confused shame. She walked off, wringing her hands, then turned abruptly and came back to him and pulled his head roughly to her body, soothing him, but he walked well apart from her back to the cottage.

In the evening she and Anton had their dinner in the bedroom and Jeppe ate in the kitchen. Afterward she called to him. "Will you go in to him?" she asked. "He wants to read to you. There, that's a good boy."

He went into the bedroom, holding his breath against the smell. Uncle Anton lay way down beneath the covers, very small. An old red book was in his hands. Jeppe sat down on the edge of the bed, clattering something with his foot. "What's that?" he asked.

"A bedpan. Now, Jeppe, do you like H. C. Andersen?"

He did not know. He was given the book so that he could look at the illustrations. One picture was of a white horse flying over the tops of snow-laden trees, pulling a sleigh in which sat a queen in white fur and a crown of stars. Another showed a mermaid with flowers in her hair, standing by a scalloped sea, looking at a sleeping youth in a blue and gold tunic. Jeppe pointed to the second illustration, and Uncle Anton began to read.

"The Little Mermaid. Far out at sea the water is as blue as the loveliest cornflower and as clear as the purest crystal. But it is very deep—deeper than the anchor has ever reached; many church towers would have to be piled one upon the other to reach right up from the bottom to the surface. Down there live the sea folk . . ."

"Oh!" cried Jeppe, since he had seen the sea that day. And he added importantly: "It's more green than blue."

Uncle Anton nodded and went on. His voice was faint, and he had trouble keeping the book straight up. On the second page he fell asleep, and Jeppe sat there regarding the book patiently. The smell had ceased to bother him. After a while Rosa looked in. Her face broke into a smile. "He's fallen asleep," she whispered, and after taking the book from her husband's hands she led Jeppe from the room. He asked her if she would finish the story for him, and standing, she read it to the end. He could not follow her, she went so fast.

Every morning when he woke and stuck his head out the window there was something about the smell of sea and heather that made him noisy. He went to the piano and struck chords; he jumped on one foot around the room. This behavior stopped soon enough. Rosa would come in and seize him by the wrists. "Quiet! Quiet!" After she was gone he would stick his tongue out at her until the roots hurt. Then he would attend to his tasks. He collected the eggs from the shed out back, he swept the living-room floor, dusted the wood stove and the piano, and watered the potted plants. Except for these duties he was free, but he was not supposed to go away from the house in the morning. Anton came into the room at ten o'clock, and just before he came in Rosa would go up to Jeppe and say, "Come now, Jeppe, let's have a smile." And he would stand there as the bedroom door opened, his eyebrows knotted with confusion, a smile on his lips.

His uncle's piano playing grew shorter and slower every day. And now he had a cane. The first day he used a cane Rosa looked at him and said, "You don't need the cane."

"I do," he said.

In the evenings Jeppe went into the bedroom to be read to. It was the same story Anton had started the first night. Sometimes he would read a few sentences with long pauses in between, and then put the book down and rest. A breeze from the window would flutter the leaves of the open book and ruffle his blond hair, which lay in flat, jagged tiers, inexpertly cut by Rosa. Sometimes the book slipped from his fingers, and he turned his head madly from side to side on the pillow and cried for Jeppe to leave. Sometimes he would not read, but would talk a little, asking Jeppe if he was helping Rosa, telling him to be a good companion to her. The boy would look at the book in his uncle's hands and nod. But there were times when his uncle was very funny, making jokes, and imitating Per by pulling his lips down over his teeth and bobbing his head. Once when he did this, Jeppe jumped across the bed to tussle with him, and his uncle gasped sharply, his eyes lit up with pain. The boy scrambled off the bed, but his uncle called him back, saying, "Don't be frightened." But after a while he said, "No, you shouldn't be here at all. Go out. Go out!"

But Rosa insisted that they be together in the evenings while she caught up on her household tasks, and when she came in and found her husband asleep her face lost its hardness, and she took Jeppe away almost gently.

Outside his companion was Per. At first he tried to avoid the old man, having been told not to listen to him, but it was useless. And then, the boy almost looked forward to seeing him and listening to him, if only he would not hold his hand so tightly. They would proceed down the road together. "See this old road?" the old man always began. "It has no name, none at all, but Sea Road, which is neither here nor there. Now, what's to keep them from calling it Per Norden Road? Tell me."

Jeppe could not answer that. Sometimes he would reply, "Well, why don't they then?"

The old man would stop stone still at his companion's ignorance. "Why *should* they? What've I ever done for a road to be named after me? Only messed about with hay and manure. And besides, they don't like me. Nay, boy, nobody likes me, and that's a fact." He would begin to walk again. "Aye, it's a fact. You, for instance, do you like me?"

"Yes," Jeppe would answer.

The old man would stop again. "Nay, you don't. Think it over and come clean. You don't really."

The boy would then shrug doubtfully, his fingers hurting.

"Of course you don't. That's how it is, boy."

Once Jeppe asked him why he wanted a road named after him.

"Why, when I'm gone, who's to remember me otherwise?"

"I would," Jeppe said.

"Nay, you just pass the time of day with me."

"Anyhow, where are you going?"

"Ah, into the ground," he grunted.

In the forest Per would chew his tobacco, sitting among the wild roses of the ruined church while Jeppe played. The boy took one of the tattered life preservers off a cross and laid it on the ground and sat inside it, as though it were a boat. "I'm sailing away!" he cried. Per would get up and plod among the crosses, bending over now and then, hands on hips, to read the faded lettering, and straightening up with some comment. "I remember the day they buried you, Captain Bohr, you old scoundrel. Embalmed in akvavit you were . . . Anna Hansen, you had a behind on you, you did . . ."

"What, are there people here?" the boy asked, stopping his play.

"Aye, in the ground, where else?"

"The ground?" he asked.

94

"Aye, aye," Per said impatiently. "There's the folks above and the folks below. I'll be going under soon enough, and here! Here where nobody ever comes. They'd never think to take me to the big one in Hjørring where Hans Norden lays with a marker tall as a ship's mast. Nay, it's here it's got to be."

"What do they do down there?" Jeppe asked.

"Why, they never do a thing," Per said, shaking his head. "Never a thing."

"Let's dig down!"

"Ah, never. You're disrespectful, boy. Come away."

These people in the forest interested Jeppe. When he was there alone he put his face close to the sand and called down and listened. He dug surreptitiously, keeping an eye peeled for Per, but gave up after a while. He conceived of the people as sitting in a little room in chairs, snoozing.

One morning, when his uncle rested in the living room by the window, Jeppe said suddenly, "What are the people in the forest like?"

"What forest?"

"The one by the beach, where the people are in the ground."

"Oh, the old cemetery," Anton said.

Rosa burst in from the bedroom. "Go outside and play, Jeppe," she said. He withdrew into himself at her look and jumped to his feet.

"Do you go there often?" Anton asked him.

Jeppe nodded, edging toward the door.

"What's it like?"

Rosa put her hand to her head. "Go outside, Jeppe."

"Tell me," Anton said, "I haven't been there for a long time."

"It's all green," Jeppe replied.

"Go on."

"There are wooden sticks in the sand."

"Wooden sticks? They're crosses, Jeppe."

Rosa went back into the bedroom, shutting the door behind her.

"I used to play there, too, when I was a boy," Anton said.

Rosa seemed even angrier after that, Jeppe did not know why.

One day a man came and drove off in the light blue car. Jeppe was wary about asking questions on any subject, so he waited until he saw Per to find out why the car had been taken.

"So they sold the machine," Per said, nodding his head over this tidbit of gossip. "There's no use for it anymore, is my thinking. And they can use the money, aye, that they can. Well, it's too bad. Your uncle, he was that proud of it. Him and her, they rode all over the countryside, proud as two pigeons. Things was coming good for him. People thought a deal of him, just a farm lad worked his way up to engineer in Hjørring. Things was coming good, and see him now, and her a stone, poor creature. Them two were a pair ever since they were your size."

"Could I have my hand back for a minute?" Jeppe asked. As he flexed his fingers he said, "What's the matter with him? Is it the croup?"

"Would that it was," Per said, taking Jeppe's hand back, and whispering in his ear, "It's what they call the bone cancer." Straightening up, he added thoughtfully, "They never had such a thing in my day."

"He won't play the piano anymore."

"Nay." Then he turned to the boy. "What do you ever do in that house?"

The boy shook his head.

"It's a selfish thing. She wants you to cheer him, and he wants you to cheer her. It's too big a job for a wee lad. You ought to come and live with *me*, I wouldn't set you down to such a task. Tell me, wouldn't you like that?"

Per lived in a bare little room in the cottage of his niece and her husband, a pious, ascetic couple whose life was a damp lament over their son who had gone to rack and ruin in Aarhus. Per's sympathies were with the son, and he needled them mercilessly.

"They'll turn me out soon," he said. "There's no doubt in my mind. They don't like me, I don't know why, but there you are. But you and me, boy, we could find a little place up by Skagen where the fishing boats is, and we two could have a jolly time."

For a while Jeppe was prepared to go with him and asked endless questions about Skagen, but the thing never came to pass.

Summer turned to fall. He sat around with the red, tattered book and looked at the story his uncle never finished, running his finger over the lines of words. Once he had taken the book to Per. "Finish it, Per," he had whined, "I want to know how it ends."

"It's a fairy tale. They all end happy."

"I knew it! Oh, finish it."

"All right, then," Per had said, but he had a great deal of trouble with the words and soon enough lapsed into the subject of Per Norden Road. Jeppe had then brought the book to the Carlsens, Per's niece and her husband, and asked them to read, but Per had looked at him with such fierce eyes that he had taken the book and gone back home.

The days were growing cold. He gathered wood for the big stove in the corner. The sea was gray; the smell of salt water and heather faded. In the forest the roses withered, and as he poked around the ruins he picked the last surviving ones and brought them home. When Jeppe came into the bedroom with the roses the doctor was there. He was a frequent visitor these days. A week ago he had attached a tube to Anton's arm, under the sick man's protest. Now Anton made no protest as the doctor checked the tube and the bottle to which it was attached. He lay there with his eyes half closed. He moved as little as possible because of his bedsores, and Jeppe had come to think of him as almost a statue under the covers. Rosa stood at the foot of the bed. The lines in her face had deepened; she had grown gaunt, and so silent that whenever she spoke Jeppe was startled. She saw the doctor out and returned as Jeppe laid the flowers on the medicine table.

"Where are they from?" Anton asked in his small voice. "I didn't think anything was growing now."

"They're from the cemetery," Jeppe replied, using the word for the forest that his uncle had told him to.

His uncle reached over for the flowers with his left hand. His right arm and shoulder were bound up. A few weeks earlier Rosa had bumped against him in her sleep and the shoulder had snapped in two. His screams had awakened Jeppe, and he sat straight up in his couch, his eyes wide, as Rosa came running in, her white nightgown a blur in the darkness. "Stay there!" she hissed, colliding with furniture as she sought the telephone.

It was dawn when the doctor came, and Jeppe saw him sleepy and disheveled, standing in the doorway silhouetted against the chilly pink sky. "You weren't to sleep in the same bed together!" he snapped at Rosa, adding less gruffly, "My dear girl, he is a soda cracker." Rosa looked up at him. Her cheeks were gouged where she had torn at herself. From then on she slept on a cot by the bed.

Picking up the flowers, Anton said to his wife, "Put them in water."

She took them silently.

"Don't throw them out," he said, and she stopped in her tracks, as though that were exactly what she had intended to do.

"Heather is nicer," she said. There were a few vases with heather in the room.

"No, I want these," he said.

Jeppe stared at the roses wonderingly. There was nothing special about them. Rosa, too, looked at them, her eyes half shut, as though against a painful light.

"Put one small bubble in this tube . . ." her husband asked. She turned on her heel and left the room. Anton closed his eyes, around which the skin was dark, as though rubbed with soot. He could not bear to be shaved often, for his skin had grown very sensitive, and there was a dark stubble on his cheeks. His hair, though clipped regularly, looked too heavy for his head, which seemed very fragile.

Jeppe went outside. There was a new man to be seen around these days, a dotty old fellow Per's age, a onetime carpenter who had come to live with his son in one of the nearby cottages. He and Per had hit it off at once, and the new man, Egon, hung on his companion's every word, his mouth agape. Jeppe would walk at the side of the two men, his head lifted to catch their words.

98

Sometimes he pressed between them, and Per would say, "Get on, now, boy."

Today the sound of a hammer came ringing down the road on the wind. Per sat at the foot of a telephone pole, chewing, while Egon worked beside him. Jeppe went up to them. "What are you doing?" he asked listlessly.

"Take a look," Per said, pointing to Egon, who was hammering a sign to the pole. The letters were heavy and black.

"What does it say?" Jeppe asked.

"Per Norden Road," the old man read, slow and loud. "Per Norden Road." He stood up, hands on hips, and stared at the sign, his eyes narrowed with satisfaction.

"Will it do?" Egon asked, stepping back and looking at Per.

"It's a bit crooked."

Egon set to work again. Per walked back and forth, looking at the sign from different angles.

"It's a good sign," Jeppe said ingratiatingly, dogging the old man's heels.

"How do you know? You can't read."

Jeppe thought again. "Egon's a nice man."

"Nay, he's a ninny."

"Let's us two walk."

But when Egon finished with the sign the two old men walked off together.

Jeppe wandered back to the forest, where he sat looking down at the sea. The sand would be cool to the touch, the water numbing. The waves spread, thinning, up the hard part of the beach, leaving great, foam-ringed arcs dark as the deepest corners of the forest. The sea folk, he thought, would be shivering today. But how could he know? He had never gotten that far in the story. Still, it was a happy story—Per had said so—so they probably had their part of the ocean heated. He turned to leave and saw Rosa among the trees.

She was sure to have come to tell him to play elsewhere. She did not like the forest. She might push him against a tree as she had against the shed. "I don't come here often," he lied, keeping his distance. She glanced at him and walked around the crosses.

She had not put on a coat, and she looked cold. He crouched in the sand; she walked around and around slowly, her hands clasped across her billowing apron. After a while he grew bored and slipped away. As he came out from the trees he heard a sob such as he had never heard before, like something coming up out of the earth, dark and jagged. He walked quickly away, and then, under a cloud-burst, he ran. When he got home she was walking slowly down the road in the rain. She wiped her face with her apron when she came in, and went into Anton's room.

That night she seemed different to Jeppe. Her eyes were no longer like blue stones knocking hard against things. They lingered, some-times on his own face; they seemed moist and almost asleep. The next morning she told Jeppe to bring Per to the cottage. Anton talked to the old man in his room, and then the old man went off on the bus to Hjørring. He came back that afternoon with some packages.

That evening Rosa washed Jeppe in the kitchen sink and then wrapped him in a towel and combed his hair. "Ah, the snarls," she sighed, tugging patiently, patiently, until he almost fell asleep. His clothes were in a sad state. She basted the more obvious rents and helped him dress. Then she brought her own good clothes into the living room and dressed in a corner. When she came out she wore a green velvet dress and a string of pearls. Her hair was neat; her lips were red. She took him into Anton's room. Anton was not interested in them, it seemed, and stared up at the ceiling with half-closed eyes. In the crook of his arm were two small packages. Finally, he looked at his wife and nephew. Rosa took the packages and handed one to Jeppe. The boy undid the gold ribbon, trying to conceal his delight, for he felt a smile was somehow out of place. Inside was a wristwatch. His face flushed with excitement, and a gasp broke from his lips. Now Rosa opened her package and held up a narrow silver bracelet. She put it on carefully while her husband watched her hands.

After a long while she said to Jeppe: "Kiss Anton good night."

The boy pressed his lips to his uncle's cheek, thanking him, and went into the other room to bed.

The next morning Rosa woke him. "Anton is gone," she said. "You must go over to the Carlsens' and stay there today."

He dressed, whispering, "Where has he gone?" But she stared out the window, looking plain and tired in her green velvet dress.

He stayed at the Carlsens' all day. They read to him from the Bible, answering his questions about his uncle's trip with words he did not understand. Per sat in a corner saying "bilge" and "rot" now and then. Once Per examined the wristwatch. "It's a fine watch he gave you," he said. "You'll grow into it in time." It was very large and weighed Jeppe's wrist down. He sat watching the hands move with their unbelievable regularity as the Carlsens read on and Per made faces at them.

The next day Rosa sewed his clothes up properly and put him into his coat. She herself wore a black dress, a black coat, and a black veil, which was just now thrown back over her head. There were people in the house, relatives and neighbors. One of them, a great-aunt from Hjorring, took Jeppe aside, fed him peppermints, and hushed him when he grew loud, for the press of people excited him.

"Will you read to me?" he urged.

"This is a solemn day, Jeppe," she replied. "I can't read to you. Besides, there isn't time."

But he slipped away from her and went into the bedroom for the book. Rosa stood alone in her coat and veil. She looked at the stripped-down bed and the tube and the bottle. "You understood better than I did, Jeppe," she said.

He crept toward the table where the book lay.

"We must go," she said.

"The book . . ." he faltered.

She took him by the hand and led him from the room, lowering her veil. There were cars parked before the cottage, and he and she got into the back seat of a large black one. In a moment the procession began. It went along a narrow paved road to a small village by the water. Children ran up and down the cobbled streets, yelling. Fishing boats bobbed alongside a net-strewn pier. Jeppe wondered angrily why he had never been told that this place was nearby. All this time he could have hiked over here and played.

The car stopped before a little church against which leaned a great anchor, partly embedded in the ground. Inside, the church was bare and uninteresting, but a model of a sailing ship hung from the rafters, and this Jeppe consumed with his eyes. Everyone, in perfect silence, seated himself, and the priest in his great white ruffled collar began to speak. Jeppe looked covertly around, having had enough of the sailing ship. Per and Egon sat nearby, dressed in black suits almost purple with age, their wooden clogs exchanged for regular shoes of leather. They both had mean scratches on their faces, and looking more closely, he realized that the usual gray stubble on their cheeks was gone. The Carlsens sat a good distance from the two, their faces sad but composed. He looked down at his lap, where his hands lay crossed. Whenever the priest paused he lifted the watch to his ear and listened. He had learned that if he wound it every once in a while, it would not stop. It was so large, the glass so thick, the metal so hard, that it would no doubt last forever, always ticking; even if it were submerged in water or run over by a car it would probably continue to tick, though of course, he would never expose it to such cruelty. He wound it again now.

There was a large, long box in the corner that the priest bowed his head to whenever he spoke of Anton, and just when Jeppe felt tendrils of itches curling through his body six men rose and carried the box outside. He and Rosa and the rest followed. It had begun to drizzle. They got into the car again and drove back the way they had come, leaving the pleasant little village with its boats and children behind. He looked out the rear window until they rounded the bend; then he turned reflectively to Rosa. "If the boats go out today will the men use umbrellas while they fish?"

"I don't know," she said from under the veil. She was so strange beneath that black cloth. He tried to make out her face, but it was like some odd fish, faint and frightening under water. Drops of water splashed from under the veil onto her coat front, sparkling in the gray light.

They came to the cottage but did not stop. They passed the sign saying "Per Norden Road." "Have you seen Per's sign?" he asked, but she did not look.

Finally, they stopped on the road where it became deeply rutted and overgrown. The drizzle was light, but people opened their umbrellas when they got out of their cars. Rosa was offered an umbrella, but she moved on as though she had not heard and plodded behind the priest and the box. "Jeppe," she cried, and he hurried after her.

The forest was wetter than the road. The sand was soggy, and the leaves dripped steadily, making a soft tap-tap-tap all around. Someone had replaced his toys, the life preservers, on their crosses, and they hung there glistening in shredded curves in the dimness. Someone had dug out a large rectangle in the sand, and here the priest went, holding his hands in prayer before him.

It was unbelievable, Jeppe thought, that all these people should be here in his forest, and he was torn between pride and jealousy. He ached to ask someone if they would come like this from now on, but as he fidgeted, Rosa took his hand. Her grip was soft and loose, as though her fingers were rubber, but as the minutes went by the fingers tightened until his hand hurt as much as when Per in the old days had held it.

The priest addressed the box, calling it Anton Nikolajsen, his uncle's name. It came to him then that his uncle was in there. He drew back sharply and scanned the faces around him. Everyone was looking straight at the box. He wished to see the trees part into a great door opening on the heaths, but they remained where they were, their thick branches intertwined like arms all around. His eyes swept from cross to cross, then shut tightly. Presently he heard a scraping noise, and his lids crept apart. He watched with horror as the box was lowered into the earth.

Then they were leaving, walking silently through the wet sand to the road. Rosa wished to walk home, and she and Jeppe went together down the road as the others climbed back into the cars, which passed them slowly, one by one, their motors soft.

Jeppe looked unceasingly at the black veil. After a while Rosa took her hand from his and lifted the veil back over her head where it rose behind her in the wet wind.

"Uncle Anton?" he asked.

"Yes, he's at rest now. He's asleep."

"There, in the forest?"

"Yes."

He swung his eyes down to the road, shuddering.

"We'll come back tomorrow." Her voice was flat but gentle. She stopped walking. He was still looking down, so that she could see only his brown, dropletted hair. "Jeppe, I'll always be grateful to you." She put her hand on his head.

He could only think of the hole in the sand. His mind crept toward the memory and veered away and crept back. He put his hand to his mouth.

The cottage was filled with people. The ladies made food and brought it into the living room, where card tables were set up. Jeppe ate nothing. He sat in a corner, looking at his watch.

The next day, when the house was empty again, Jeppe told his aunt that he felt sick; he did feel a little ill, but he pretended he was worse than he was, puffing out his cheeks tiredly, and touching his stomach. He did not want to go back to the forest. She put him to bed on the couch and went there alone. He lay on the couch, playing with the watch. The cottage was very quiet. He remembered the village he had seen the day before, but the thought of sneaking over there to play disturbed him, just as the thought of the forest did. He wished to forget yesterday entirely.

In the evening Rosa urged him to eat; she had made him a surprise dessert, a baked apple, crisp and sugary. She was kind to him, and even sat with him on her lap until it was time to go to bed. It was as though the sun had come out, but soon enough the sky would darken again and she would scold him for making noise, and give short, faint answers to his questions. The book was now in the bookcase, and he considered asking her to read to him, but she had read so fast that he said nothing.

Now she was busy again—both visitors and people on business

came in the days after the burial, and she seemed relieved to see them, for when she and Jeppe were alone she often stood by the window, just looking out. He would go outside and play along the road. He saw Per and Egon walking and talking together, but knowing that they did not wish to be disturbed, he kept his distance, following the black hens around, moving the watch up and down his wrist. He thought to himself that Per should be very happy now that he had a road named after him, but the old man seemed the same as ever. He wondered what could make people happy.

October passed, and it began to snow.

One afternoon when he came into the cottage from his play, he found a visitor sitting on the piano bench with a cup of coffee on her lap. The face meant nothing to him, but by the bright colors of her clothes he knew she was his mother.

"Here is Anne-Marie," Rosa said to him.

The woman put her cup and saucer on the bench and looked Jeppe up and down. "Well, little man, do you know me?"

"You're Mama."

"You see," she nodded to Rosa.

Jeppe hung his coat in the closet and came back into the room.

"Say hello," Rosa told him, her eyes resting thoughtfully on her sister.

He walked across the room and stood looking at the woman.

"What, haven't you been taught any manners?" she laughed, and took his hand and shook it. Her face was oddly colored—the eyelids were blue, as though painted with watercolors, and the mouth was a glowing pink-white. Her hair was piled very high on top of her head and looked hard to the touch. She drew him to her and kissed him. He rubbed the lipstick off his cheek.

"You'd better put your slippers on, Jeppe," Rosa said. "Your shoes are wet."

"We'll have to go soon if we're to catch the bus," Anne-Marie interrupted pointedly.

Rosa turned to Jeppe. "Your mother wants you to go back with her."

"To Paris?" Jeppe said.

"What strange ideas the boy has," his mother said, lighting a cigarette. "No, to Odense maybe. Or Aabenraa. I'm not sure."

"You move around like a gypsy, you never keep in touch. You might have been dead for all we knew," Rosa said.

"But I'm not, you see."

Jeppe had sat down to unlace his shoes.

"Can't he undo his shoes yet?" Anne-Marie asked. "See how slow he is."

"I've had little time to help him . . ."

"Oh, of course. Poor Rosa, it was a terrible thing for you. And Jeppe must have been such a bother."

"No, you mustn't think that," Rosa said. "I thank God that I had him."

Anne-Marie slipped down to the floor beside Jeppe and undid the laces in a wink. He remembered when Per had helped him with the shoes.

"I'm glad he was good," Anne-Marie said, standing up and glancing out the window. Outside, Per and Egon walked along the road, bundled up against the cold, Per talking away as usual. "Is he still alive?" she asked, "He was a hundred when I left. It's the mean ones that live forever." She sighed. "What will you do now without Anton? Or the boy?" She waited, her eyebrows lifted.

"Without the boy?" Rosa asked slowly, and then her voice grew hard. "You can't just come back when it suits you and ask for him. A year from now you'll drop him somewhere else. I have no patience with you."

"I think you have no patience with anyone," Anne-Marie said softly, "least of all with children."

"Ah! Let him be the judge of that!"

Anne-Marie looked at Jeppe. At the hardness in his aunt's voice he had hung his head tiredly. He stared down at his watch. "Have you seen my watch?" he asked his mother. "I found it."

"You never found it," Rosa said. "Anton gave it to you. Why do you lie?"

"I don't know," he whispered truthfully, pushing the frightening memory of his uncle away.

"Anton was fond of him," Rosa said to her sister. "He was good to him, he read to him . . ."

"He didn't," the boy blurted.

"Well, shall I?" his mother asked. "Come, where's the book? I love to read to nice little children."

With great precision Jeppe took the book down from the bookcase and handed it coolly to his mother.

"No, you're not to read it," Rosa said to her sister.

"You're cruel to him," her sister murmured.

"*I* will read to him. I have all the time now, all the time." She looked down at Jeppe. "I'll read to you."

" 'The Little Mermaid,' " he whispered to his mother.

"Put the book back, Anne-Marie," Rosa said. "It was Anton's since he was a child. And stop pretending. So things are hard just now, and the state will give you a little money if you have your child back to support . . ."

Jeppe looked resentfully from his aunt's face to the closed book. Anne-Marie stood up, still holding the book. "Are you coming with me?" she asked softly. He ran quickly to the closet and came back with his shoes. "Sit down and I'll put your shoes on," his mother said.

Rosa stood looking at Jeppe as though dazed. "No, I don't understand," she breathed, her fingers at her lips. "No, I really don't . . ."

"It's the boy's own choice," Anne-Marie said briskly, lacing up the shoes.

"Boy! He's not even a boy, just a baby, not yet six . . ."

Anne-Marie stood up and got Jeppe into his coat.

"Are you crazy? Do you think you can do this?" Rosa ran to her sister and dealt her a hard slap on the side of her face, at the same time grabbing at Jeppe's arm. He dodged her, plucked the book from his mother's hand, and ran out the door, flying down the road in the opposite direction of the forest, darting past Per and Egon, paying them no heed. Looking back, he saw his mother running out of the cottage with her coat and boots in her hands, and Rosa running after her in her slippers, bare-armed and bareheaded.

"Per!" Rosa's voice came faintly on the wind. "Stop Jeppe!" The old pair turned as one, their hands cupped around their ears.

"What is it she wants?" one asked, and the other shook his head.

The two women were farther apart now, Rosa falling behind. "Per!" she cried again.

But Per was staring at the rapidly approaching Anne-Marie. "Why, it's the little chippie come back from the wars," he said, and as she passed he doffed his cap and bowed low.

"Come, Jeppe," she said, yanking on her coat. "What timing. We'll just make the bus." He fell in alongside her. She muttered as they hurried along, cursing the snow that drenched her thin shoes.

Jeppe paid no heed to her. He held the book against him, and he could feel his watchband pressing into the old red binding. "To-gether," he murmured, looking at them. Then breaking into her muttering, he said to his mother: "You will read to me on the bus. And not fast." The words came out in a breath that hung like white steam in the bitter cold.

"Yes, yes," she said impatiently.

"If you don't," he said evenly, "I'll go away and you won't get any money."

She gave him a glance of surprised amusement.

The snow began to fall again. The flakes settled between his arm and the book, and he brushed them off carefully as he ran. He could hear Rosa's voice on the wind, hollow and distant: "Where? . . . What address?" then in a wail: "Jeppe!"

He looked around. Far back on the road stood the two old men, black against the whiteness. Ahead of them, no longer running, but plodding heavily along, shaking with the cold, was Rosa, her white apron flapping in the snowy wind. Her arm was lifted high, waving in great arcs. All around her were the white heaths and, beyond, the leafless forest. Happily, he spread his fingers in a wave and hurried on.

Monsieur Scream

He was a highly excitable young man of seventeen, with a pale and prematurely old face. He came floundering out of the bus with his easel, paint box, rolls of canvas, and suitcase—six feet two inches of barely fleshed bone clad in sandals, heavy cord trousers, striped red jersey, and black beret, all smartingly new.

There before him lay the village with its dribbling stone fountain, its little streets paved with real cobblestones. He swung around in an exhilarated circle, dropping several items with a clatter.

An old man sat in a nearby doorway, embroidering. His needle paused in the air. Some small boys playing by the fountain stopped to squint.

"Will you carry my things?" the stranger called in correct but horribly accented French. "I'll give you twenty centimes each," and the boys rushed up, each grabbing an item. Towering over them, the youth pointed down the street to a small whitewashed building with a faded awning bearing its name. "Hôtel Poste, *mes enfants!*" And off he strode, filling his lungs with heat, dust, and history.

"Are you from Paris?" asked one of the boys, running to keep up.

"Oui," the youth cried over his shoulder. He had changed trains in Paris.

"Are you an artist?" yelled another.

"Oui," he sang out, already hurrying to the door of the hotel café, where he paused to dig out some coins for his entourage. Then he sprang inside. A man in a net undershirt was working behind a counter.

"I am James A. Skrimm, monsieur," the youth greeted him in French. "I wrote you last month from Chicago, Illinois, U.S.A., to reserve a room for me?"

"Ah, Monsieur Skrimm," the man cried pleasantly—he pronounced it Scream—and he shook the extended hand with warmth. "We are closing."

"Closing?"

"Oui, we're leaving on our summer holiday."

The boy's face underwent a jolt, as if it had been socked. "But there's no other hotel in Bemiarle, is there?"

"Non," the man replied cheerfully. "We're only a village. You go to Vichy, it's a big town with a lot of hotels."

"But I don't want to go to Vichy . . ." He turned slowly around and looked at the café. It was as he had pictured it, the windows hung with yellowed lace, the walls done in faded brown paper; and along the molding lay wine bottles swathed in the tricolor, to be opened when their respective owners returned from military duty. Some of the bottles had gathered dust since the Franco-Prussian War.

"Tant pis," he said manfully, and went back outside. But there he was greeted by a clamor from the boys, who were racing off with his gear, urging him to follow. He did so, and was led along a narrow unpaved street, where eventually they stopped before a door.

"Mon Dieu," he breathed, looking at the stones in which the door was set. "This is the old city wall!" He was growing excited again, but the door was pushed open on a room filled with chairs facing a small television set. Sweeping the room with a twig broom was a short, aproned woman with frizzed black hair. Three little girls were straightening the chairs.

The oldest boy went up to the woman. "He would like to stay here, madame."

She gave James a short look. "He has to have a hostel card. You know that, Achille."

"Oh, but I have one!" James cried, his face filling with light. And he dug into his wallet and withdrew a clean yellow membership card, which he thrust into the woman's hand. "I never thought of checking for a youth hostel here," he said, beaming.

The woman glanced impatiently at the card. "You don't want to stay here. There are no comforts."

"Oh, I don't care about comforts. How much is it?"

She scowled up at him. "Five francs a day. For how long?"

"How long will the Hôtel Poste be closed?"

"Hôtel Poste?" she cried. "The Darmanches? They're going for a whole month to Normandy—as if they could afford it, the *poseurs!*"

"Then I'll be with you a month."

"A month!" She threw her hands up. "No one has ever stayed that long. Come see the dormitory."

All of them—the boys, the little girls, and James—followed her through a dark passageway like a mine shaft and up a flight of stone stairs to a small landing. There the woman pushed open a door with her foot, disclosing a large bare room. Five iron cots with moldy straw mattresses stood against the once whitewashed stone wall, now scarred and streaked. The wooden floor was littered with dirty straw. Everything, even the light bulb hanging from the ceiling, was thick with dust.

"It is not what you expected," she said with gloomy pride.

But James was already at one of the windows.

"The light's perfect. And look—there's the monastery!" Down the street stood a long gray building with a church at one end and a round tower at the other. "My father stayed in Bemiarle once, in 1938," he told the group, turning around. "He's a painter, too. He painted a picture of that monastery."

The oldest boy, Achille, was peering out the window. "That's not a monastery. It's an apartment house. I live there."

"It used to be a Dominican monastery," James told him, taking his easel from the boy and unstrapping it. "In the fifteenth century the monks were bricked up in the cellars to die of starvation. There must be fifty skeletons down there right now."

Achille, eleven, with dark, serious eyes, was looking at him with interest.

"For a week you could hear them yelling and screaming," James went on, "then—silence!" He unfolded the easel and set it up.

"Pay me by the day," the woman said, sticking her hand out. "Then you can leave any time." James gave her five francs. Pocketing it, she herded her daughters out the door ahead of her.

"That's Madame Pinippe," Achille said as the door slammed. "She hates hostelers."

"Why? It's a hostel, isn't it?"

"*Oui*, but she doesn't like them in the kitchen. Or the recreation room—that's where her Tele-Club meets."

"Isn't the place supposed to be for hostelers?"

"*Oui*, but she doesn't care."

"I hate television anyway," James said, untying the cord around a sheaf of stretchers. "And I won't be using the kitchen, I'm going to eat at a café."

"There is no café, now that the Hôtel Poste's closed."

The youth frowned at this, but a moment later lost himself in his stretchers, which he banged together at right angles on the floor.

"Are you famous?" the youngest boy asked.

"Well, yes and no," James murmured through his banging. "What is fame?" Now he held the stretcher frame up and reached for a roll of canvases. But suddenly he set the frame aside, overcome with fatigue from his journey. He flopped down on a cot, which flew with dust and straw.

"Aren't you going to paint?" the boys asked.

"Not right now."

Their interest was fading. With a burst of energy, pummeling and tripping each other, they disappeared out the door and down the stairs. James closed his eyes in the abrupt silence. His home in Chicago rang with the voices of five younger sisters, his father's art students, and his voluble father himself. It seemed to James that he had longed for silence all his life. Now it covered him like a sweet syrup.

A noise like thunder woke him to darkness. He leaped up and flailed around for the light bulb, yanking the string and producing a little pool of dim light. The thunder roared on, pierced by greetings

and scraping chairs, and now he divined that it was the sound of
many feet rumbling across the room below. As he stood listening
his stomach clenched with hunger. He was reluctant to leave the
little pool of light, but he forced himself across the dark room to
the landing, and groped his way down the stairs to the black passageway. Fighting down panic as he felt blindly along the wall, he came
across a door handle and propelled himself into what he hoped
was the kitchen. He switched on a light. The room held a king-
size bed with a satin counterpane, and a sleek, modern dressing
table. He turned hastily around as he heard footsteps behind him.
Little Madame Pinippe stood in the doorway, her arms crossed.

"I thought I'd have to keep an eye on you. What are you doing
in here?"

"I was looking for the kitchen," he said nervously.

"The kitchen is not to be used after seven o'clock."

"I didn't know. I haven't eaten today."

"I can't help that," she said, uncrossing her arms. And stepping
over to him, she reached vigorously up to the sleeve of his jersey
and ushered him out, turning off the light on the way. "And if
you go into my bedroom again I'll have my husband thrash you!"
she said, walking off.

"Wait!" he cried, but she opened the door of the Tele-Club room
and slammed it behind her, leaving him alone. Turning in the black-
ness, he began stumbling back over the uneven floor, his hands
feeling along the wall until they came to another door. He opened
it to a crack, and with a rush of gratitude stepped out into an
alley.

Gradually the pounding of his heart subsided, and he became
aware of music issuing from a small window some six feet from
the ground. Walking over to it, he stood on his tiptoes and looked
in. Cowboy music and pistol shots blared from the small television
screen. Every chair in the room was occupied; some of the viewers
sat on the floor.

Suddenly the figure of Madame Pinippe shot out of a chair. "You!
You American, get away from that window! It is four francs to
watch!"

His face burning, James crept back inside and up to the dormitory. He forced a chair tightly under the door handle, then got down on his sharp knees and looked under every cot, though it was too dark to see anything. Finally, leaving the dim light burning, he lay down on one of the cots, fully clothed, his stomach still gnawing, and tried to sleep.

The next morning sunlight drenched the dormitory. In the wash-room he dashed his face with a few rusty drops from the tap, and ran outside, where a cart drawn by real oxen came rumbling by. Looking in all directions, smiling at everyone he passed, he hurried down to a shop and bought a two-foot loaf of bread, eggs, powdered coffee, and an aluminum pot, and hurried back to the hostel.

The door stood open to the kitchen. It was a small stone-hewn room with a contemporary stove and shelves crammed with wine bottles, canned goods and jars of pickled beans. From rows of hooks hung pans, ladles, and meat cleavers. Madame Pinippe was washing lettuce at a tin sink, her back to him.

"I'm going to make my breakfast, madame," he said. "I've brought my own pot." And he held it up.

"Monsieur Scream," she said, turning around, "it is my duty to ask you to leave. You have abused every rule."

He stood silent, trembling.

"When my husband left for work this morning he came back and said he saw your light burning from the street. Do you realize how costly that is? The dormitory light must be out by nine o'clock. You have abused that rule. You have also broken into my bedroom, and you have sneaked free television entertainment at my expense. These things are not to be tolerated. You must leave."

"I haven't done anything wrong—I've paid—I had a right—in fact, it's—" But he could not bring himself to say that it was she who was abusing the rules, using the recreation room for commercial gain, investing her upkeep money not in the dormitory but in her private furnishings. He had only the courage to say: "It's not a decent place to sleep, the dormitory—"

"*Au contraire!*" she flew back. "It is you who are used to luxuries.

You Americans, you expect the Palace of Versailles in poor Bemiarle! Nothing is good enough! Ah—cook your eggs!'' Wiping her wet hands on her apron, she strode from the room, turning around in the door. "And that outfit of yours—no one has dressed like that for fifty years!''

Releasing a breath, James set about making his breakfast. He had just pulled a chair up to the table when the oldest daughter, a girl of nine or ten, came in and sat down opposite him.

"Bonjour," he greeted her uncertainly.

There was a long silence.

"I'm James Skrimm. What is your name?''

"Henriette,'' she said without enthusiasm.

"I have an aunt named Henrietta,'' he said after another silence, breaking off a chunk from his loaf of bread. "She lives on a houseboat.''

The child's eyes flicked from his hands to his mouth as he popped the crust in.

"If you're hungry,'' he said, suddenly picturing Madame Pinippe withholding food from her children, "you can have this.'' He thrust the loaf under her nose. She recoiled.

He put the loaf down and started eating his eggs, unnerved by her silence. "Do you have a pet?'' he asked at length.

She nodded.

"A dog? A cat?''

"A dog.''

"What's its name?''

"Noir.''

"That's a nice name. Is it a nice dog?''

But she was tired of answering questions. She looked at the table, bored.

"What are you sitting there for if you don't want to talk?'' he asked.

"I have to watch you. You're not to steal anything.''

"Steal?'' He sat back, knocking the coffee cup to the floor, where it broke neatly in two.

"That's our cup. You must pay for it.''

"Put it on the bill!" He crammed the last of his food into his mouth and stood up.

"You must wash up after your meal. There's a fine of two francs if you don't."

Swiftly he washed and dried the plate he had used. When he was done the child said, "My mama says you must scrub the floor of the Tele-Club. Every hosteler has a duty."

He went to Madame Pinippe and coldly asked for the necessary equipment. She gave him a wooden bucket, a sliver of soap, and a rag. "Do a good job," she said. "Otherwise there's a fine."

He set to work. The scrap of soap was useless; all he could do was liquefy the dirt, leaving it in whorled patterns. He was fined two francs directly he was done.

Upstairs, smoldering, he took out his ball-point pen and some notepaper, and wrote a detailed letter to the main hostel in Paris, whose address he found in his hostel handbook. Then he took the letter down to the post office, a hole-in-the-wall where one sleepy man with a drooping mustache sat. After that he felt relieved, and stretching in the warm air, he walked off in search of scenes to paint. Down by the fountain he ran into Achille and his friends.

"I saw you in the window of the Tele-Club last night," Achille said. "Madame Pinippe was furious."

"I don't pay attention to her."

"Really? Everybody else is afraid of her."

"*Quelle sottise,*" James said with a laugh. And flinging his arm out at the village, he asked the boys if they would give him a guided tour. "What a place!" he marvelled as they walked. "Do you realize how lucky you are? No traffic? No smog?"

"No nothing," Achille said.

"Bemiarle's a medieval glory! Look at your fine old church over there. Look at those stained glass windows. Look at that old archway."

"Tell us about the cellars," Achille said, "the skeletons of the monks."

And as they walked through the village into the surrounding fields, James again described the maddened priests pounding their fists against the bricks.

"I think my apartment must be exactly over them," Achille said with dark pleasure.

The fields were lime green, lazily bounded by crumbling stone walls. Tall poplars stood in pools of bellflowers. A distant rustic bleating of goats could be heard. "My God, it's peaceful," James sighed.

"Dull," Achille answered, picking up a large stone and staring at it. "It's Mère Signac's skull!" he cried.

His friends wheeled around.

"It's just a stone," he said, throwing it down and turning to James. "She was over ninety years old, she lived in a shed with a goat, and walked around the hills talking to herself. Then one day she disappeared—nobody ever saw her again."

"We think she died over there," one of the boys said, pointing to a forest. "The foxes probably ate everything but the bones."

James gave a small shudder.

"It scares you?" Achille asked with surprise.

"Quelle sottise! It's very interesting. Why wasn't she ever found? Didn't anyone look for her?"

"Ah, *oui,* the men searched for a day, but it's a big forest. Besides, if they found her they'd just have to go to the expense of burying her." He picked up another stone and threw it. "Anyway, I think Madame Pinippe killed her."

The others scoffed at this.

"No, really, she might have had some money hidden on her. And Madame Pinippe got wind of it and got her up to the hostel and killed her with a meat cleaver and stuffed her into the loft."

"Look at the goats," James said, pointing, but his companions persisted in their morbid talk. He concentrated on the green rolling hills. His father had stumbled upon the place during a walking trip when he was little more than James's age. He had stayed at the Hôtel Poste until he ran short of money, then moved into an abandoned barn that had bats hanging from the ceiling, but he was happy. It was in Bemiarle that he painted his first good pictures, had his first all-night drunk, and enjoyed his first amorous adventure—a wild little farm girl with green eyes.

His father never tired of telling these things, and he was as powerful a raconteur as he was a painter; not only did his work hang throughout the great museums of the country, but he was a sought after professor at the Chicago Art Institute. Even at home his students flocked around him, enthralled by his unusual personality. He smoked four packs of cigarettes a day and sometimes went into rages during which he would kick his easel down. That was temperament, said James's mother, who was very quiet and did little else but have babies. When James was small he begged for some paints, and he had been painting all his life. But though his father raved over his students' work or condemned it passionately, his son's efforts left him indifferent. One day he even advised the boy to prepare for a career in the business world. James only worked the harder, yet more and more often he would suddenly smear everything out with his fist and have to start over.

He had planned on Bemiarle since he was thirteen, taking every odd job he could find, and later in high school throwing himself into his French course. At the end of four years he had enough money for his round-trip ticket and six weeks in Bemiarle. He informed his parents. His mother said, "Heavens, no, James, you're too young," but his father drowned her out: "Nonsense, look at the size of him." And his mother had said, "It's not size that counts. Besides, he's far too nervous." And his father had snapped, "Nonsense. Let him go." James's heart had swelled, but then his father had ruined the moment by saying, "What're you going to do there?" and when James replied, "Well, paint," his father had looked at him with pity that he covered up with a shoulder clap.

But now, as he walked along, his father's attitude had no significance in the lush rolling countryside. *"À bientôt!"* he yelled to his friends, and raced back to the dormitory for his equipment. Having carried it up a slope overlooking the village, he studied the maze of roofs and towers, and in high spirits began to build the scene on his canvas. Sweat poured into his eyes, he smoked one Gauloise after another.

In the afternoon, when the sun was at its hottest, Achille climbed up to him with a newspaper. "You'll get sunstroke," he said, draping it over James's beret, and he sat down under a tree and fell asleep.

They parted at dusk. In the dormitory James laid the canvas on a cot and regarded it thoughtfully. Then he was on his knees, rubbing the paint into a blur.

It was evening when he went down to the kitchen and boiled some eggs for dinner. Henriette soon appeared at his side, this time with the dog, Noir. It was a huge, queer-looking beast, black except for a large white spot on its head, like a plate. It slobbered over to James, lifting its head for a caress.

"The only decent member of the family," he murmured, patting it. "Well, pull up a chair, Henriette. Keep your eyes peeled."

Henriette did so, shoving the dog away as it licked her arm with its lolling tongue.

"You're a miserable brat," James could not keep from saying as he took his eggs from the pot.

Henriette considered this. Then she said, "At least I don't look like an idiot."

Bitterly stuffing the wet eggs into his pockets, James left the room. Noir followed him, and he invited it into the dormitory, where it sat down with a dog-smile on its face.

"Yes, you're decent," James muttered, and the animal's presence made him feel more cheerful. When he had eaten his eggs he took out his notepaper and wrote a letter to his parents. Subtly pointing out his stoicism, he made everything much worse than it really was, adding broken windows and rats, and describing Monsieur Pinippe, whom he had never met, as a demented giant; but he was painting well, and putting his pen to his lips, he conjured up a group of village girls who stood around his easel watching him work. Hunched over his notepaper, he almost scribbled himself into a warm satisfaction with his lot, and at nine o'clock he stuck the chair under the door handle, pulled the string of the light bulb, and fell promptly to sleep. The dog guarded him all night.

In the following days he painted without stop—the monastery, the old archway, the hills, even a portrait of Achille.

"*Alors,*" he said, stepping back from the finished canvas and gesturing for the boy to look, "what do you think?"

"Is that me?" Achille asked, grinning with self-consciousness. "Is that how I look?"

James wiped his hands on the paint rag. "It's not the resemblance that counts. It's the character."

The boy looked more closely.

James waited. "Don't you see the essential Achille there?" he urged. "The spirit of Achille?"

Achille looked a little longer, then shook his head.

"Well, what *do* you see?"

"I don't know. A face. Perhaps."

Tightening his lips, James removed the canvas from the boy's gaze.

But he continued to take Achille along when he painted in the hills, because if he went alone he sensed Mère Signac's white bones gleaming through the grass wherever he looked, and he would turn around and hurry off, his paint box banging against his thigh. With Achille along he did not have this problem, and sometimes he brought off three pictures in one afternoon.

But alone, at night, his fears returned; he thought he heard odd noises—footsteps and moans—and he would lie frozen on his cot. He was bothered very much by the landing, where stairs led up to the loft. He bought a box of candles, and every morning he climbed up to the loft entrance and stood there, stretching his candle as far into the gloom as he could, to assure himself that Mère Signac's skeleton was not protruding from the old wicker basket that stood there. Unfortunately he could not summon up the courage to do this at night before going to bed, when it would have made more sense. He got very little sleep.

The second week he ran out of canvases, and took the bus into Vichy to buy more. He used those up in a few days and bought still more. He saw that he was painting too fast, too nervously, and suddenly he didn't like any of it.

By the beginning of the third week he wished he had gone to Paris instead. He had been proud of ignoring Paris for an obscure village, like a world-weary traveler, but now his solitude was becoming unbearable. There must be something about him that kept the villagers at a distance, though he always cried *"bonjour"* and smiled his most dazzling smile. As he sat by a candle reading a paperback biography of Van Gogh he ached to join the television audience downstairs, but he was prevented by the thought of placing four francs in Madame Pinippe's palm. Every evening he waited in vain for Noir to come back and keep him company.

One night there was a whine at the door, and he gratefully let the dog in. It thumped its tail and licked him, and seemed to disperse the sinister elements that hung in the dark corners. When he blew out his candle James fell asleep for once without any difficulty. But he woke with a stupendous start, his eyes boring horrified into the dog's bulk on the cot opposite, where, outlined by the moon, it sat staring at him. Suddenly it leaped down and rushed straight for him. He reeled off the cot, and as the creature fell on him he went sprawling across the floor with a scream.

It was some time before he moved. Noir sat beside him, thumping its tail. James shakily extended his hand and patted the white spot on the dog's head, which was merely a white spot, not a monk's tonsure. "I'm going mad, Noir," he whispered. He led the poor animal from the room, knowing that he would never let it through the door again.

After that he stayed awake every night, sitting on the floor inside a ring of glowing candles stuck into some empty wine bottles. He bought a small hunting knife and kept it in his lap. Only when the sun came up did he try to sleep. The paint on his palette hardened; the canvases gathered dust. His single thought was to last until the Darmanches returned. Then he would have two full weeks of decent living, and he would paint with all his faculties restored. This knowledge comforted him, and he felt that if only he could bring the fist of justice down on Madame Pinippe before leaving his plight might be almost bearable. But though he kept checking the post office for a reply from the main hostel in Paris, and even nursed the hope that the Parisian officials would suddenly appear in the flesh before their defective employee, nothing happened. He wrote another letter, and another, and it seemed to him that Madame Pinippe sensed his machinations and treated him with more scorn than ever.

"You are not happy here," she remarked one morning as he

scrubbed the Tele-Club for the eighth time. "You are haggard. You do not sleep well up there, you are afraid?"

"Afraid? I sleep like a log."

"Then look sharp," she said with a glance at the rag he was dragging in circles. How beautiful it would be, he thought, to push her head into the bucket of dirty water and hold it under. But he lacked the strength. Dark circles hung beneath his reddened eyes, there was a tremor in his hands, and he was plagued by bouts of nervous diarrhea.

Having finished his labor and paid his fine, he went upstairs to sleep. He had turned three cots on their sides and propped them around his own cot, and now he climbed over the ramparts, flung himself down on the eroded mattress, and closed his eyes.

But as usual he was too tense to sleep. All day he tossed and turned, his skin scratched red by the protruding straw. As the afternoon closed he lay staring up at the crumbling plaster of the ceiling. "She's up there," he said aloud, "in the loft," and he saw, very clearly, the white bones of Mère Signac's fingers emerging from the old wicker basket.

"This is impossible!" he whispered, clutching his head, and he climbed over the ramparts and thrust his face out a window into the cool gold of the evening. A boy was walking behind some cows, lazily switching their rumps. Peaceful mooings drifted up to his ears, along with the hollow clunking of cowbells. In the distance lay the soft green fields and hills. James's puffed eyes rested gratefully on the innocent scene. Just then, below him, Madame Pinippe came out the side door, meat cleaver in hand, and headed for the backyard where chickens and rabbits were kept.

"Out for more blood," he whispered, withdrawing his head from the suddenly tainted air. Yawning and rubbing his eyes, he puttered with his painting equipment, softening brushes with linseed oil and blowing the dust from his palette, keeping everything in good order for the day the Hôtel Poste reopened.

That night, during the Tele-Club gathering downstairs, there was a knock at his door. He was sitting inside the ring of candles, his knife in his lap, trying to concentrate on his Van Gogh biography.

"Qui est là?" he cried, springing up with his knife.

"Achille!"

"Un moment, un moment," he called, hiding the knife under a canvas and hurriedly dismantling his fortress of cots. Then, going to the door, he tried to remove as noiselessly as possible the chair he had jammed under the handle. *"Entrez,"* he sang out, swinging the door open.

"Good news—the Darmanches are back! They came home a week early!"

James slapped his sides, speechless.

"They asked if you were still here. You can move in tomorrow."

"I'll move in tonight!"

"You can't, they've gone to bed—but they'll be open at ten in the morning. I've got to get back downstairs," he said, turning and hastily feeling his way back down. "It's Sherlock Holmes."

James closed the door, laughing and walking around the room, too excited to sit down. When the shock of the good news had worn off, he rubbed his hands and began to pack his suitcase. Then he stacked his paintings and tied them with a cord, and got all his equipment together. He sat down on his cot, jiggling his foot. At eleven o'clock the Tele-Club departed with its usual thunder, and the ensuing silence was so thick that he imagined he could cut a slice out of it, like a succulent melon. He had not replaced his barricade of cots or stuck the chair back under the door handle, but he no longer cared. All his fear had loosened up and flowed away. He pictured the small whitewashed hotel room where he would crawl between clean sheets, and the café where he would eat glistening green salads and soft cheese. He felt all his drive and talent gather inside him, readying to flow through his brushes. He would leave as soon as the sun came up, and sit in front of the hotel until it opened.

He began pacing back and forth. Now and then he would throw himself down on the cot and try to sleep, then get up and pace again. At five o'clock, when the first gray light of dawn touched the room, he grabbed up all his gear, and, stumbling under its weight, made his way to the landing, where he turned and gave the dormitory a farewell look of cheerful disgust. Then, glancing up at the loft, he stood motionless, his lip between his teeth. He set his load down and climbed swiftly up the steps. Without hesitating, the floorboards creaking under his feet, he crept through the loft's gloom toward the big wicker basket.

"Let her be there," he whispered exultantly.

He was almost to the basket when his courage faltered. He stopped for an instant, then plunged ahead with one long stride that sent him crashing through the rotten floorboards to his waist. Madly flailing his arms, he overturned the basket on top of him and a mass of moldy garments smothered his face. He tore at them, screaming like a beast in agony.

Almost at once the nightgowned Pinippes had rushed up the stairs to the dormitory, their eyes half shut with sleep.

"*Sacre bleu*, do you see what he's done?" Madame Pinippe cried, pointing up at the long thrashing legs. "He's ruined my ceiling! Come down, come down, you great fool! What are you doing in my loft! How dare you! Pull him, Émile!"

"I'll pull him up from the loft," said Monsieur Pinippe, a stooped, bald man with an enormous drooping mustache, which he pinched nervously.

"The loft's not safe, you'll fall through too. Pull him, I say!" She fetched a chair for her husband to stand on. "And stop that screaming!" she cried, shaking her fist at the legs.

The three little girls stood in a line, faces lifted, mouths open. Monsieur Pinippe got up on the chair and grabbed James's kicking legs. "*Voyons, voyons,*" he soothed over the screams. "It's not far to drop, I've got you." He gave a great tug and James popped out of the ceiling, still screaming, pulling the man with him to the floor.

"Ah! Ah!" Madame Pinippe cried, beside herself. "Do you realize what you've done? What an insolence! That fine ceiling that has withstood storms and bombs for five hundred years! Oh, the costly damage!"

"I'll just throw a couple planks across the hole, Geneviève," said Monsieur Pinippe, patting her arm. She shook away from him.

"A hundred and fifty francs' damage, and it will never be the same! Oh, stop that screaming." She gave James's cheek a slap. He looked around him, then up at the hole.

"You've had a bad fright, my boy," Monsieur Pinippe said, and through James's wheeling mind came the knowledge that he was looking at the postmaster.

"Pay up at once," Madame Pinippe told him. "That's the second time you've broken into my property. Come, hand it over, or must we have you arrested? A hundred and fifty francs."

James dragged out his wallet and with floundering hands gave her the money. A pack of neighbors, awakened by the commotion, arrived on the landing and stood gazing in.

"Ah, *oui*, it's a fine thing!" Madame Pinippe shouted to them. "He's fallen through my ceiling! Come in and see it, completely ruined. I knew he was crazy from the start." She turned to James. "Now be off! And if I see you again I may yet have you arrested!"

James wobbled out to the landing, amassed his belongings, and labored down the stairs with them. Outside, bending every few feet to retrieve a dropped item, he progressed haltingly away from the village, until at last, from the empty dormitory windows, his figure had dwindled to nothing in the brightening day.

The House of Angels

May 27, 1954—Two minutes past midnite so it's my wedding day, I should be getting my beauty sleep. But I haven't written anything down for a long time and I won't have time when I'm married, so this will be good bye. Babe's asleep on the cot, I've got a newspaper stuck against the lamp so not to wake him, I keep thinking what's going to happen to him.

I know he got off to a bad start with his name, he came along last, number nine, and they just called him Babe, like they just called me Sissy, but when I was ten years old I gave myself this name I liked, Sandra, and I asked Babe what name would you like? He said Donald, I don't know where he got hold of it, and I started calling him Donald, but he said it didn't count that I'd just call him it, so I said when I grew up and went to Kansas City I'd take him along and he could start off fresh there being Donald, but he said it would be too late then. Nothing satisfies him, like if he was awake now I know he'd be wishing I wasn't even here in my rightful room with him.

We're not alike. I'm blond and attractive, not to sound vain, where he's puny and redheaded. He was the runt of the litter and he was hanging onto Ma all day, even when she went down to the outhouse, and we'd have to come and drag him away, but she didn't favor him. For one thing she was too tired to be bothered, and for another I don't think he was our Pa's child because the rest of us were all blond like peas in a pod, and it used to grate on her when Pa said, For a tired woman you sure get a few things done,

127

but he didn't really care, I think he was short on brains. I didn't get my brains from Pa. None of we kids got past the eighth grade, but I was always writing diaries and stories and things, and now I have finished up my high school diploma at nite school. I believe in self betterment, and it was me who took pity on Babe and tried to install him with my philosophy of life and call him Donald and everything, but it never took. All he really wanted to do when he wasn't hanging onto Ma was to sit on this sagging old bed in the kitchen that he shared with Earl and Brother, with this old crummy blanket over his head, and daydream and pick fleas off the cat.

Pa died in '48 and our Ma went the next year with a growth the size of a cantaloupe, it was what made her so tired. I came here to Kansas City and went to work at Woolworth's in the hardware section, and Babe was sent to the County Home on account of being under eighteen, but he never liked the place, he said he didn't like the building. Last year when he turned eighteen and I turned twenty-one he got let out in my care and I got him a room down the hall from me and got him work as a busboy in a cafeteria, but he dropped things all over and they fired him. Then I got him work as an usher in a movie house and I thought it would be wonderful because he could watch the movies, but he said he didn't like the building, and also he didn't like the candy counter girl, he said she made eyes at him. I got mad then, it was the most modern show in town with big mirrors and murials on the walls, and I also thought he should be grateful if the candy counter girl made eyes at him because god knew he wasn't exactly Laurence Olivier. I tried to install him with my attitude, I told him he ought to look on the bright side and treat the candy counter girl to a terrific evening on the town but he said there wasn't a girl alive he'd treat to a terrific evening, anyway he got fired for having b.o.

All this time I wasn't exactly a wallflower, but I'm very choosy, I believe a man should have good manners. A lot of men start cracking their knuckles if a girl gets enthusiastic about anything but them, they can talk their heads off about sports or just hanging around some billiard room and you're supposed to hang on every word even if you're bored to death, and if you start to say, Well I had an interesting experience the other day, a lady came into hardware who looked exactly like Ingrid Bergman they start cracking their knuckles. I've passed up a lot of dates to great places because of that. My fiance has got good manners and he's intelligent in his own way, he's a garage mechanic, his name is Don Lemoyne, and in a few hours I'll be Mrs. Donald R. Lemoyne. Babe has never liked Don I think because of the name, he begrudges anybody else having it, also he doesn't like Don because Don keeps telling him he ought to join the army. But I know the army wouldn't want Babe because besides not being very smart his feet are flat, I mean like a penguin's. But Babe says he doesn't want to join the army because he doesn't like army buildings. What the h---, Don says, buildings shmuildings, he thinks Babe's crazy, he has also pointed out that Babe has taken advantage of me, and I have to admit this is true. But if I don't watch out for him, who will? None of the other kids. I don't even know where they are anymore except for Brother and Viola, and Brother has been in the state asylum for six years and Viola married high up and only has me over once a year when her husband's away on business, and never Babe. Because on top of everything else Babe's dirty, in fact it's the worst thing of all, he never takes a bath, he says he's afraid of a chill, but the real reason is that he likes dirt. I think the world is too clean for Babe, that's why he's so unhappy. Ma was a dirty housekeeper, it sounds mean to say but it's true, I was glad to get away but I think Babe misses the mess.

But what I was getting to is where Don always says Babe should join the army, I always thought he should fall in love, love makes you put your best foot forward not to mention how optimistic it makes you feel. So I made Babe clean up and introduced him to a couple of my girlfriends but he never opened his mouth and when I asked him afterwards why he was so rude he just shrugged. Don't you ever want to fall in love and get married, I asked him, and he said who cares about love? Someday you'll eat those words, I said, when you fall in love and you're so filled with it you're not fit to be around, don't worry it happens to everybody. It won't happen to me, he said, and to tell the truth I didn't really think it would either. I was just wishing it would so he would change his ways. I was getting fed up with him. On top of being dirty and a wet blanket he was out of work so much I had to pay his rent half the time. Once when I mentioned this he said he would gladly find some other room because he didn't like my building anyway, well this building, it's not new but at least it's clean and there are venetion blinds instead of torn shades, so I said Who are you not to like this building? But you can't talk with him, he drives me out of my mind. But the thing is I've always felt sorry for him and his hair even began to go thin last year and he's got little wrinkles around his eyes already and just nineteen years old.

He looks like life has passed him by, especially when you're in the middle of preparing to get married and full of plans, we're just going to City Hall and no honeymoon til Don's vacation in July, but I bought a white suit and shoes to match, not to mention packing and everything because we're moving into an apartment next week. I guess in a way I thought I'd meet somebody more up my alley but I never did in the three years I've been here, and Don has got a lot going for him, he's steady on the job and is nice about things other men might not be, like making frames for my movie star pictures out of folded cigarette packages, that's not simple. Anyway, when you're a bride-to-be, Babe looks all left out and empty, a stranger would say to look at him, What if he died, he wouldn't have lived at all. But that's the funny thing because he finally did have a love affair and when it ended it nearly killed him. He's been laying on that cot like a corpse for four days, ever since it ended.

It started with sometimes he liked to take long walks by himself and once I followed him because I wasn't sure what he might be up to. He walked over to the slummy section of town but he didn't even stick around the normal part, he went to the part that was being torn down for new housing, what a horror, just rubble all over the place like the newsreels of the Korean War, but there were some buildings left standing here and there. He went up to one and drank it in, it was an old rooming house with a sign that said *The House of Angels* because of these two plaster of paris angels outside an upstairs window, they had bird droppings on their heads and they were white there but the rest was gray and mildewy looking, and they looked loose, like they were ready to fall down, the whole house did, it gave me the creeps.

One day after Babe lost his latest job as a hotel dishwasher I gave him his rent money for the landlady and when I came home from work that nite he was gone with the money and he had left a note for me saying, Don't be worried, I am going to be very happy (only he didn't spell it like that, he can't spell).

At first I was so boiling mad I didn't care where he'd gone but after a week I got to worry and on my day off I went to find him, and I went first thing to that Angel House. An old man about ninety-five years old answered the door stinking of beer even though it was in the morning, he was dirtier than Babe ever was and with brown stumps for teeth and long yellow fingernails like horn. I asked for Babe and sure enough he jerked his thumb up and said room nine, and I went inside practically having to hold my nose, it smelled of damp and garbage and beer all mixed up. Upstairs I knocked on Babe's door but nobody answered so I walked in and there he was laying on this crummy bed with a smile on his face. Hello Babe I said, but he didn't answer, he didn't even look surprised to see me. It was a terrible room, brown wallpaper hanging in tatters and linoleum on the floor with big holes in it and a dirty sink in the corner with a half naked hula doll hanging on the wall next to it, I can bet Babe didn't put it there, and the bed sagged in the middle almost to the floor and there weren't any sheets, just an old threadbare blanket. This was the room behind the two angels and he had pulled up the window for a view of their heads and all the rubble in the distance.

Babe, I said, you ran off with the rent money, how could you, you were never dishonest.

I couldn't help it, he said.

You had a nice room and good dinners with me on my hot plate, why would you run off to this awful hole?

He said it wasn't an awful hole.

It is so, are you blind or what? I asked.

He said, If you don't like it you can go.

I was surprised, he never used to have a quick tongue, and I looked him over careful. There was something funny about his face, better, I don't know what, but his clothes were the worst ones he owned, a gray tee shirt with billions of holes and pants all ragged at the pockets, he was barefoot too and his soles were black, you pick up an extra lot of dirt with flat feet. He was going downhill fast.

I told him that.

I'm not going downhill, he said and he ran his hand over that old blanket like it was silk. He said, I want you to leave me alone, I'm happy here.

Well you can't live here forever on that money you took, I told him.

He said the rent was cheap.

I should certainly hope so, I said with a bitter laugh, but sarcasm is lost on Babe. Anyway, I told him, they're going to tear it down.

He said, They won't tear it down. Mr. Olafson, that was the old man downstairs, told him that they wouldn't.

All he wants is for some silly fool to pay him rent until they do, I said. Why don't you use your head Babe, when they put up the new housing do you think they'll want a stinking house like this in the middle?

It's not a stinking house, he said and he was mad. He was touchier than I ever saw him before.

Well I can't stand it, I said, I feel dirty all over and I'm going.

Good, he said, and he went over and looked out the window like a king looking down at his gardens and goldfish ponds.

I stopped at the kitchen downstairs, I won't even describe it, and I said, Mr. Olafson is it true what you told my brother Babe that they're not going to tear this building down?

Who knows sister, he said to me, I live each day like it comes. He was punching cockroaches on the wall and saying Gotcha! each time, it gave me the creeps.

When Don came over the next nite I told him everything and asked him to go over there and try to get Babe to move out. He

came back later and he said, Sandra it beats me how you who are
so clean and high-minded can be related to that kid, he was sitting
on the bed wrapped up in a blanket with just the moonlight coming
through the window and those crazy statues outside and he jumped
up and yelled For Christ's sake who said you could come barging
in here, like I'd interrupted him in a big clinch with Rita Hayworth.
I never saw him act like that, he looked like he was filled with
electricity.

Did you talk to him? I asked.

How could I talk to him, Don said, he run me out of the room.

My feeble brother Babe, he ran you out of the room?

He had some bread and a breadknife and he threatened me with
the knife, oh I could have easy taken it away from him but I thought
why bother? I tell you Sandra I think we ought to sic the authorities
on him.

What kind of authorities, I asked.

Authorities from an asylum, he said.

That made me mad, but I was mad at Babe too. I let things slide
for awhile then about two weeks later on my day off I went there
again just to see if he had improved any or slid down further.

Ain't (he still says ain't) you ever learned not to come barging
into a room, he asked me, and when I plumped down into this
crummy old chair he said Watch how you treat that chair.

Do you realize we could have the authorities cart you away, I
asked him, but he paid no heed, his eyes were roaming around
the room like it was the face of some girl. He had plenty of whiskers
now, they're red, and he looked dirtier than ever but he looked
good too, like he had filled out. I said, How come you look like
you filled out?

He said Mr. Olafson and him ate good, he said Mr. Olafson didn't
make skimpy little salads like me and just a chop with all the fat
cut off, he made big pots of stew.

Cat stew, I said sarcastically.

Rabbit stew, he said, Mr. Olafson got a rabbit hutch out back.

Ugh I said, didn't you get enough rabbit stew when we were
kids? Besides, he's not supposed to have rabbits inside the city limits.

We ain't inside the city limits, he said, slow like a priest, this is the house of angels high up in the sky.

You're talking crazy now Babe, I said, he gave me the creeps, but I have to admit he looked good when he said it. As long as I could remember his eyes were those sleepy kind of eyes but now they were bright like two blue lights and I thought gosh he has nice eyes after all.

But I kept to my aim and I said, Look I've come to install you with some sense, no don't roll your eyes and look bored, it isn't healthy for you to sit here doing nothing all day in this filth, how long do you think it can go on?

Always, he said like a lovesick goon, there was no reasoning with him.

I had brought him some carrots and bananas and a carton of cottage cheese and I gave him the bag even though I was hurt by what he had said about my salads and chops, they are very tasty and nutritious, but he didn't even open the bag and I bet he never did. But I told him I was going to come every single week til the place was torn down and bring him decent food.

He said Don't bother, but I did, every week on my day off I brought him fruit and vegetables, also I brought him sheets and a clean blanket, five bars of soap and a towel, he never used any of it.

Once when I came he was sound asleep so I snuck down to the kitchen and got a bucket and mop from Mr. Olafson, he said, What the h--- do you want with those, sister? but I ignored him. That mop was as dry as a bone, I bet it hadn't seen use for ten years, well I filled the bucket with water from Babe's sink and started mopping the floor when he woke up in a split second. I never saw him act the way he did then, he came leaping out of the bed and he grabbed that mop and tried to break it across his knee, only he couldn't, so he threw it down and yelled, Sandra never come back here and try to louse up my life! And suddenly I was glad he had fallen in love even if it was only with a building and even if it didn't make him cleaner, only dirtier. At least like Don said it gave him some electricity.

So I said, Honey I don't want to louse you up I want to help you but if you don't want me to I won't come anymore.

That's fine, he said, Thank you very much Sandra.

It was the first time I ever heard him be polite, will wonders never cease I asked myself as I went out.

I kept my promise too, I never went to visit him anymore.

He lived there nearly four months on that rent money he didn't pay our landlady, I don't know what would have happened when he ran out of money but before that could happen they tore the place down. On one of my first visits I stuck my phone number on Mr. Olafson's kitchen wall with a tack in case Babe was ever sick or something, and four nights ago Mr. Olafson called up and said they were going to tear the house down the next morning and Babe wouldn't leave.

I got Don to drive me out and there was Mr. Olafson with all his things piled in a rickety old car, ready to leave. He took us upstairs, he told us Babe had locked the door but Don is strong and he butted his shoulder against it til it broke open. Babe was sitting on the bed with his blanket around him and that butcher knife Don told me about in his hand. What's this Babe, I said, you want to be torn down with the building tomorrow?

Leave me alone, he said.

Put that knife down and come with us please Babe, I said as sweet as I could, you can stay with me tonight and I'll set up a cot for you, but he didn't even let me finish, he just shouted Leave me alone again.

Don got mad and he said Do you realize how you're upsetting your sister? She's getting married in a few days and she's keyed up enough as it is.

But Babe paid no heed to this, he just stuck his chin out, and then Mr. Olafson said he had to get going and he looked at Babe and he said, Listen here I don't know why you want to stay on in this dump but you better get a move-on.

Babe scrambled halfway across the bed. Dump! he yelled, how can you say that, you been here longer than me, eight years, how could you say that?

135

I guess it struck him odd that Mr. Olafson didn't hold the house in the same esteem he did, maybe he thought because Mr. Olafson was as dirty as he was that he looked at things the same way. But I could tell that Mr. Olafson didn't care much about anything, he just gave a shrug and walked out.

I was cold standing there and there wasn't even any light on, I made to turn on the light but Babe jumped up with his knife so I didn't. I whispered to Don to take the knife away but he said, Now Sandra we've got to go careful, and he pulled up the chair for me and he sat down on the floor, and the moonlight was coming through the window and everything was quiet and creepy.

We sat there in that room all nite trying to talk sense into Babe, I was fed up with both of them, practically more with Don. Once I got so impatient I made to take away the knife myself but Babe was wild, he didn't respect it that I was his own sister and he said he'd cut me if I took another step, then I guess Don was ashamed so he tried a couple times but only halfhearted, then he started being cautious again. What do you think you're gaining, he asked Babe, you'll have to leave when the wreckers come.

They won't come, Babe said.

You're living in a fool's paradise I told him, they'll come any time now. It was getting light when I said that, my god that room looked awful in the grayness, even Babe looked gray, he was gulping in the room like a glass of wine somebody was going to snatch away from under his nose. I was so fed up I could have killed them both, I think the only reason I stayed all nite was because Don kept saying, Come on Sandra let's go.

When the sun was all red I said, Babe you've got to come on, the wreckers will be here any minute. No they won't, he said, and I began to believe him because it got to be nine o'clock and ten o'clock and nothing happened, the room was bright with sunshine and all three of us looked like death and we all hated each other so much it wasn't even funny. I hate to think about it but I called Don a coward and we began to yell at each other, forgetting all about Babe, and then suddenly a couple of men walked in.

This place is supposed to be vacated, one of them said.

Don't we know it I yelled, that's my brother over there, he won't leave. Babe held the knife up like he had been doing all nite but they walked over to him and one of them snatched it out of his hand in a wink, it was as simple as that, I gave Don a dirty look but he was already going over to help them yank Babe off the bed. Babe turned over on his stomach and held onto the mattress and they all three went to work on him, I really hated to see it, they had to pry him off and he was yelling bloody murder all the time but finally they got him off and as they dragged him out of the room he kept trying to grab things along the way, the chair, the sink, the tatters on the wall. I followed them downstairs and I wondered how we'd ever get him into the car but when we got outside he suddenly gave up like a horse that's just been broken, he got into the car as quiet as you please and we drove away and he turned around and looked at the house til it was out of sight.

I put my arm around him and I said, Now we'll go home and have some breakfast and you can stay with me for a few days. I accepted it that he couldn't ever be happy in a normal place, might as well let him have it his own way, so I said Listen honey we're going to find you a nice dirty room in the slum district.

He looked me right in the eye and he said It won't be the same.

For Christ's sake a room's a room, Don said.

You marry Sandra, Babe said, why did you choose her instead of somebody else, is anybody else the same as her?

It was the most intelligent thing I ever heard him say.

But Don said, It's not the same thing, Sandra is a person, and he began saying very nice things about me. I admit all nite in Babe's room I came close to breaking off with Don but now I realized I had been under a terrible strain, besides we already had the ring and the license and the girls at the store already gave me a kitchen shower.

We got Babe up to my room and set up the cot and he fell right down on it and closed his eyes and Don took me back out to the car and he said, Sandra you can't take him to a room in the slum section, it wouldn't be a normal healthy life, he'd fall to pieces and die young, you can't let him do it. Besides, there's the rent, you know he can't hold a job. Well after he left I thought about it and it sounds mean to go back on my word to Babe but Don is right, so what we're going to do is day after tomorrow take him back to the County Home, it's only for kids under eighteen but if they can't take him they'll turn him over to some other place. It sounds hard but there's nothing else I can do, a year ago I wouldn't have done it but then I still had hope for him. Now you can't even get him off the cot, it's like he was dead and laid out, except he moans and groans. But yesterday I came home from work and he was gone, it scared me but pretty soon he came back with a sack. What's in that sack Babe, I asked but he just shoved it under the cot, so when he was asleep I dragged it out and snuck a look. Inside was the head of one of those angels, close up the eyes were funny looking with no circle or dot on the eyeballs so that you got the feeling they were staring but you didn't know what at. I put it back in the sack and shoved it under the bed again.

I've got to end this now, it's four A.M., I'll look all fagged out at my own wedding, but I can't sleep and it's not that I'm keyed up, Don said I was keyed up enough as it is but I'm not, that's the funny thing. Maybe I should have waited longer for Mr. Right to come along, somebody who made me feel different inside like Laurence Olivier makes me feel, but I read in a magazine that that's infatuation, and Don is clean and clear headed as well as being steady on the job but I keep waiting for some big feeling. But we've already got the apartment, we're moving in next week, it's not too cute or anything but I'm going to fix it up, I've got a knack, and then as soon as we can afford it we're going to move into a brand new tract house, nobody else would ever have lived there before, no old dirt to wash away, and I can see myself sitting on the front lawn with a baby, it's not exactly exciting to work in hardware at Woolworth's all your life, and as far as movies go they're always happening to somebody else, I want something to happen to *me*, something big that sticks me up in the clouds, and here it is only seven hours til I'm Mrs. Donald R. Lemoyne and I'm not even keyed up. But I read in that magazine that every girl starts wondering if she's doing the right thing just before the wedding, it's natural. I ought to stop writing now, I'll look like something the cat dragged in, anyway the lamp is flickering on and off, it's a bad connection. Babe just woke himself up, he cries out in his sleep.

Glad Offerings

Uribia is one of the most pleasant resort towns on the Mediterranean coast of Spain. The sea is green, the beach white, and the Hotel Costablanca as large and modern as any. Yet, because the town is remote, buttressed by the vast and barren Sierra Helada, it escapes the usual hordes of foreign vacationers. It is the Spaniards themselves who enjoy Uribia.

All this information Rudy Drexel acquired in a characteristic manner. Instead of going to a tourist bureau when he and his wife arrived by jet in Madrid, he loped down the main avenue observing people until he spied a fierce-looking, mustachioed gentleman, politely stopped him, and asked in fluent Spanish where he went on holiday.

"We're going to Uribia," he told his wife as they walked away from the man. "It's a place where Spaniards go—we won't run into a lot of Americans."

"He sure talked a lot," Peg said. "I thought you said Spaniards were reserved."

"There's a difference between talking a lot and being informative. If you understood the language you wouldn't jump to conclusions." But he was annoyed with the man for parting with such an abundance of facts to a stranger. Rudy cherished a Spanish image of noble brevity. The man should merely have looked at him, seen the light in his eyes, and said: "Uribia."

"You don't really mind, do you?" Peg was asking. "Afterwards we'll go wherever you want—into the hills, whatever. But just one week at a really nice place first. I mean—it's my honeymoon too."

Rudy nodded, but to himself he said, It's *my* graduation present. He had just graduated cum laude in Spanish studies. He prided himself not only on his command of the language, but on his knowledge of the people, gleaned from his vast reading. He had no interest in cities and resorts—it was the villages he wanted, the scorched earth, the relentless heat. Sniffing at the unexpected briskness of the late-afternoon air, he felt affronted, and wrinkled his nose.

It was a long nose, under which the mouth sat crammed with protruding teeth. His body was slight, with a thin, tender neck. His blond hair was thick and tousled, his skin tea-colored, like a farm boy's. He looked wolfish, hungry, and walked with a loose roll, eyes alert.

"Now. We wire the hotel in Uribia for a reservation. Then we go to a bank. Then we catch the train. Third class."

"Can't we stay and see Madrid first?" Peg asked. "And why do we have to go third class?"

He did not answer. He was thinking of where he wanted to be— some tiny, secluded village, a cluster of rugged mud houses where boys practiced the kneeling *molinete* with a stick and old shirt, and where austere, black-shawled women wove at looms in doorways. There would be a cheap *fonda,* and simple meals alongside battered old Loyalists with scars like white medals on their flesh.

He looked at Peg walking beside him. His parents called her a gamin—a kindly term for unsymmetrical features and no figure. Thin as a stick, even now, three months pregnant. On campus she had worn torn jeans and a wild natural, which, much to Rudy's delight, had scandalized his family when he brought her home for a visit. But now, bride and mother-to-be, she had gone all conservative. Her blond hair sat like a shining little cap above her protruding ears, and she wore a stylish summer dress. Somehow it made her look twelve years old. She hurried alongside him in flat shoes. They were exactly the same height if she wore flat shoes.

"I'll take care of your money," he announced, stopping.

"But I want some spending money of my own!"

"I'll handle the finances. You don't speak the language."

With a sigh she handed him the money.

But at the bank she grew furious. He was cashing all his traveler's checks. "You can carry cash around in Spain," he told her, stuffing his wallet with bills. "Spaniards are straight. Besides, I don't want to be bothered with cashing checks and all that crap."

He sent a telegram to the Hotel Costablanca, and in the early evening they boarded an all-night train for Alcoy, where they would transfer to a bus for Uribia. They sat crushed together on a wooden bench in a crowded, stuffy third-class carriage. As it began rattling across the plains, which were soft with dusk and gratifyingly sultry, Rudy cleared his throat and made his first overture to the people of Spain.

"Hace mucho calor," he said.

Yes, they replied, it was indeed warm. He asked about the towns they passed. They answered courteously. He told them he was Bulgarian—it sounded better than American. They nodded graciously. He complimented them on their countryside. They thanked him. Then the conversation faded, and everyone sat quietly except for a man in a grease-stained bright blue gabardine suit who made vivacious faces at a small pig in a peasant woman's basket.

Peg's eyes had closed, and now the jet lag hit Rudy, too. A few minutes later they both were asleep, leaning together. Once or twice during the jolting night Rudy awoke, then dozed again, dreaming. Once he dreamed that he was in the presence of El Cid, who leaned down in a brilliant blue cape and touched him with a whispered benediction. When the train pulled into Alcoy at eight the next morning he woke with a smile and stretched. The other passengers all had disembarked along the way, and with one of them Rudy's wallet. He stifled a scream and leaped onto the station platform, where he collared a soldier from the Civil Police. "He was wearing a blue suit!" he cried, forgetting his Spanish. "He must have waited till everybody got off and then he stole my wallet. I thought he was El Cid! I decently took him for El Cid while he stood there picking my pocket!"

He had to repeat the story in Spanish. Then he and Peg were led to the police station, where he gave a full account of the incident. When they came out Peg was crying.

"Don't go all to pieces," he said, fighting tears himself. "We won't think about it yet. We'll go on to Uribia, and then we'll think about it."

"And how do we get there?" she wept, turning on him.

"I've still got a couple of bills in my other pocket," he muttered.

As the bus chugged over the great barren hills Peg blew her nose and put her handkerchief away.

"Do you realize what we'll have to do, Rudy? We'll have to turn right around in Uribia. We'll have to wire your parents for train fare back to Madrid and take the first plane home. It's just lucky the plane tickets are in the suitcase, or you'd have lost them, too. Our whole trip, right down the drain!"

Rudy did not answer. He sat quietly with his hands folded in his lap, a picture of repose. But Peg could see his pulse beating in his throat, and occasionally his long nose gave a frantic twitch.

He was looking at the magnificent landscape, unable to enjoy it for the lump in his throat. If Peg said another word he would strangle her. But she was silent now. And after a while he felt her hand on his. "He probably wasn't a Spaniard at all," she said. "He was probably a Moroccan."

Uribia burst upon them like a travel poster, awnings bright, bougainvillaea rampant, streets filled with Spanish vacationers in dark glasses. The fact that he saw no American tourists failed to hearten Rudy: in the morning he would have to wire his parents, and as soon as the money came he would be back on the dusty bus, gone before he had arrived.

At the hotel they were dealt a further blow. There were no rooms available; the season was at its height. They spent the entire day tramping with their suitcases from one whitewashed pension to another. Every room was taken. Finally, toward evening, they found themselves on the outskirts of town. The houses were a warm mud color, huddled together on narrow streets that led down to a brown shale beach, where a few fishing boats lay. "This is more like it," Rudy said, brightening. Some boys directed them to a *fonda*, a building of pocked, blue-plastered adobe set on a steep incline of dirty steps. The door opened onto a gloomy dining room with benches and bare wooden tables. They set their suitcases down and stood waiting, exhausted. Presently a woman came into the room, followed by an elderly cat.

"Buenas tardes," she said, moving gracefully on thick, hairy legs. She wore a pair of run-down slippers over striped ankle socks, and a faded housedress encompassed by a transparent plastic belt. Her face was as badly pocked as the walls of her *fonda*. The cat leaned against her legs, and she picked it up, chirruping, *" ¿Cómo estas mi querido Contento?"* It replied with a deep wheeze, and she kissed it between the ears. Quantities of the animal's fur had fallen out; its eyes were runny; its mouth was almost toothless.

Rudy asked for a room for the night, and the woman led them up a narrow tunnel of stairs to a hot, cramped room with a bed, a table, and a wardrobe on which was pasted a large decal of Minnie Mouse. She shifted Contento to her left arm and took a pencil and a pad of paper from her pocket; she wrote down the price of the meals and the room. Then she introduced herself as Señora Ciervas.

"Señor Drexel," Rudy said with a polite bow, and indicated Peg. *"Ésta es mi esposa,* Señora Drexel."

The woman smiled with surprise. "You look too young to be married," she marveled. "Why, I took you for brother and sister. I thought, where are these children's parents?"

Rudy's nostrils taunted. "Man and wife, señora," he stated with dignity, holding up Peg's hand with its wedding ring. This threw the woman into a fit of laughter. Then, touching them both gently on the cheek, she went out. A few minutes later she returned with their suitcases. She told them they could eat whenever they wished.

"I don't want to eat," Peg said when they were alone. "That cat ruined my appetite. Rudy, you'd better go out and wire your parents."

"It's too late, the telegraph office would be closed. Anyway, we just got here. Do you really think I came all the way to Spain just to turn around and go back?"

"What *else* can we do?"

"I'm thinking. Don't yammer at me."

They sat down on the bed, which was like a slab of concrete, and were silent as the room grew dark and Minnie Mouse's bright smile disappeared.

"Well?" said Peg at last.

"Let's get out of this oven."

With darkness, the streets around the *fonda* had grown festive. Children ran; dogs barked; water gushed down the gutters. All the houses were patterned with lighted windows, and radiated a rough inner activity. Rudy forgot his stolen money, almost forgot Peg. He was perfectly happy just walking around breathing in the atmosphere.

It was almost midnight when they returned to the *fonda*. Several people sat eating, but the dining room was silent except for the sound of Contento wheezing among the tables as he stayed on Señora Ciervas's heels.

"You must be hungry now," she told the couple, beckoning them to a table. "Sit down and I'll bring the food."

Peg looked at the cat, then at Rudy. He took a seat decisively, pulling her down next to him. The cat stood there, its threadbare tail hanging to the floor, its rheumy eyes half closed. Then it wobbled after Señora Ciervas into the kitchen.

"That cat turns my stomach," Peg whispered.

But Rudy was assessing the other diners. They all were men, all dressed in dark, shabby, unmatched trousers and jackets, hair combed straight back, eyes serious about the food. Now and then they glanced at the two foreigners. Presently Señora Ciervas returned with a plate of fish in a black sauce, Contento behind her.

"How old is your cat anyway?" Rudy asked, trying to conceal his annoyance as she set the plate down with her thumb well into the sauce.

She beamed down at the animal. "He's seventeen years old, the darling. He used to be sleek and quick, but now he's almost blind, he's lost his voice. He is so old, my poor darling."

"He looks diseased," Rudy murmured.

"Oh, no," she protested, picking him up. "Old he is, but not diseased. See, no sores. And he's clean as a clean plate. I keep him clean."

"Why don't you get a young one?" Rudy asked.

"What do I want with a cat? They're good for nothing."

"Isn't Contento a cat?"

She shrugged. "I suppose so."

Rudy started to eat. "You ought to put him out of his misery."

"He isn't in misery. He ages peacefully."

She kept standing. Rudy felt bound by the Spanish tradition of courtesy to ask her to sit down with them. He assumed that she would refuse, but she accepted, a smile creasing her pitted face. She remained at their table throughout the meal, rising now and then to bring in the other courses, all savorless fish dishes.

She had been widowed for twenty-two years, she informed them, and ran the *fonda* alone. "Why should I pay someone else to help when I can do the work alone?" she asked Rudy. "Money isn't that easily come by." She made little profit, and most of it went to the church. She had a sister who was a nun. She herself had not felt the calling; she had married instead. Her husband's name was Antonio. He had fallen from a scaffolding in his thirty-second year, God rest his soul. Though not blessed with children, it had been a happy union. She wished the Drexels a happy union, too. "In the United States," she asked with indulgent eyes, "do they all marry as young as you?"

"We're twenty-one," Rudy said shortly. He wished she would stop harping on their age. He wished she would stop talking altogether. But now she was questioning him about American food; Hollywood; his family. He looked at the other diners. If she weren't there, blocking him off with her chatter, they would accept him as one of them. But it was only when he and Peg had finished their dessert of two undersized oranges that the woman bade them a cheerful good night.

They lay sleepless on the stony bed.

"You've got to send a wire in the morning," Peg reminded him.

"I like this place," he mused aloud, "except for her. She's no different from the landladies back home. All she needs is a bunch of plastic curlers in her hair."

"Well, I *don't* like the place. The food's awful, the bed's hard, and the toilet's outside. And that cat turns my stomach. I thought you said Spaniards weren't gooey—I've never seen anybody gooeyer than she is about that thing."

"I can't help the odd exception," he said irritably. "Look, let's not talk. I'm trying to figure things out." He turned away from her on his side. Fortunately Señora Ciervas would not present the bill until they were leaving; that gave him some time to turn around in. Of course, the police might catch the thief and return his money, but that was unlikely. With a shiver, he pictured himself telling his parents face to face that he had cashed all his traveler's checks and immediately been robbed. And what fantastic story could he conjure up to tell his friends about his speedy return? But worst of all, he would be forever burdened with the memory of having been exploited, ripped off, he, who loved Spain so deeply, and carried his brotherhood like a glad offering.

In the morning he ignored Peg's renewed plea to send a wire. They had *café con leche* in the dining room; then he led her out to explore the neighborhood by daylight. At the vegetable market he struck up a conversation with one of the vendors, an old woman in a shawl, who spoke in an open, direct manner, yet managed to give the impression of parting with nothing. "That's how Señora Ciervas should be," he told Peg as they returned to the *fonda* for their bathing suits. He wanted to swim down at the little shale beach.

But the brown, lukewarm waves were listless, tamed by a long breakwater, and Peg found the shale uncomfortable to lie on. They returned to their room and slept through the broiling afternoon.

In the evening they sat down to their meal, and Señora Ciervas once more joined them, flowing with information and questions.

This routine went on for three days. Then Rudy allowed Peg to nag him into trying the large beach by the hotel. They began spending their afternoons there. The sand they stretched out on was soft and white as bath powder, and the lively sea a Technicolor green. Around them sprawled dozens of prosperous city families reeking of suntan lotion, whose children sliced the air with screams and shouts. "We might as well be at Miami," Rudy muttered. "Look at them, what do they know about their own Spain right around the corner?"

"They know enough not to be there."

"Christ, you're hopeless. Don't you get *anything* from the *fonda?*"

"No," she said, with a longing look at the Hotel Costablanca.

"Well, I do." But he was not being truthful. What he got from the *fonda* was mainly frustration. There around him sat the unvarnished citizens of Spain, eating in a holy silence from which he was excluded. Singled out as the American tourist by the Ciervas woman, he was fawned over, spoken to without stop, forced to watch her coo at the bedraggled creature in her arms. First a grease-stained El Cid, now a blathering tablemate. And Peg. Out of place as a milk shake. There was nothing he could do about her. Or the seed growing inside her. She had wept and developed black circles under her eyes while he, feverishly lost in his preparations for finals, had groaned and shelved the problem until suddenly it was too late for the abortion that had floated around his mind. Now she was happy. She loved him. And she was born to pregnancy. She had not suffered a moment's queaziness, not one dry heave. Her eyes were brighter and her color rosier, that was all.

At the beach he fell in with some youths from Madrid, and he would race them into the breakers, flapping behind them like a wet hen. Afterward, his thin limbs dripping, he would bend down for his towel and Peg would glance up with a smile, looking like a peeled twig in her bikini, while he averted his eyes from the voluptuous beauties on the sand.

At four o'clock the beach crowd drifted back to the hotel, and Rudy and Peg would wade back along the water's edge to the shale beach, and trudge up the street to the *fonda*. If they wanted to wash the salt from their hair they had to ask Señora Ciervas for a kettle of hot water, and soon she had a kettle boiling every afternoon. One day, when Peg asked where she could wash some clothes, Señora Ciervas plucked them from the girl's arms and washed them herself. She fell into this habit, ironing them, too, with a huge black iron that stood on the stove. Peg insisted that it was too much work for her, but she could never wrest the iron from the woman's hand. Even the drip-dry things were ironed. Every other day they would find their limp, sweat-stained clothes hanging neat and fresh in the wardrobe. Rudy said that this service would show up on the bill, but Peg told him she had a feeling it wouldn't.

Ten days passed, each one with a more precarious flavor. Rudy refused to send a wire home and knew that Peg dared not send one herself. Somehow he was certain that he would come up with a strategy that would allow them to stay the three months they had planned on. In the meantime, he put up with the sleek crowd on the beach, and at the *fonda* he continued to eat fish in black sauce without a nod of response from the other diners. He grew more and more hateful toward Señora Ciervas and her ruinous pet, two ugly things cleaving to each other. He could hardly bear the woman's voice as she rattled on about the price of fish, the few movies she had seen, the various aspects of Contento's character. There was not a spark of dignity in her, not an ounce of intelligence. Her personality extended to the decorations of the *fonda*. Every room, she told them, was graced with a Disney decal. She had bought them once on a trip to Valencia. Apparently she thought them modish.

The outhouse stood behind the building in a tiny patio of baked earth, and at night the Drexels were obliged to go down the stairs and through the *fonda* to the patio in total darkness. Peg was afraid someone would leap at her from a corner, but rousing Rudy, she could never get him to accompany her. There was nothing to be afraid of, he told her; besides, it was a refreshing experience going through the dark *fonda,* emptied as it was of Señora Ciervas's voice.

One night, having visited the outhouse and walking back across the patio, Rudy noticed Contento lying there. He remembered that Señora Ciervas said it sometimes slept outside on a pillow when it found her room too stuffy for its sinuses. It lay so still that he wondered, hopefully, if it was dead. He went over to it and, crouching, touched its shabby flank. It gave a characteristic wheeze and flicked its tail. Rudy sat motionless for a moment; then he slipped one hand around the thin neck and gave a massive squeeze. The cat struggled for an instant, then went limp. Rudy stood up, brushing his hand off on his pajamas, and went back into the *fonda*.

The next morning, before he and Peg were out of bed, there was a knock at the door. *"Pase usted,"* he called out sleepily, and Señora Ciervas came in with dragging steps, her eyes swollen.

"My Contento is dead," she said brokenly.

"¿Qué?" asked Rudy, sitting up with a great show of surprise.

"When I took him his breakfast he lay dead. His little tongue was out." She stood wringing her hands.

"What's wrong?" Peg whispered to Rudy.

"It—it was God's mercy, señora," Rudy said nervously, wondering why she had come to him with the news. "He was old, and God gave him rest."

"Oh, God is kind," she agreed with a sob, sinking into a chair, where she sat with streaming eyes.

"What's *wrong*?" Peg insisted, pulling Rudy's pajama sleeve.

"Last night, how did my little sweetheart seem then?" the woman asked through her tears. "When you kneeled by him?"

"I?" Rudy said with a start. He felt his face flame.

The woman's swollen eyes grew puzzled. "I sat by my window, I couldn't sleep. Certainly it was you I saw. Do you say it wasn't?"

"Certainly—certainly not," Rudy stammered, flushing more deeply.

She sat silently regarding his face. Her swollen eyes narrowed slightly.

"I saw him lying there, and—I went over to pet him." If only his face weren't on fire. And now his nose gave a sharp twitch. To offset it he smiled—too sharply. The woman remained silent.

At length she said, "And he was all right then?"

"Certainly!" But he was covered with confusion. He should have said the cat seemed ill. If only Peg would stop pulling his sleeve. If only the woman would stop looking at him.

"You never petted him before," she said, getting slowly to her feet. "Why should you pet him then?"

"I—I just felt like it," he said faintly, but beneath her steady gaze, his eyes dropped.

Again the woman was silent. Then, in quivering tones, she said, "You did away with my little Contento. Under my very eyes, while I thought how kind you were to sit with him."

And suddenly she rushed to the bed, grabbed Rudy by the arm, and flung him to the floor. As he struggled to his feet she beat his head and shoulders, screaming, while Peg wailed from the bed. He was terrified, yet his humiliation was almost greater than his terror—it was unbearable to be flung about and beaten up in your pajamas, to be spat upon and screamed at in your bare feet.

"You're making a terrible mistake!" he cried.

"I have made no mistake!" she cried back, and flung him to the floor again. He tried to scramble under the bed, but whichever way he crawled she blocked him with violent kicks. Then, with one final kick, she whirled to the wardrobe and flung it open with a crash. Tearing out armful after armful of clothes, she threw them to the floor.

"Out! This minute! This minute!"

Rudy had leaped to his feet and run to hide behind the bed, where Peg lay sobbing into her pillow. He stood trembling, unable to move or speak. Señora Ciervas kicked her way through the clothes to the door, where she turned.

"I will wash your room down with lye! I will scrub the table you ate from! You never stayed here, I never spoke with you!" She opened the door. "You do not exist," she said in a whisper, giving them a last glimpse of her terrible face. The door slammed behind her.

"What happened?" Peg wept. "Oh, Rudy, what happened?"

Despite his throbbing bones, Rudy felt a wave of relief at having escaped the bill. "It's some crazy mix-up," he said. "We've been kicked out."

"But why . . . ?"

"How do I know? Her cat's dead, she's gone off her rocker." With shaking hands he began to dress.

"But what's it got to do with us?"

"I don't *know*. She's off her rocker. Come on, Peg, get a move-on."

Wordlessly Peg took the rest of the clothes from the wardrobe, slowly shutting the door with its grinning Minnie Mouse. When she was dressed and packed she asked dismally, "What about the bill?"

"We don't have to pay," Rudy said shortly.

"Why not?"

"I don't know."

They carried their suitcases downstairs and through the empty dining room. Outside, they started walking toward the center of town. Peg was crying again.

But Rudy had been jarred from his lethargy at last, struck by inspiration. "Listen," he said, walking more rapidly, "we're going to the telegraph office. I'll wire home saying that you had an appendicitis, or better yet, some foul-up with the pregnancy, and you're okay now but the money's been used up on the hospital. They'll be worried by now anyway, wondering why we haven't written. They'll have to send us more money, they'll want to. And we can start the whole trip over again, the way we planned."

"Why did she kick us out?" Peg asked, wiping her eyes.

"I don't know."

"Did she blame us for the cat dying? How could she do that?"

"I don't *know!*"

"It sounded like she was accusing you."

He tightened his grip on the suitcase handle. "I told you, the woman's gone off her rocker."

"I heard you get up and go down to the outhouse last night. Did you see the cat then or something? Was it sick? Did you talk to her then or something? I don't understand."

"I don't either. Forget it."

"She was so unhappy and so fierce," Peg murmured.

"Forget it."

"I can't. It's horrible, leaving like this. Why did she accuse you?" She stopped in the street and put her suitcase down. "Tell me, Rudy. You never tell me anything. I want to know."

He set his suitcase down with a thud. "For God's sake, all I did, I came out from the outhouse and I saw the thing lying there, and it looked, I don't know, dead or something, so I went over to see. And she's apparently sitting there looking out her window, and afterwards she just *assumes*—"

"Why? Did you touch it?"

"Yes, sure I touched it! To see if it was okay!"

"I can't imagine your caring."

"Well I did!" But under her scrutiny he felt a sharp return of his earlier flush, and he turned his face away.

"Was it dead?" she asked.

He hesitated. "Yeah, it was dead. It was already dead. Come on." He bent down and picked up his suitcase.

"Then why did you act so surprised when she told you about it this morning?"

"That's great! My own wife accuses me!"

"No, but you did. And you looked so nervous. You looked scared to death."

"That's just great!"

"Oh, Rudy, you didn't really kill that poor old cat?"

"Poor old cat? You were the one who was always throwing up over it. What are you bitching about?"

"You did," she said softly. "Christ, Rudy."

"Christ Rudy nothing! I told you, I didn't do anything. It died of natural causes." He walked on and paused. "Come on. Come on, Peg!"

She picked up her suitcase and followed him. He could hear her crying again, quietly. The town was just awakening, the air was already warm but still fresh from the night. The telegraph office had not yet opened, and they sat down on the front steps to wait. At the end of the street they could see the green water bordered by its dazzling white beach. A few striped umbrellas were already up.

"It'll probably take a day or two for the money to get here," Rudy said. "Are you game to sleep on the beach tonight? It'll be warm." Peg did not reply, but blew her nose long and disconsolately. He reached over and gave her knee a reassuring pat. "And don't worry about food. I've got enough left for some sausage and rolls." Then he leaned forward, toward the green sea, clasping his hands around his knees. The crisp white shirt that Señora Ciervas had washed and ironed the day before stretched across his knobby spine.

The door behind them opened. "You stay here and keep an eye on the luggage," he said, getting up.

But she followed him inside. "We'll wire for train fare back to Madrid. That's all. Write it down, Rudy." And suddenly, flashing out her hand, she tore a button from the white shirt and threw it stingingly in his face.

The Famous Toboggan of Laughter

"Whenever I see a picture of the Eiffel Tower, it always reminds me of Paris."

I didn't bother answering. I didn't like her. Anyway, she was already past me, halfway down the boat deck. She was always in a big hurry, Mayo, never waited for a response. She was reckless, too. The first day out she climbed halfway up the ladder to the pilothouse just for laughs, and having only one arm, she almost fell off. Every night she drank with the drinkers or smoked pot with the pot smokers, stumbling into our cabin at dawn and making extra noise for the benefit of our other cabinmate, a retired missionary woman in her seventies. Mayo was my age, nineteen or twenty. I made no pretense of liking her, but she seemed to be the star of our student crowd even though, or maybe because, her rudeness was breathtaking, the kind that hits you in the solar plexus. There was always a lot of laughter and stomping of feet around her. Even Miss Shatswell, our cabinmate, seemed drawn to her.

Miss Shatswell had melancholy eyes. Her long, thin hands were full of condolence. When she spooned up custard or soup at the dining table she seemed to be soothing a great culinary flaw built into the universe. When she looked out at the ocean she seemed to see only the ships that had sunk and the sailors that had drowned. She always dropped dark quotes from Ecclesiastes.

Watching us play shuffleboard, she would tell the loser compassionately, "The race is not to the swift, nor the battle to the strong." When a stout Frenchman sat down on a folding chair and broke it Miss Shatswell hurried over to him as he tried to fix it, and said with feeling, "That which is crooked cannot be made straight." And once by the pool she singled out Mayo in her bikini, looked at the stump of her arm, and, with her eyes moist, told her, "That which is wanting cannot be numbered."

There was a silence around the pool. Then Mayo barked, "Pull the nails out of your hands, lady," and jumped into the water with a big splash. Her friends clapped, but Miss Shatswell's gentle smile was unperturbed.

In the Cherbourg customs shed, at the end of the crossing, I saw Miss Shatswell threading her way through the crowd toward Mayo, and I saw Mayo's eyes narrow. The old lady looked at her for a moment; then her special smile filled her face. It was the most radiantly pitying smile I ever saw. She laid her long fingers on the girl's shoulder.

An obscenity burst from Mayo's lips. Still smiling, Miss Shatswell melted back into the crowd. She was on her way to the Passion Play in Oberammergau.

I was on my way to Paris for the summer between my junior and senior years at college. I found the cheapest room I could near the Place St. Michel, and went out to the cafés. Within a week I had met enough interesting people to keep me busy. The sun shone, and everything was fine. Then a sullen, clammy rain began to fall.

One day I saw Mayo again. She was coming down the street toward me under a big black unbrella. I crossed the street, but she crossed, too.

"What time is it?" she asked peremptorily.

I consulted my watch. "Three," I said, and she walked off leaving me with my arm in the air. I saw her again a few days later as I came out of my hotel room, but this time she didn't speak. The third time I saw her was in Notre Dame Cathedral. She was eating a pomegranate and spitting the seeds on the floor. It was cold in the church.

"He must have had rheumatism," she said, coming over to me.

"Who?"

"Quas."

"Who?"

"Quasimodo. The Hunchback," she said loudly, adding, "*Jesus,* it's cold." And tossing her pomegranate core into the open shoulder bag of a nearby tourist, she sauntered out, pausing to give a skeptical glance at the rose window.

The next day there was a knock at my door, and Mayo walked in with a newspaper under her arm.

"Shooting a picture down on the Costa Brava. Want to be an extra? *Extras,*" she shouted into my surprised silence. "And don't look at my arm, anybody can pass in a crowd scene. It's some crazy American picture shooting in Spain for tax reasons. You're wondering why I don't wear a prosthesis."

She had taken off her coat, and was wearing one of the slightly soiled sleeveless blouses she favored, exposing the stump, which was three or four inches long and very white.

"I don't like those hook things, and artificial hands get discolored. Satisfied? Or now I guess you want to know how I lost it. Right? Okay. Went for a ride a couple years ago. Car rammed into me. I was thrown out on the road, the arm stayed in the car."

For the first time since I had met her I felt that my look of cool dislike was out of place. I searched for something to say, but came up with only, "Gee."

"Great dialogue!" she snapped, adding, "Does it disgust you? The stump, I mean."

I nodded. "The way you always draw attention to it, to shock people."

"That's tough. Now look, page six." She shoved a week-old London tabloid under my nose.

"Do you go in for this kind of journalism?" I asked, feeling the cheap print smear under my thumb.

"Myself, no. But the concierge doesn't care what quality he hangs in the WC. From the Manchester *Guardian,* which goes a long way, to the flimsiest Fleet Street yellow sheet. Never a French paper, always English. He's either an Anglophile or an Anglophobe, hard to tell which."

I could tell she had practiced that one, and I found myself giving a proper audience smile. I didn't like her, yet she did have something.

"I don't want to go to Spain," I told her, giving the paper back.

She shrugged, going to the mirror and taking a tube of lipstick from her bag. "Gotta meet a guy. Big Hungarian. Wears a cloak. Very smashing." The lipstick gave her face the only color it had. It was a small heart-shaped face with regular features. The skin under the eyes was gray, as though she had stayed up every night since puberty. The eyes were gray, too, with long lashes. She was pretty, but she didn't strike you as pretty.

"I don't remember your name," she said, blotting her lips with the back of her hand.

"Judith. How did you find me?"

"Saw you come out of this hole once. So I asked downstairs for the American girl with the big nose. No problem."

I touched my nose. "You're really a charmer."

"Whenever I see a picture of Madrid, I can't help thinking of Spain," she said with a smile, going out the door. She came back a minute later. "You don't like me, do you?"

"Does anybody?"

"Oh, you'd be surprised," she laughed, and shut the door.

A few days later I received a note from her.

"Dear Judith," she wrote, "I've contracted an amusing chest cold and can't go out. Have you changed your mind about Spain? I was in San Sebastián once with this guy, Terrance. It was winter, lots of fog. We went up this big hill on the outskirts. There's a posh white restaurant at the top, and a crazy amusement place called the Grand Labyrinth. We almost died in the Labyrinth, it was so terrific. But I want to go farther south now. Reconsider. Mayo."

I bought some fruit and went to her address, finding a surprisingly high-class pension. Her room was large, messy—books, clothes, and pomegranate cores strewn everywhere—and filled with a dozen American students. I had interrupted a girl who was reading aloud from a small English-French phrase book, seated on the edge of the unmade bed, her clear pink face shining like a nun's. I took her for the type whose washcloth would have a neatly printed little name tag sewn in the corner.

"These are useful phrases for the visitor to France," she explained
to me, and read on in a warm, tremulous voice. " 'This is not what
I asked for. It is too hot. Too cold. Help! Fire! Thief! Who are you?
I shall call a policeman. I am hungry; tired; ill . . .' "

Ignoring the laughter, Mayo was walking around the room looking
for something. "Move over," she ordered the girl on the bed, and
she found what she was looking for, a bottle of cough medicine.
"Seat must be as numb as your head," she muttered. The girl gave
her a charming smile. I suppose what was beginning to fascinate
me was the predictability of Mayo's obnoxiousness. I wondered
when, if ever, she would slip up.

When the group left she slammed the door after them. "Met
that ass in a bookstore once and can't shake her," she said. "Today
she brings up a bunch of rubbernecks I don't even know. Know
her type. Crooked seams offend her. But not on me. Vulgar language
offends her. But not from me. Thinks she's a goddamn angel of
mercy."

"Here, I brought you some fruit," I said, and she took the bag
and flung it down on the table.

"What'd you come to Europe for anyway?" she asked.

"I don't know. I wanted to see Paris."

She shook her head angrily. "I don't know what the hell I'm
doing here."

"You must have been here before. You mentioned San Sebastián."

"Hell, I've been in Europe a year. Lived in London first. All the
time I was there I had this fantastic desire to be in Dublin. So I
went. Had a ball. Met this guy Terrance. He had blond hair, a
brown mustache, and a red beard. Colorful guy. And he had this
thing for San Sebastián. So we went. We had this fantastic time.
Greatest time of my life. He was a very smashing guy. At first.
But he got to be a bore. Too possessive. So I ditched him. I had
this fantastic desire to be in Paris. And my family said I was frittering
my time away and withdrew my allowance. So I had to go back.
You've got parents?"

"Sure, of course I've got parents."

"You oughta have mine. My mother's always cutting off my allowance so I have to come home. Then she hangs on me and tells me how she worries about me. I bet. She wishes I'd been totaled, like the car, instead of leaving an arm in it. Anyway, I persuaded them I'd get into the Sorbonne. I've got this fantastic IQ. But Paris is dead in the summer. I want to go to Spain."

"I want to stay here."

"What for?"

"I told you, I like Paris. Besides, I've made friends here."

"So have I. God, have I got friends."

"Frankly, I'm surprised."

"*I'm* not." And she said cheerfully, "But you—you really don't like me, do you?"

I reflected. "I don't know, in a way I guess I wouldn't be here if I didn't."

She shot me a furious and disappointed look. "I thought you were different. Angel of mercy! Try to be honest for once in your Christian middle-class life. Don't put me on. Don't tell me you like me."

"Don't worry," I told her, "I *do* think you're obnoxious. I'm only here because I find you interesting. I mean your approach to life. As a person I dislike you. That's the truth."

"That's better," she said. "Anyway, you're in the same boat. That's one ugly nose."

"I'm taking my fruit back. Your parents are loaded, buy your own." And I took the fruit and left.

I came across her occasionally after that in cafés. She was usually with a group of friends. She now wore an artificial hand made of plastic. It was yellowed and dead-looking. When people were introduced to her she always shook hands with that hand, and watched their faces as their fingers came in contact with the cold plastic. Her friends always laughed, and this relieved the stranger, who would laugh, too. Then she stopped wearing it; I guess the novelty wore off.

One evening a few weeks after I had taken my fruit back she appeared at my room. It was very cold and damp.

"Come to Spain," she said. "None of this crappy cold weather."

"I don't want to go to Spain. Leave me alone."

"Well, I'm going," she said.

"Good for you."

"I'm going down to that movie they're shooting. I want some excitement."

"What do you want more excitement for? You always seem to have a lot of people around you."

"On *their* terms, baby, *their* terms." She was silent for a moment. "I'm leaving tomorrow. I want to leave this with you, this I cherish." She pulled a slip of green paper from her pocket and handed it to me. I looked at it.

WILL YoU HAVE SoME FUN?
If so, Ladies a nd Gentlemen,
Come In a nd See The
    GRAND LABYRINTH
A Voyage to Italy a nd Egypt
The Sun Bath
The Invisible Man
oRPHEE IN HELL
A LoVE AFFLICTIoN
A Midsummer Night's Dream
THE FAMoUS ToBoGGAN oF LAUGHTER
A nd other merry entertainments that
    everybody
Should not fail to visit the
    GRAND LABYRINTH
everything in it is amusement, joy a nd
    gaiety.

"That's the place you mentioned in your letter," I said. "In San Sebastián."

"That's right."

"What do you want me to have it for?"

"I don't know. I might get killed in Spain or something."

"Why should you get killed?"

"How do I know? Christ, don't you know anything about accidents? Nobody expects an accident."

161

As she went to the door she paused. "Everybody thinks I've had lovers for years. But I'll tell you something—I only had a lover once, last winter, in San Sebastián."

"That multicolored Irishman?"

"Yeah, Terrance. He was smashing."

"I thought you said—"

"I know, I know, I wound up hating him. He suffocated me with his ardor."

"Oh."

The door closed.

After she had gone I realized she had finally broken her predictability and forgotten to be obnoxious.

She was back in nine days. She was sunburned and she looked good, and she was not obnoxious.

"How was Spain?" I asked.

"A gas. Only the picture was canceled."

"You didn't get killed, anyway."

"Naw, I didn't get killed."

She paced up and down my room.

"Every time I see a picture of the Colosseum," she said, "I'm always reminded of Rome."

"You're going to Italy."

She stopped her pacing. "Everybody in this world is a Miss Shatswell."

"Who's that?" I had forgotten.

"I don't care if they're French, Spanish, American, or what, they're all Miss Shatswells. Now I'm gonna go meet the Italian Miss Shatswells. What the hell." She turned to me. "Well, I've got to zoom, got to meet a guy, a big sculptor . . ."

"Very smashing?"

"You've still got the Grand Labyrinth, I hope?"

I found it for her. "It must mean a lot to you," I said, "that little piece of paper. Don't you want me to keep it for you till you get back from Italy?"

"You might be gone by then." She gave it a long look. "I'll tell you something, that's where I had my affair. With Terrance. Right there in the Grand Labyrinth, right under the Famous Toboggan of Laughter."

"You did it in a crowd?"

"Naw, of course not. It was winter, the place was deserted. Just this old caretaker puttering around. He opened the place up for us, and we had it all to ourselves. There was this fantastic foggy, silvery light coming through all these little windows, I can never forget that light. And I was standing there, looking at the Famous Toboggan of Laughter, and it was all lit up by that light. It was the most beautiful thing I ever saw. All in a second we got down under it, under the table." She stuffed the slip of paper into her bag, gave a quick wave, and went out the door.

I spent the last two weeks with friends at a youth hostel on the Bay of Biscay, near Bayonne. The day before I left Paris I received a postcard of the Colosseum from Mayo. On the back she had scrawled: "Whenever I see a picture of the Vienna Opera House I can't help thinking of Vienna."

I decided that if I got the chance I would make a pilgrimage across the border to the Grand Labyrinth for Mayo.

It turned out that we went into San Sebastián several times—it was only a few miles from Bayonne. The weather was so hot that it was only our last time there that I got up the energy to detach myself from my friends and take the bus to the outskirts, to Mount Igueldo, where the Grand Labyrinth was located. There were few people aboard the funicular that ran to the top.

I walked over to the small building and found "Grand Labyrinth" painted over the door in blue letters. Sitting by the door, an old man in a black uniform with gold braid was dozing. I asked for a ticket, and he woke with a start. He took my money and gave me a ticket and, with a deep, courteous nod, watched me as I went in.

The room was as uninteresting as a dentist's waiting room. In it were a half dozen neatly spaced tables, each with a cardboard box on it. A series of small windows ran along the walls and the sun poured through them.

The old man had come inside and was leaning against the wall.

"Enjoy yourself, señorita," he said. "Take your time and see everything."

I walked over to the first box. One side was removed, to simulate a theater stage. The old man announced loudly, "The Sunbather."

Under a painted yellow sun, lying on her stomach, was a nude lady shaped like a tube of toothpaste. A fly sat reflectively on one buttock.

"Look at the next one," the old man said. There was a huge joke in his voice, and I looked with interest at the next box, entitled "The Invisible Man." The floor of the box was painted green, the sides blue. There was nothing in it.

The old man chuckled and moved from his station against the wall. He followed a few paces behind me as I went on, reading each caption aloud and waiting for my response.

" 'A Love Affliction,' " he announced.

I looked at the small figure of a lady whose paper hair had turned green with time. She held a bent cardboard knife to her bosom.

"Look at her face," he urged.

Her mouth was drawn down to her chin, her eyebrows were fiercely knotted, and a chain of faded blue tears decorated both cheeks.

"She looks very unhappy," I said.

"And so she should. She is suffering from a love affliction."

The next box was "The Famous Toboggan of Laughter." Several tiny, well-bundled figures sat on a small blue toboggan made of cardboard. The little faces were all but consumed by enormous smiles expressing the very ultimate in excitement and delight, and the tails of their caps all stood straight out to indicate that they were going at a great clip.

"You like this one?" the old man asked when I had looked at it for several minutes.

"Yes. It's very happy."

"I think it's probably my best."

"Did you make these scenes?"

"Every one."

"That's quite an accomplishment."

"Go on, señorita, look at the rest." And as we walked along he said, "Nowadays it's all cinema and television. Who cares for the Grand Labyrinth? You're the first person to buy a ticket in three days."

"Still," I said, "your fame has spread. I heard about the Grand Labyrinth in Paris."

"Did you?" he asked, his eyebrows going up. "Did you really?"

"Yes, the person who told me was very enthusiastic."

"Who was the person? Not a Frenchman. The French are the worst—jaded."

"No, an American."

"Ah, an American. Like yourself, señorita, if I may presume. Much is said against your countrymen, but I have always found them to be soulful. What did this one tell you, precisely?"

"She was very enthusiastic about the Toboggan of Laughter."

"A woman of taste. Was she a woman of taste?"

"Well, she's well read, intelligent."

"Tell me, was the memory fresh, or had it lingered for several seasons?"

"I think she'd been here about eight months before, in the winter."

"In the winter? But the Labyrinth is closed in the winter."

I had completed my tour, and somehow I was anxious to leave before he recalled Mayo. "Thank you very much," I said. "Your Labyrinth has lived up to all my expectations."

"In the winter it is closed," he repeated, and paused for a moment. "But wait—wait. Your friend, does she—forgive me for mentioning it—does she have only one arm?"

I nodded.

"I remember her very well. Indeed, it was in the winter . . . in January, during the fog . . ."

"She mentioned that," I said, approaching the door.

"I was outside . . . I came around the building from the garden, not able to see a foot ahead of me for the fog, and all at once I ran right into them . . ."

"Them?" I said, stopping. Then perhaps Terrance wasn't a fantasy. I realized that was what I had really thought.

"She had her sweetheart with her," he said.

"Did he have a red beard?" I asked.

"A red beard. Imagine crashing into them unexpectedly, a man with a big red beard and a girl—forgive me again—with only one arm. It gave a jolt."

"And he—he wasn't a nothing sort of fellow, was he? He was big and good-looking?"

"Oh, he was a good-looking boy, very tall, with fine eyes."

I looked back at the Toboggan, at the floor beneath it. "And he liked her? He seemed to like her?"

"He couldn't take his eyes off her."

For a moment I could see the fogged, silver light coming through the windows, and felt the winter stillness.

"And they spent a long time in here?" I asked.

"Over an hour. They were so interested they wanted to stay on, so I went back to the garden. When they gave back the key I saw that they had been very impressed."

"They were, they were." I smiled.

"They cheered up my whole winter," he said, following me outside. "You tell her that if you see her again."

He seated himself before the door again. I waved good-bye, and he waved back, ending the gesture with a little salute. I went back to the funicular, feeling suddenly, unaccountably sad.

The funicular clanged to a stop at the bottom of the hill, and the few tourists got out and stood on the corner to wait for the bus. I could picture Mayo and Terrance standing on this very corner waiting for the same bus.

After twenty minutes the bus finally drew up, the same one I had come out in—ancient, rattling, packed to capacity as all Spanish buses—and we jammed our way aboard. I struggled toward a strap and stood hanging onto it, and all I could see was Mayo pushing through the crowd with her stump, forcing a gap between her and Terrance. I saw her fixing her narrowed eyes on his fervent ones, and seeing in them the fire of pity she saw everywhere in this world of Miss Shatswells—only stronger, hotter, more unforgivable than any before.

Water Music

Captain Toshiro Kasahara was fifty-eight, the age at which all Japanese merchant seamen must retire. When he stepped off the ship in Yokohama this time it would be for good. The last voyage was the usual: Yokohama, Hong Kong, Singapore, Genoa, Rotterdam, Hamburg, Liverpool, Los Angeles, San Francisco, and Yokohama. The freighter had carried no passengers the first part of the trip, and it had suited the captain, who was a solitary man. But in Liverpool they had taken on two American passengers, a woman of sixty-five and a youth of nineteen, traveling separately. The third day out the captain put aside his pleasant anticipation of a solitary Japanese dinner, and met his obligation.

The two passengers looked up from the table when he entered. He was tall for a Japanese, heavily built, with shoulders so developed that they seemed to have consumed his neck. The back of his head was flat as a board, and innumerable small white scars showed through the black hair, giving the effect of a moth-eaten bear rug. The skin of his face was covered with pockmarks.

He sat down and introduced himself, saying a few words of welcome. He spoke a correct but halting English, pausing for long moments to compose the sentences in his mind. When the woman passenger spoke, her words were so rapid that he could not distinguish one from another. She herself seemed not to listen to what she said. As he ate he nodded now and then, which was what he did when a conversation was of no interest. The woman, Mrs. Graham, a widow, was youthfully dressed and coiffed; she wore an off-the-shoulder evening dress and her short bluish hair was arranged in soft waves around her face. Her white, well-manicured hands were still lovely, and she left them unadorned, to speak for themselves. She herself spoke incessantly, her eyes moving around the captain's face as though it were a portrait in a public gallery. She thought him remarkably ugly, but what was more remarkable was his lack of charm. He had neither the smiling graciousness expected of his race nor the talent of appearing interested, which the unattractive so often cultivate.

She was disappointed, not only with the captain, but with her fellow passenger, who had now rudely interrupted her to ask the captain if he wrote *haiku*. Though Mrs. Graham did not know what *haiku* was, she was gratified to hear the captain answer briefly in the negative and ask the steward, in the same breath, for more water. The young man, Howard, turned back to the voracious disposal of his food. Mrs. Graham recovered the floor and continued her description of the food she had eaten in Paris, the trains she had used in England, the leather goods she had purchased in Florence, the services she had received at Cook's. Howard marvelled at the lips that seemed to operate without her notice, like tapping fingers.

It had been a disappointment to find that she was the only other passenger aboard. He had gone to England after half a year's study of French in Paris, and had intended to take a passenger ship to New York, where he would fly home to Los Angeles. But then he had decided it would be more interesting to go by freighter through the Panama Canal. He had pictured a group of unusual fellow passengers—people of individual, perhaps eccentric temperament; world-wise, ocean-loving travelers with tales from Alexandria, Rangoon, and Vladivostok, one of whom would perhaps be a young woman both mysterious and unattached. He had not considered that the time of year, January, was unlikely to result in a full passenger list.

Mrs. Graham had also looked forward to a dozen companions, preferably her own age. She did very nicely in her own age-group, where she was often thought to be fifteen years younger than she was. It made her act like a young girl who walks with careless grace before her elders, looking for admiration from the corner of her eye—an affectation Mrs. Graham detested in the young.

Howard had no affectations, she realized, but he was objectionable enough without them—bumptious, intense, wrapped up in himself. He treated her with an offhand courtesy that made her feel dead and shoveled under already. And she couldn't stand his music. He sat for hours on end in the smoking room hammering on the piano. He seemed to be working on some original composition, but it wasn't very good.

"Have you heard our little composer?" she asked the captain, forming her words with exaggerated clarity, for she wanted an answer.

"I have heard the piano for two days," he replied.

"God," said Howard, "I hope it doesn't travel all the way up to the bridge."

"My cabin is on the deck above," said the captain, nodding at the ceiling. "Over the smoking room."

"I'm sorry. I hope it doesn't disturb you."

"It does not disturb me."

"It doesn't *disturb* you?" said Mrs. Graham. "You're being polite, Captain."

"It does not disturb me," the captain said, and having finished his dessert, he rose from the table and said good night.

"Well, it disturbs *me*," she said when he was gone.

"How? You can't even hear it. Your cabin's way down the end of the passageway."

It was true that in her cabin the music was barely audible, but it was not really the sound of the music she objected to as much as the thought of the boy sitting there pouring his feelings into the keys as though his life depended on it. He was ridiculous. But instead of being amused, she found herself perturbed. She put it down to the strangeness of the sea.

"It wasn't as though you were a pianist," she said, flicking her lighter under a cigarette as Howard leaned across the table with a match.

"I think the steward wants to clear up," he said, blowing out the match.

They arose and went into the adjoining smoking room. Mrs. Graham opened the glass case in which the ship's library was kept. Spreading her feet apart for balance, she looked with dashed hopes at the titles.

"Most of it's Japanese."

"It's a Japanese ship."

She withdrew three old *Saturday Evening Posts* and turned around carefully. The chairs slid back and forth, straining at the chains with which they were attached to the floor. The room seemed cold and disheartening. "I'm going to bed," she said.

In her cabin she changed into her nightclothes and climbed into the bunk with the magazines. After a while she stopped reading and looked at her watch. It was only eight-thirty. She could have wept with boredom, and the thought of four weeks of the ship and the sea filled her with dread.

From the darkness of the rocking stern came a deep muted sound like the groan of a dying beast. The dim mast light swayed from side to side. Howard already knew the ship well. He liked to walk around at night in the dark sound of the waves crashing. The thought of the freighter alone on the watery vastness, cleaving through mountainous swells, filled him with a powerful joy. He climbed now up to the bridge, exulting in the sway, which increased with each ascendant deck, and hung over the rail with the wind ripping at his clothes. After a while he turned and looked at the pilot house, where a faint green light shone through one of the portholes. He made his way over and looked in. The room was black except for the radar set, which gave off the green light. The captain stood looking down at the radar, his face dimly defined by the light; it looked like the pitted limestone head of an old Buddha. He gazed unblinkingly at the radar set, absorbing the ship's roll so expertly that he seemed one with the vessel. Then he moved away, and the first mate emerged from the dark periphery and took over.

Howard went back to his cabin, took a hot shower, and sat down at the table in his bathrobe. Opening a notebook, he dug his pen into the paper and scrawled "Impressions of the Sea," and began making copious notes.

On the fourth day out the weather grew calm. By the seventh

day it was hot. The officers and stewards changed into their white summer uniforms; the fans were turned on, the crew began chipping rust from the stern and prow, and painting the booms. The air was filled with the sun's flashing—from the shiny white accoutrements of the ship, the curved bodies of the leaping dolphins, and the sea itself, which glittered like chipped glass. Mrs. Graham and Howard spent most of their time in the passengers' area of the boat deck. Mrs. Graham had dragged a deck chair to a shady corner, where she sat in a sun dress, her hair caught in a net, her face carelessly made up, reading magazines or writing letters. There was nothing to write about after she had described the food (Western and excellent), the effectiveness of her seasick pills, the discomfort of the rough seas, and the sameness of the calm. She put her pen down and looked out. The dolphins held her attention for a while. So did the flying fish, skimming the water like small worried birds. When their novelty wore off, she watched the sailors with their hoelike implements, scraping the rust from the gray surface, and painting over the raw patches with red lead. After that, another coat of gray would be applied, and then the salt spray would begin its corrosion again. It seemed to Mrs. Graham a futile job. She looked out at the flat sea again. No other ship broke the line of the horizon. Here, at its heart, the sea told of nothing but empty time. Each small wave, rising with blue insolence and catching the sun for a second, was lost the next, as totally as if it had never existed. In every direction, as far as the eye could see, these small risings and fallings repeated themselves, yet the sea went nowhere; it stood still, like a rippling flag pegged to the ground.

She closed her eyes for a moment; then with concentration she returned to her letters and magazines.

Every day Howard sat astride the rail in a pair of red swimming trunks, holding a rope attached to a canvas container which was used to bring up seawater to be tested for its temperature. It hopped along the surface like a rabbit until it got a gulp of water and sank into the greenness, down where the freighter churned up foam that billowed like white thunderheads just below the surface. Howard would draw the container up, swinging it in diminishing arcs, and tip it over his head. The water ran icily down his hot back and chest, making him feel hard, invulnerable as a ship.

"Sometimes you don't act like a young man almost out of his teens," Mrs. Graham commented as she watched him pour water over his head for the third time one morning.

"Really?" he asked, not caring, and leaped off the rail to the deck. Throwing himself down, he opened his notebook and began writing as if possessed by demons.

Now he would be lost in his writing, and Mrs. Graham would forget about him again; then suddenly he would leap to his feet and stride back to the rail, squinting and craning his neck. He was an alarming person to have around, beginning and ending each activity as if to the accompaniment of trumpets. He must believe himself to be the exact center of the universe; it was as if not one wave rose, one dolphin leaped, or one sailor coughed but that it deserved some reaction from himself. It was the eternal busybodiness of youth, and it filled her with impatience. Again she would turn away, and he would dissolve from her mind, only to startle her afresh with a cry directed at the flying fish. If at last he departed it meant only that he had gone down to the smoking room and that there would now be music.

It poured through the open doors and portholes like heavy smoke, groping and urgent, full of inexpertise and crashing chords. She had once watched him through the door. There he sat in his red trunks, his hands crashing down on the keys, his head flying back when a chord was particularly expressive. He looked so silly and somehow pathetic that a rueful smile had formed on her lips. These sounds he made with such intensity reverberated through the room, but they faded on the waves, and the ocean rose and fell with its enduring indifference. She turned away suddenly. Later, in her cabin, she took a cool shower, the steady drumming of which soothed her.

The journey seemed long to Mrs. Graham, who sat with half-shut eyes in her deck chair, and for Howard, who clattered fascinated through the hot blue days, but it was going quickly for the captain.

172

He spent more time than usual on the bridge, where he watched the water stretching as endlessly as the sky. He had never spoken much, he spoke less now.

At dinner he noticed that Mrs. Graham no longer gave vent to long, uninteresting descriptions of her trip. She picked at her food. The boy ate with enormous appetite, delivering himself of great enthusiasms about the sea. Mrs. Graham had once cut him off with her own impression: "It's very big, and very pointless." The remark had struck the captain as clever, and he had laughed aloud for the first time. Mrs. Graham had been pleased, but Howard looked at him with disappointment.

Day after day the piano music rolled through the stifling air. Only when they reached the Panama Canal did it cease. Howard was occupied with searching the brown waters for alligators, straining his eyes at the small tropical islands dripping with moisture, and waving at the crews of passing ships. When he took his eyes from the Canal it was to scribble in his notebook, or to sit halfway down the stairs to the shelter deck, where the Canal crew—exotic blacks in orange trousers held up by frayed rope—had slung hammocks for the afternoon siesta.

Mrs. Graham, too, had grown excited as the tide slackened, the shores closed in, and the locks drew into view. Each time the smooth water obediently rose or fell, and the great locks opened, strong and quiet, she had felt more heartened.

She had smiled at the captain on the bridge, and he had lifted his hand in reply. Sometimes his silence, his opaqueness, had seemed to conspire with the endless sea, the long hours, the inflated boy, to make the trip intolerable for her. Now her resentment toward the captain faded; he was only a cog in the efficient machinery of the Canal.

That night she and Howard stood on the deck, watching the last lights of the locks grow distant. Earlier the Canal crew had disembarked, climbing down a rope ladder to a small launch. It had sputtered away in the choppy water, and the ship had moved on. Now as she and Howard stood at the rail the lights slowly faded from sight and were gone. She kept the picture of the Canal in her mind as the ship headed back into the dark sea. She thought of the green shores whose dense growth was efficiently cut back by machetes all year around, and of the great locks that opened and closed in response to a human hand in a tower nearby, and of the vessel pulled along by cables to the pleasant accompaniment of busy shouts. All her excitement had died away now, but she felt, for the first time aboard, a strong, smooth optimism of the sort she ordinarily possessed. It seemed to her that she might enjoy the remainder of the trip.

"Will you do me a favor, Howard?" she asked, turning to him in the dark. "Will you stop playing the piano?"

"What for?"

"Because it disturbs me," she said as kindly as she could. "I mean, you can play the piano anytime—"

"I won't feel like this again," he said, looking out across the water.

"—whereas, I'd like to enjoy the trip, too. I wouldn't even mind, if only you wouldn't play so hard."

"I can only play hard."

"Nonsense. Why is everything you do so terribly, terribly important that it can't bear the slightest change?"

He did not reply, but said good night and left her.

He was the same as ever the next day, sitting on the rail, splashing himself with water and yelling down to the flying fish. Watching him, Mrs. Graham felt powerless and tired, and she steeled herself for the inevitable. But in the afternoon, when he usually played the piano, she saw him wander down the stern, instead, and lean against the rail. She sat back with relief, and looked at the dun-colored coast of Costa Rica. Small coastal ships now rode the water, and gulls swooped overhead.

The days unrolled clear, musicless, a little cooler. They passed Nicaragua, El Salvador, Guatemala, Mexico. The coast of Baja California was pearl white. She threw a sweater around her shoulders in the mornings when she went on deck, and in the afternoons did a little packing in her cabin. The evening meals were filled with her resumed chatter.

"Tomorrow, Los Angeles," she said, as they drank their after-dinner coffee. "It will be wonderful to step on dry land again. Not that it hasn't been a lovely trip"—bowing her head at the captain—"but a whole month on a ship, it gets on your nerves. Won't you be glad to have a rest when you get to Japan? You will get one, won't you?"

"I will," he replied.

"Of course, you're used to it. You must have sailed for years. Twenty, thirty years?"

"Forty-one years."

"Good Lord. Good Lord, so long to be on the sea."

"You no longer play the piano," the captain said to the boy.

Howard shrugged.

"I asked him to stop," Mrs. Graham explained. "I'm afraid I'm not as polite as you are, Captain. Or maybe I'm just more sensitive to noise—"

Howard sat forward. "Noise? That was *music*—" But now, suddenly, he felt embarrassed, remembering how hard the sea had hit him. He must have played like someone demented, out there, in the middle of the ocean, but it had seemed beautiful, more beautiful than anything he had ever heard. He rose and roughly shoved his napkin into its ring, not lifting his eyes to his table companions'.

"Well, if it was music," said Mrs. Graham when he was gone, "he wasn't much of a musician."

"No," the captain agreed, and she looked at him with gratitude, almost with friendship, and her words flowed faster. When he had finished his coffee he excused himself, but she detained him with some questions about disembarking. Then she could keep him no longer. She picked an orange off the table to take to her cabin.

The captain spent most of the night on the portside of the bridge, where he stood at the rail in the wind, looking out at the water. Around midnight he saw the boy come out on the boat deck and stand, as he, at the rail. A moment later the boy had gone, leaving behind a memory of the urgent, groping music that had daily touched the captain with something as great and deep as the sea itself.

Inside

The pond was deep green, almost black, so solid and still that if you imagined a rusty can or a handful of change at its bottom you could not see them as gently embraced by a liquid, but stuck fast in the stone gut of a boulder, just as the bodies in Pompeii had crouched till decomposition, their very pores one with the frozen lava. She dipped the toe of her shoe into the water, lightness shattering the illusion of solidity, and as the toe withdrew, dripping, her vision followed, floating up to rest among the water lilies which lay scattered across the pond, pale as the skin of the dead. As though, she thought now, a miniature Armada had sunk, and all the bodies risen to the surface.

"The Armada," she said, and started along the path to the museum. The park stood lifeless in the afternoon fog, the misted trees looking at nothing, the benches empty, wet, and waiting, like riderless horses with their heads down. But here, in the bend of the path, a newspaper had been spread on the beaded green boards, and a couple sat bright as neon in the mist, a blue windbreaker on the man, a fuchsia coat on the woman, the gaudy fuchsia that some sallow, dull-witted women wore, believing that the threads of the fabric crept in under the neck to the pallid cheeks, where they stopped, massed, and became a blush.

"Are you staring at me?" she whispered, walking by them; and stopping, she repeated the question more loudly. "I'm curious to know," she added, trying to strike the right note of friendliness, sincerity, and respect, since they were old enough to be her parents.

"If you were staring, you must have a reason."

"I beg your pardon," the woman said with dignity.

It never did to put them in categories. Gaudy clothes always led you to expect a rude, direct answer or a bald scowl of irritation. You were prepared for either, but this glacial poise was as jolting as the reaction of the frail old lady she had once found staring at her as she waited on the corner for the light to change. Confronted with the charge, the old lady had said: "Who the bloody hell are you talking to?" But you could not give up when so much depended on it. Her lips trembling in a smile meant to be disarming, she had told the retreating old ear, "I don't mean to be offensive, but I do wish you would explain your reason." The woman had walked off rapidly, as though she had been touched by a leper.

So she had hung back, burning with shame.

She felt the shame again, standing on the wet path before this couple who looked at her with such disdain. No, the coolness was not out of place after all, she thought through her shame; it was the impregnable self-absorption of the cow or the camel. Cows, ferrets, apes, or bugs, that's what they always came down to. Knowing this, why did you feel such shame before them?

"Do I look peculiar?" she forced herself to ask, nervously smoothing her hair. Twisting around with sudden hope, she looked to see if she had inadvertently sat on a candy wrapper in the bus. She had once seen a man walking down the street with a Hershey bar wrapper stuck to the seat of his trousers. Then someone had pointed it out to him and he had removed it. A simple procedure. If someone would just tell her in a few words why they stared at her she could do something about it. But the couple was leaving the bench, casting her a united look of dislike.

"Cows!" she shouted after them. "Camels!"

The fog was thickening. Weekday fog was usually thicker in the park than weekend fog, since there were fewer people around to dissolve it with warm breath. If she breathed lightly the fog might harden into ice and form an igloo around her, a compact one with just enough room inside for a polar-bear rug and herself. But a distant pinprick of sun broke through the vision, allowing a long, thin ray like a golden needle to enter her eye. The sky was an even gray, but the sun, full and southern, would be in the museum.

"It isn't as though I were unintelligent," she told herself, feeling better, and continuing along the path, "as though I wandered aimlessly around parks. I have a destination." Again she felt the back of her skirt, but she had definitely not sat on a candy wrapper. She touched her hair suddenly, for she had often seen girls walking along filled with self-satisfaction, even arrogance, ignorant of the fact that their hairdos had been torn by the wind into the most laughable messes, with all the lacquered ends sticking straight up like dead twigs. But her hair, glossy and coiled, did not have a strand out of place. In any case, it was not her appearance they stared at, much as she would have liked it to be, since an appearance can easily be altered. "Not that I'd *want* to alter my appearance," she thought. Her suit was smart, of heavy wool, moss green, the same color as the lawns as they crept under the low, sweeping protection of the dark firs. She wore a single strand of pearls. Alligator shoes and bag. A well-balanced, quiet ensemble very much like her features, which were symmetrical, pleasing, and even at the worst of times perfectly composed. The whiteness of the pearls was repeated in her small teeth, the green of her suit in her eyes, although her eyes were lighter, like leaves on a windowsill with the sun shining through them. It seemed to her when she saw those eyes in the mirror that her skull should be flooded with light. "Like a Mediterranean grape arbor," she thought, approaching the museum. It was true that Father had always called her the Andalusian Beauty, but there was a mocking tone to the remark, reminiscent of his compliments to stupid Martha, the cook. No, she was not all that dusky, or all that beautiful; she was somewhat dingy and ovine, a sheep tethered in the smog. Still, she was better-looking than most girls. She had only to look around her to see that. It was a fact that when you walked down the street or rode on the bus you were mortified as a member of the human race to see so many ugly men, women, and children. They came in all sizes and shapes and hues, like so many discards; this one had horrifying legs like a stork, so stiltlike that the next one could have run between them wearing a top hat, so small was he, like a cruelly inbred lapdog. Each one by his close proximity cast his neighbor into glaring subhuman relief, making shams of the wristwatches and earrings, the spectacles and folded newspapers. Thankfully she seldom went out.

The area where the museum stood was just as deserted as the wilder parts of the park. The last of a group of shivering tourists was climbing into a sightseeing bus, and now with a low groan the bus moved slowly down the road and out of sight. Only she and the statuary remained: two wildcats at the entrance, farther off a sphinx, a monk carrying a cross, and Goethe and Schiller with their arms around each other's shoulders. Late at night the two deceased men climbed down under cover of the fog, and with their stone feet ringing against the macadam like the Anvil Chorus, they walked along deep in discussion, joined, one by one, by the sphinx, the monk, and the wildcats. Goethe would force the wildcats to heel, and press the sphinx for its innermost thoughts, while Schiller offered to help the monk carry his cross. If you rode inside one— Goethe it would be, for despite his opinion of himself as an Olympian divinity while carrying on like any ordinary skirt chaser, in contrast with Schiller's kinder, more normal character, you would choose the greater writer—it would be like riding inside a suit of armor, with your point of vision startlingly high, for the statues were very big; and the heeling wildcats would strike their stone tails against the legs, making sparks fly into the night.

She walked before the double statue and lit a cigarette, gazing obliquely through the smoke at the figures' feet. It was such a beautifully realistic piece of work that it might have been cast from a mold of the two writers while they stood in some Weimar studio breathing through a straw. Wonderfully lifelike. She looked at Goethe's face, which looked back at her with its hard, stone eyes.

Abruptly she stamped out her cigarette and walked away. After all, she did not need them, with all their *Sturm und Drang,* and their Gothic cathedrals and low-lying gray northern fog. She had visited Germany as a child with Father and old Aunt Charlotte, who, poor soul, with a face like an unborn calf's, always had a splitting headache because foreign languages upset her. "They put up a wall by speaking these foreign languages," she complained, fanning herself wildly in the Latin countries, and half strangling herself with her muffler in the North, and Father refused to translate anything for her, but just grew more disgusted the more confused and complaining she became. She was none too bright, but she had the money. Germany had been gray and bronchial; Aunt Charlotte had hacked away, pressing her white hankie to her mouth and rolling her eyes pitifully over its edge. Spain had been lovely. They had left Aunt Charlotte at the hotel in Madrid, suffering from dysentery, and had first gone to Seville and Granada and then up the Costa Brava. She remembered the towers and the sound of bells, gardens of flowers and a sweetness in the air, and above all the sun scattering every shadow with its great rush of light. It might have gone on forever except that Aunt Charlotte recovered and met them in Barcelona, where she made a thin little scene about the nursemaid Father had hired in Seville.

The museum, though not crowded, was more alive than she had expected. A whole flock of schoolchildren was being led down the main hall, their shrill voices resounding against the walls. She stiffened, knowing from experience that children were the worst; they were bold beyond belief, deprecative to their marrow, and maddeningly protected by the license of innocence, so that even when your temper got the best of you, you had to smile and pretend you thought they were sweet.

"Look at *her*," one cried now. They looked. She narrowed her eyes and began to smooth her skirt. The teacher, a young man in a rumpled suit, was looking too, smiling, tactfully pointing to a picture behind her.

"It's one of Picasso's ladies with two noses," he said. They tramped by, each one staring in her direction, and under their massed glance she felt her eyes falter; she pretended to look for something in her bag. The hall quieted as they went around the corner, thankfully at the opposite end of the visiting collection from Spain, and she expelled a shaky breath, concentrating on the treat ahead of her. The paintings. The only painting she remembered from Spain was Velázquez's "Las Meninas" at the Prado in a room by itself. The colors were soft, airy, and an old priest had sat on a bench, nodding, his face bathed in the mellow sunlight. She had crawled up beside him and fallen asleep while Father stood before the painting with a notebook.

Immediately she bought her ticket and stepped into the room she was startled. The pictures were all dark, like so many bruises along the walls, and the faces, the centers of the bruises, were sickly, pale. "But why should I be surprised?" she asked herself. "I'm well acquainted with Spanish art." She had forgotten that. "I forget from one minute to the next," she accused herself, and focused her mind on the rich mosaic of her education: the battles of Salamis and Tanagra, the Han Dynasty, the Florentines, the Bloomsbury Group, the Vorticists, hundreds more stretching into the horizon, all laid there piece by piece by Father, who had tutored her so patiently. At will she could perceive whatever facts she wanted, yes, it was true, and doing so, she silently recited the succession of the Roman Popes, breaking off with Martin V, for what was the point? Better to concern herself with the Spanish decline, since it was hanging so palpably from the walls before her.

It was a poor selection. There were few Velázquezes, and those were all of Philip IV. She walked beside the somber, phlegmatic Habsburg faces with their prognathous jaws settled on immense collars yellowed with age. Why did you come to an exhibit like this when the Spanish Habsburgs had always disgusted you with their sorry court of fools and freaks, their stupid egoism? Postpone a dentist's appointment, ignore the beginnings of a cold, and take a bus all the way out here in the fog where you happily clink down fifty cents, just to stand before these proud, lackluster eyes that made you want to weep?

Anxiously she considered her face, but it wore a properly absorbed gallery expression. She glanced covertly at the other visitors, an elderly couple harshly conversing in what sounded like Dutch, a dirty-looking boy with a big beard, a girl about her own age, but desiccated and tweedy, and a man in a black overcoat. All were facing away from her but the boy. He stood near her, fingering his beard.

"Are you looking at me?" she whispered.

"What?" he said loudly.

"Sh, don't be offended. Just tell me what you're staring at."

He regarded her with intelligent eyes and leaned toward her ear with a smile. Nervously she inclined her head to his beard.

"I'm sorry, but I wasn't staring at you," he said.

"Don't tell me *that*," she whispered back bitterly. "Just tell me the truth. *You* have nothing to lose . . ."

"Why should I stare at you?" He shrugged, and moved off.

"Sheepdog . . ." she hissed after him, and he turned and smiled a casual, benign grin at her as though she were an idiot. A fire of shame rose in her but went out at the sight of a small picture in the corner. She walked over to it. It was only by one of Pacheco's lesser students, and it was somewhat flatly rendered, but the colors were gay, the whole thing was drenched in a sun of dripping butter.

"Tchk, tchk," she clucked softly, her nose almost touching the canvas. She could see the spidery cracks in the varnish, spreading across the small dancing figures dressed in rose and sapphire and lemon. "Tchk." She was trying to crawl through one of the cracks. Make ready, prepare the music, she was bringing the castanets.

"That's a stupid thing to try to do," she admonished herself, stepping back from the picture. "It's not my métier, I've never danced."

She felt exhausted. There was a bench in the middle of the room, and she sat down on it and put her hands in her lap. The Dutch couple was departing, still talking loudly; the beard was gone. The tweedy girl and black-coated man, at opposite ends of the room, weren't looking in her direction, but all Philip IV's dull, hooded eyes were trained on her. She gazed back uncomfortably, then lowered her eyes and looked up quickly to see if he was still staring.

She got up and stood before his portrait nearest her, looking deeply into the dark pigment of the eyes, the color of wet coffee grounds hardened to granite. Withering under the gaze, she thought in a tapering hope, you could bore into them and lie there just under the surface, unmoving, unseen . . .

She went back to the bench and sat down again, facing the other wall. Immediately her palms began to prickle, and the hairs rose along her neck. Though she was looking straight ahead, she was aware of a pair of eyes boring two holes through the side of her head, an outright murder compared to the usual laceration. She swung her eyes around and met those of the man in the black coat, who had seated himself next to her. He was staring in an almost theatrical way, one eyebrow raised, as though he were waiting for her to react.

"You're staring at me," she said, fighting down a feeling of hysteria. If he denied this most open, calculated stare she would go mad.

"I always stare at attractive girls," he replied.

Usually the men who indulged in that particular evasion were bent, bewhiskered derelicts who leaned against the walls of bars, looking, looking; they never said "attractive girl," they said "dame" or "broad" or something worse, with a blurred, insulting edge to their voices. There were exceptions, of course; sometimes a clean-cut, vapid young man with hair like an army brush would say it, using a pleasant, vapid term, looking hopeful and unsure, so unsure, in fact, that she would rush right in, feeling extremely confident, and say, "No, don't worry about all that, go right ahead, tell me what you're *really* looking at," at which he would grow confused and retreat. But this man was neither young, like the vapid ones, nor scruffy, like the others. He was middle-aged, well dressed, with scholarly horn-rimmed glasses, and his voice was relaxed and unequivocal. She sat very still, trying to decide which would be her best approach, for she must be careful and not scare him away. You could never tell what would put them off, even when they met you halfway, like this one.

She had once met an elderly Englishwoman in the park who had admitted to staring, explaining that it was because she was reminded of her daughter, who looked and walked just the same way. The woman had been quite friendly and had gone on to say that her daughter had been a brilliant but rather lonely girl, and she had worried about her a great deal, and then the girl had up and married a thrice-divorced journalist with one arm . . . she had been unhappy and had left him . . . she had gone to France . . . had taken up painting . . . then she had undergone a serious heart operation from which she had not yet recovered . . .

She had listened intently, realizing that the daughter was a front for a subtle and elaborate code explaining herself. One arm . . . France . . . heart operation . . . she had been so excited and so surprised (for she had never expected to be told in the form of a code) that she had swept caution aside and demanded the answer outright. "What's the key to the code?" she asked once, twice, and the third time the woman had hurried away.

She had decided later that it had not been a code, that the woman had been testing her. If she had not butted in and irritated her, the woman might have got down to brass tacks and told her the truth. They were all very touchy. But this man looked more amiable than anyone who had heretofore held out a promise. She decided to take her cue from his attitude, and she leaned back, smiling sleepily. "You think I'm attractive, then," she said.

"Mm." His eyes were narrowed, yet he looked humorous and casual. "You look like Beatrice d'Este."

"You think so?" she replied, trying to look as humorous as he. "But I've never cared for her profile."

"What should I say? Hedy Lamarr? Elizabeth Taylor?"

She shrugged gracefully. They were movie actresses, beneath contempt. "Father called me the Andalusian Beauty."

"Oh, then, by all means, the Andalusian Beauty. You come around here often?"

"When there's an exhibit of special interest." She wondered when he would finish with the nonessentials. It was a strain to be so smiling, so relaxed. Yet it seemed to be working; he was still there.

"My name's Maurie House," he informed her.

"Maurie House." She giggled. "What a name." But laughter might irk him. "It's a nice name," she amended. And so it was. She saw him laid out in rooms inside, anterooms filled with books and paintings, glass sun porches with potted flowers and literary magazines, and one great room in the center with his heart throbbing on an Aubusson rug. But it never did to put them in categories; it was true that at first glance he looked bookish, but there was something that was incongruous with his appearance. He was too forward, that was it . . . most unbecoming for a man his age, he must be fifty. Was he "on the make," as old Martha used to grunt about Father? Martha was ancient, stupid, and horribly snobbish, the way some servants become, surpassing their masters. She was very thick with the doorman, who told her that the taxi drivers did a "regular trade" with Father; it was not just gossip, all you had to do was look at his laundry, the shirts smeared with lipstick and splashed with liquor. Only Martha was blatant enough to mention it. She believed in the divine right of kings, but only if it was put to use well within the boundaries of propriety. Father would bristle at her grunted criticism and snap in his imperial voice, "Get back to the kitchen, Martha," and she would go, somehow mollified . . .

"I asked what your name was."

"Charlotte Beasley," she replied quickly. "Inez," she added. "It's my middle name, I prefer it."

"Charlotte is nicer."

"Charlotte reminds me of my aunt. I was named after her. You wouldn't have liked her, she was an old bat. A dim little chip of a woman, hypochondriacal, subservient, and totally superfluous."

But he was not very interested.

Of course, he knew all this already; he knew everything about her, even her name; it was part of their maddening protocol to ask what they already knew. But if he wasn't even going to pretend an interest what sort of conversation should she try?

"How would you like a drink, Charlotte?" he asked abruptly.

"No, thank you," she replied automatically. His eyes were narrow and moist and humorous, not even disappointed. Underneath her purse her hands fled together in alarm. Now he would leave.

Remember the Englishwoman in the park who had gone on for fifteen minutes about her daughter; it had seemed a ridiculous preamble when she thought it over, but apparently it was necessary; they had to play with you first, as a cat plays with a mouse, and you had to go along with them. She had failed with the English-woman.

"I have changed my mind," she told him candidly.

He looked her boldly up and down and got to his feet. "Right," he said.

They walked toward the door, passing the tweedy girl who stood lost in thought before a hideous Bosch, her stomach and beak nose thrust out, like a severe hen. Father always said it was a rare woman who could combine intellect and charm. At the door she gave Philip IV a backward glance of triumph and spite, and followed Mr. House to the entrance.

"Father always said it was a rare woman who could combine intellect with charm," she told him as they walked down the steps. "He said I had neither of them to combine."

"He was wrong," Mr. House said shortly.

"You remind me a good deal of my father."

His face fell a little, and he shrugged. Perhaps it was the wrong thing to say? Most men would be happy to resemble Father, or at least Father intimated as much, and it was very likely true; he was without peer intellectually, he was handsome, or if not handsome at least large, imposing, regal . . . although this man was not regal. But he appeared to be growing more regal now; his look was no longer humorous, but serious, contemplative . . .

"How old are you, Charlotte?"

"Twenty-two," she replied as he opened the door of his car.

"You look younger, you know . . . I'm thinking maybe they won't serve you at a bar. What about—"

"Oh, we needn't go to a bar." Why waste time driving to a bar? And it would be too noisy to talk in anyway. "Right here in the car is all right."

But he looked quite startled by this. It was a mistake to hurry them, even if you were going mad with impatience. "Whatever you think best, Mr. House," she added with forced sweetness.

"What about my apartment?" he asked, giving her a quizzical look as he started the motor.

"Whatever you think best, Mr. House."

They drove out of the park into the traffic. Now and then he glanced at her. It took all her energy to conceal her nervousness, but she was doing an excellent job, lying back against the seat with a lazy smile.

"Tell me about yourself, Charlotte," he said.

"Oh, you know all about me," she replied, and again she knew she was going too fast. They wanted to take their own sweet time, to tell you on their own terms . . . that's how it was, there was nothing to do but wait.

"Do you live with your family?" he asked.

"No. Aunt Charlotte died years ago, and Father died last year, and Martha went to stay with her sister. Martha disliked me."

"Do you go out very much?"

"No."

"Don't have a steady?"

"No."

After the preamble came the questioning, apparently. She answered with great alertness, knowing that he would compare the answers with the truth.

"You do this sort of thing often?" he asked.

"Yes," she confessed, "I try to."

Again he looked over at her. "You make it sound like a duty."

"I suppose it is, a duty toward myself."

He returned to his driving with a shake of the head. She stared straight ahead, waiting intently.

"What do you do for a living?" he asked.

"Nothing," she replied with dismal patience, "I have an ample annuity."

"You're really something, in this day and age."

"I sincerely hope so."

"You know," he said, turning to her, "you sound as if you'd been put in cold storage at the turn of the century."

Now he was insulting her; she didn't even need to listen to the words, it was there in the tone. All she could think of saying was, again: "I sincerely hope so." He knew very well that she had been brought up differently from most people, better than most people.

"You know very well that Father tutored me, I didn't see other people."

"Of *course*," he said, snapping his fingers, "I forgot."

He should not forget such things; everything should be at his fingertips, ready to be used in explaining the truth to her. But she dared not bring this to his attention, or he might stop the car and ask her to get out.

"What did 'Father' do?"

"He was a man of leisure. A gentleman and a scholar."

"Christ," he murmured. "Look, do you really want that drink, or what do you say we just forget it?"

"No . . . please," she said earnestly. He was putting her to a terrible test, and she was failing with every word she said. "Please bear with me, I'll do the very best I can."

"No, thanks a lot, Charlotte, you're a good kid, but it's too weird for me, you make it sound like an examination."

"*You* make it sound like an examination," she flared. "I'm only taking your cue."

"Sorry, in that case. Where can I drop you?"

"Drop me?"

"Set you off. Where do you live?"

She gave him her address, trying vainly to appear composed. Never before in all her searching had she come so very close, and now he was backing out. "You owe it to me," she pleaded, "I've waited so long, and you just as good as promised. You want to torment me."

"I don't know what the hell you're talking about."

"That's right, pretend. You're just like all the rest of them, only worse." She watched him with quiet fury. He was driving faster than he had been, and he looked nervous.

"Let's just be calm and civilized," he said. "I'll have you home in five minutes."

She whipped out a cigarette, lit it, and blew the smoke from her nostrils like a dragon. "Do you know what you are? You're a sadist. And you're a hypocrite, too, wearing those horn-rim glasses when you're not even an educated man."

"I'm not, it's true. How do you know?"

"It's in your speech, in your manners. But I should tell *you*, when you won't tell me anything."

"What do you want to know?"

"Oh, please don't play with me any longer. Why did you stare at me? Why am I stared at?"

He had drawn up in front of her apartment building, and now he leaned across her and pushed her door open. "Sorry I've got to rush you—"

She slammed the door shut and faced him. "No, I've been very patient, but now I'm tired of being put off."

"Do you mind getting out of my car?"

"You tell me and I'll get out."

"Look, if people stare at you I don't know the reason. I stared at you because I wanted to pick you up. It's the last time I ever try it in a museum."

"I *am* attractive then? Father always said I looked like a dingy sheep tethered in the smog."

"I can't help what your . . ."

"Did I look intelligent?"

"Yes, yes, you looked very intelligent."

"He tutored me all those years, and all he was priming me for, really, was for me to look after him like Aunt Charlotte. He tutored me just to show himself off, he really did, he liked to show me up, he called me mentally sterile, an intellectual mule."

"I'm sure you're not an intellectual mule. Now look, it's getting late and I . . ."

"Tell me, and I'll go."

"Look, I don't know what's with you, and I don't really care. I've got an appointment, and I've got to get going." He peered out the window. "Besides, if you make a scene, your doorman will stare. You don't want your doorman to stare, do you?"

"Why not? He always stares. Everybody does."

He began to open his own door.

"I'll scream."

He closed the door quietly and looked at her.

"You know what you are?" she asked bitterly. "You're just nothing. How dare you even speak to me?" She pulled out the ashtray and violently stubbed out her cigarette. "You could never understand anything great—and I know things that are great, things that are passionate and magnificent—oh, I used to go all to pieces when I was near him, I'd think up excuses to touch him, like picking a piece of lint off his jacket, or taking his hand to look at his watch, and it was like an electric shock. I'd sit at his feet and read the love poems of Heine and Bécquer, and I'd find myself crying . . . you know what unrequited love is like. Or probably you don't. It's terrible, but at the same time you're so happy in spite of everything. I sang in those days. I sang to him. He'd say, 'Stop it!' just when my heart was fullest. Even when I read him the poems he'd get up and move away, saying, 'You annoy me.' And yet, when I sulked and withdrew from him he'd come over and stroke my hair and say, 'What's happened to my passionate little beauty?' And then, when I responded, he'd push me away. It was like living in hell, but I'd rather have been there than anywhere else. Three times I went to his room at night. The first time I just stood there and looked at him. The second time I pulled the covers back. He almost broke my wrist in two, pushing me away, and I ran out. The third time I didn't wear anything. It was a warm summer night; I'd sat in the bathtub for an hour, I'd poured a whole bottle of bath oil into it. Then I made up my eyes like Cleopatra, very black! And I went in there to his room. He was reading in bed, and the book dropped from his hand. His face was purple. He scrambled out of bed and threw me against the wall, and he called me an animal, worse than the scum of the streets. 'Worse than those girls you won't talk about?' I asked him, and then I kissed him—the only time!—hard on the mouth, and he slapped me, and some old woman ran in. It was very quiet then, and I felt ashamed, standing there with no clothes on. I felt so ashamed. And yet there was nothing wrong with what I'd done. After all, I loved him." She was silent for a moment. "It was all so long ago, I don't even remember his name."

"It wasn't . . ." the man asked softly, "your father?"

"You're disgusting!"

"Well," he said after a pause, still softly, "I'm sorry, Charlotte, but I really have to go now." Gingerly he opened his door and came around to her side and helped her out.

"It's you I'm sorry for," she said with hushed dignity. "Someday you'll be punished for leading me on and then pushing me away."

"Good night," he said.

She watched him speed off, then walked tiredly toward the entrance of her apartment building. It was easier to get inside a real building than a painting or a statue or a man—not that Mr. House was worth getting into; some Aubusson rug, it was probably imitation Persian, cheap, curled at the edges; and the heart that rested on it was stunted and black. She looked at the building with relief. In lieu of something better, her apartment would do, with its thick walls and rugs muffling the sound of traffic and the drapes drawn against the lights from the street.

"Good evening, Henry."

"Good evening, Miss Beasley," the old doorman replied, doffing his cap. "I was staring because you looked so nice."

The Queen of the Ivsira

In the drizzling evening light, off the coast of northern California, the messgirl came out on deck and leaned against the rail, her forearms projecting over the water. It was an old ship, the *Ivsira*, rust streaked and seedy, its rails roughened with gull droppings; a Norwegian tramp registered under the Liberian flag, it worked the coastal waters from Alaska to South America, carrying anything from copra to lumber. On this run its overload of lumber was stacked high on the bow and halfway up the decks, giving off a raw, wet smell of sawdust.

With an impassive groan, like that of a dog, the messgirl stretched. She wore a white nylon dress, a white apron, and a black sweater thrown over her shoulders, which were square and hard. Her hair was gray, worn in a thin braid twisted around on top. Her eyes, gray too, set in flat cheekbones, rode the dark swells with a stolid smoothness. After a while she heard someone call her, and she went back into the pantry.

The captain stood there. He was stout, pink, flaxen-haired, the only man aboard who wore a uniform, black and shiny, with frayed cuffs and dirty braid.

"You've come down in the world, Ingeborg," he said in Norwegian.

She gave a rough nod, and pressed by him to the sink.

"The leopard will miss you."

When, until today, she had been officers' stewardess, she always swept the leopard-skin rug in the saloon and polished its eyes. "What leopard," she said. She spoke without inflection, in the flat monotone of someone unused to conversation.

"You were conscientious, Ingeborg."

"I did my work."

"But it's harder down here, less pay—what d'you want to be down with the crew for? Karen's happy enough to trade places, but I want to know your reason. I want to be fair."

Ingeborg turned around from the sink, her eyes hard. "Last night. Her eating up there."

"Ah," sighed the captain. "That's what I thought."

"In the saloon. At your table." Her eyes grew harder. "I should serve her. I'd rather be down here in this kind of dirt."

The captain nodded. "Well, it's always the same. It's what we get, having women aboard. Jealousy. Bad feelings." Then he smiled. "Shame on you, Ingeborg, at your age."

"A Gestapo mattress."

He squinted, and was silent for a moment. "You confuse her with someone else."

"We lived on the same street."

"You imagine it."

"You know what the ocean's like. Don't be so stupid."

"You forget yourself—"

"It's filthy with them. Mattresses. Collaborators. Scum." She turned back to the sink and began scraping off a plate. She heard him walking to the door.

"The war's been over eleven years, Ingeborg."

"So."

"It's time we let go of it."

"Why."

"What are they supposed to do? They have to be somewhere."

"You don't have to eat with them. Pour their wine. Light their cigarettes."

He did not answer. She heard him go out.

For the next hour she scraped, washed, and dried dishes. The pantry was the size of a closet, its walls spattered with hardened flecks of food. It smelled like a dead fish, but she had already grown used to it. When she was done she set out mugs for the night crew and, drawing an after-dinner cigar from her apron pocket, went into the crew's messroom and sat down.

The tables were covered with oilcloth, split and frayed along the edges. Blackened tin ashtrays, smoking like tar pots, were nailed through the oilcloth into the wood. Standing among them were beer bottles and glasses. Some of the crew were playing cards; others sat looking on. A little wizened Anglo-Indian half-breed turned to Ingeborg.

"Seen you talking with the old man, ma'am. Is he sending the other one back down?"

"I don't know," she said in heavily accented English.

"I hope so. She was a looker, what, Donkeyman?" He tapped the hand of the donkeyman, a giant Slav with ragged hair sticking out from under a striped cap, the seams of his face filled with grease. He was carving a piece of soap. He pulled his hand away.

"A looker, by God," said the half-breed. "No offense to you, ma'am."

Ingeborg lit her cigar.

"The old man's taken her under his wing," said a young Dutchman, studying his cards. "Pretty soon you'll hear the accordion."

"What accordion?" said Ingeborg.

"I've been on other runs with her. She's got an accordion. She plays good."

"I never seen no accordion on her," said the half-breed.

"She don't play below, she likes it above. If luck's with her she gets settled in above, then she plays loud and sweet. You'll hear."

"Maybe," said Ingeborg. "Maybe not."

The room swayed peacefully, while through the floor came the low, steady throb of the engines. The half-breed sat drumming his fingers on the oilcloth. They were thin and grimed, gleaming with heavy rings. "I say, Donkeyman, ever been to the Palladium in L.A.? Two orchestras in one room. I took a girl there once, eighteen years old, figure like a movie star. She shook like a leaf, she was so thrilled."

The donkeyman kept carving. Finished works lay at his side, small stumps that didn't look like anything as far as Ingeborg could see. But you had to give him credit for the shavings, the way each

195

one curled from under the knife like a long, unbroken apple peel.

The half-breed was looking at her. "That's a queer custom, women smoking cigars. I seen 'em do it in the cold countries, but I don't like it. It looks bad."

"Don't look."

He laughed, exposing dark teeth. "What d'you think of the mess-work down here? Pretty hard?"

She shrugged. "Work's work. Afterwards, I got my cabin."

"Hard. Needs a young person."

"The work don't bother me, mister."

"Gandhi's the name. They call me Gandhi. Small but effective."

She looked past him to the portholes. It was black outside, the winter days were short. She would go up to her cabin soon, and stretch out and be comfortable.

"Pity we're not putting into Frisco," Gandhi remarked. "Jesus, what a town. Know what happened to me there once?" he asked Ingeborg, sending up a groan from the cardplayers. "I'm going down to the hiring office when I see the most gorgeous female I ever laid eyes on, and I mean a terrific gorgeous beauty, ma'am. I ask her if she knows where I can buy me a cool glass of beer. No, she says, but I can give you one at my house. So I go home with her and we have a cool glass of beer. And you know what she does then? She locks me up in the bedroom with her. Ma'am, she didn't let me out of there for two days."

Ingeborg's eyes rested on the scrawny face. "What for."

"Use your imagination," he cackled, slapping his knee. "Use the old thinker."

"Now he'll tell you how he got knifed in Rio," one of the cardplayers said to her.

"Ever had a cold knife stuck between your ribs, ma'am? I'm at this dance hall—"

"Oh, Christ, shut up," somebody told him.

Ingeborg sat watching the donkeyman, who had reached over to a bottle of beer and was busy wrenching off the cap with his great fingers. Throwing his head back, he splashed a stream into his mouth, afterward wiping his lips with the back of his hand.

"Primitive chap," Gandhi confided to her, pouring himself a glass.

"Tell me, ma'am, signed on for long? Or maybe you're leaving us at Pedro?"

"No, Mr. Gandhi. I'm sorry." Stubbing out her cigar she got up and, with a good night to the others, left the table.

"What's a woman want with the sea anyhow?" Gandhi asked his companions, taking a swallow. "I know what a woman wants, if I don't know anything else. Damn," he sighed as the door closed, "I hope they send the other one back."

Like most freighters, the *Ivsira* could accommodate a dozen passengers, but it carried none, and Ingeborg had gotten permission to move into one of the cabins. She had never before had one like it, big, high up on the promenade deck, a corner cabin with four portholes. In Vancouver she'd gone out and bought a blue spread for the bunk, expensive, too, and she wasn't usually one to shoot her money. On one wall hung her old framed picture of King Haakon. Below it stood a sofa chair and ottoman the steward had let her take from the saloon. Here she sat every night with her legs up, turning the pages of old magazines from the ship's library, or resting with her eyes closed.

On land it was easy to tell changes in people. When she visited her brothers every few years she saw them having families, being promoted at work, moving to bigger houses, retiring with a gold watch, and now standing small and wrinkled next to their married children. On the sea it was different. Long ago you graduated from messgirl to stewardess and that was all. Nothing changed over the years—the sweeping and serving, the white uniform, the dark, cramped cabins you lived in. You went to bed at nine and got up at four thirty. Sunday was like Monday. If you wanted to live on the sea, that was how you lived, and it was a good life. But nothing changed, and you didn't know how many years had passed until it came to you that you were tired at the end of the day, and that was the only way you knew you were old.

By five the next morning she was washed and dressed and down in the galley. It was a steaming orange and silver room, with one enormous grimy porthole sealed against the spray, and a steel floor littered with pieces of lettuce and potato. The cook was slopping porridge into tureens. "Feed the bastards!" he yelled over the din. "Keep the bloody wheels turning!"

Down here the throb of the pumps was deafening. When she was a green messgirl she used to put her hands over her ears. In rough seas she had slid and dropped things, and the ship's creakings made her think it was going to break, and at night she couldn't sleep for fear it would sink. After a year she was strange anywhere else. On land everything seemed under a glass dome.

Taking the tray, she balanced it overhead on the flat of her hand and made her way up the ladders. It was five trips before everything was up, including the officers' tray, which she set in the pantry for the mattress. She could hear the mattress slapping down the passageway in her huaraches, and now she came slapping through the door, wearing her black gabardine slacks and her pink sweater with its gold thread and chipped sequins. The mattress showed nothing on her face as she squeezed by. The day she came aboard her face had gone wooden at the sight of Ingeborg; then she had smoothed her hair nervously and smiled. Ingeborg had looked straight through her, like air, then in silence turned her back on her. She said nothing now. She watched the mattress pick up the tray, and twitched her nostrils against the sweet reek of hair spray. The hair was elaborate and tinted red, the eyebrows drawn on with shiny dark brown pencil. Otherwise she was not much changed.

It was still dark outside when Ingeborg sat down to eat breakfast with the men. The lines in their faces were emphasized by the harsh electric light. The room was cold, with a cold smell of engine grease and stale smoke.

"Look how she cut the bread," she heard one of the men say through the murmur of languages. Slowly, threateningly, she lowered her coffee cup.

"You got a complaint?"

"You joking, ma'am? The other one she cut it like bricks."

"What d'you care?" asked Gandhi. "Who eats this slop anyway?"

"You better," said Ingeborg. "You need it." His hair lay in one thin strand across his skull. His flimsy wrists were hairless. It looked

like nothing grew on him. She liked to see a strong eater. The donkeyman slapped pork fat on his bread and devoured the whole
slice whole. She liked how he said nothing. Conversation was a
waste of time. You already knew whatever you knew.

After breakfast, when she had finished with the dishes, she took
the garbage bucket out to the aft deck. A mountain of bruised,
burnished clouds hung over the ship, shooting long columns of light
into the water. With a deft movement she swept the bucket up
and out. The garbage hung lit and bright in the air, like jewelry,
then fell. With a great flapping and screaming the gulls rose from
the rails and dove, skidding onto the waves feet first, wings high
and outspread. She stood for a while, watching, letting the spray
catch her face, then started back to the pantry.

There was the mattress above, shaking out a little dust rag. Having
an easy time up there where she liked it. Let her make the most
of it, she'd be back down pretty soon with her accordion and curls.
A looker? A boneless face. A peeled egg. Queer, what a man could
bring himself to call a looker. But probably it wasn't the face—
half lost anyway under all those twists and fringes—but more the
pink sweater stretched like thinnest skin around the big pointed
breasts, and the big round rear end swinging. The look of a whore,
though there was nothing wrong with whores, the ones who were
what they were. When they did wrong they paid, the way anybody
else would—like during the Occupation when some got roughed
up in alleyways for rolling with the Wehrmacht. A split lip, that
was enough. A broken neck would have been too much. Gestapo
mattresses were something else.

Back in the pantry she filled the bucket with soapy water and,
picking up the mop, went out into the passageway. What it was
like the other night, seeing her come into the saloon, slapping across
the leopard in her huaraches. And one of the officers rising to seat
her, and the captain, all pink and merry, shaking out his napkin.
There she sat, chatting and laughing and sipping her sherry, and
you were supposed to serve her. When she laughed it was a yellow
flash—the teeth hadn't done too well—but she laughed a lot, sipping
away, and then the captain, with his plump cheeks rosy, leaned

across the table to refill her glass. The other officers were in brown rolled-up shirt sleeves, but a captain dresses because he stands for his ship and his country, and his sleeve with its gold bands was the last thing you saw, even before the glass was tipped. The door slammed behind you. Let him figure it out.

Throwing the suds down the passageway, she spread her feet and began mopping. In Norway during the war she had mopped for a living, or waited on tables, trained for nothing else and land-locked for five years. The Germans were all over. They breathed your air. They flew their flag. They hammered up notices. They sat in cafés and picked their teeth with your toothpicks. You could do nothing except with your eyes, and at first your look hurt your face with its intensity, but after a while you took to looking through them as if they were air. You saw a lot of things, and there were things you didn't see but heard about. There were night visits you heard about, and that was what you thought of when you thought of the Gestapo. A night visit was fast and quiet. A door was rapped on, someone was pulled out, driven off with in a car, and never seen again. It was a simple thing. Once in a while they came in broad daylight, too, in reprisal for some underground action. She had seen that once, on her own street. They went along, and at every other house they knocked and ordered out whatever man happened to be home—father, grandfather, son—and put him in a truck. When they had a dozen they drove into the country, lined them up, and shot them. That was simple, too.

Down in the galley the cook's face was a tomato in the heat. A blackened cigarette burned close to his lips. He thrust two new-baked loaves at her for the coffee break. "Keep the goddamn mouths full! Keep the bloody wheels turning!" He would say it every time, she could bet on it—it was his relief, like the pile of butts he stood on. His mate sang loudly, drowned out by the pumps.

In the messroom Gandhi stopped by her side. "How's it going, ma'am? Not too hard on the old bones?"

"I'm not a flea. Like some people."

He only laughed and went off to wedge himself in by the donkeyman, who knocked him back reaching for the pork fat. She liked a man who did two sensible things at once. It was all right down here, even if the work was hard. She had her cabin afterward, her sofa chair and her four portholes, and that was enough for anybody at the end of the day. She stretched and poured herself another cup of coffee. Let the mattress stay above for all she, Ingeborg, cared, as long as she wasn't wined and dined at the captain's table like a guest of honor. Let the scum be kept at a distance, and her accordion be kept mute in its case, that's all she asked.

Outside the portholes a fine drizzle was sifting. Pedro tomorrow, then they would work down Mexico, Central America, South America. It would be summer there. She liked heat. She liked sitting on a blistered deck after dark, with the dark heat in the air, and the sound of the parting waves swift and soft. She didn't mind the cold, either, with the sea and sky hard as silver, and then when you plunged, day and night and everything around you slid and crashed. Sometimes she would go out and hang onto the rail as the ship rose straight into the air and came down with a cannon boom, with the water rushing white over the prow and the wind tearing your hands. Ports were all right, too, the pastry in Bremerhaven, the cable cars in Frisco, the odd native places where they howled and beat their fists on empty oil drums. But out on the sea was better.

In the pantry afterward she filled the sink with steaming water, ignoring the deep boiling bite as her hands went in. The mattress had used rubber gloves, and the plates showed it. How could you scrape a piece of hardened food with your thumbnail, or tell if the water was keeping hot? Methodically, her hands gripped and scrubbed. They were big coarse hands like a man's. Even when she was a young girl they had been big and coarse. That's how they had always been and how they were meant to be. She dried them off when she was finished, and started mopping the messroom.

There was a soreness in her back as she worked, but she tried to ignore it—funny weather, drizzly, but the sun was still around, now and then flashing a watery light into the room. At lunchtime, carrying up the trays, she was annoyed with her back, and as she ate she felt impatient with small stupid things, pushing Gandhi's bending head aside with her arm. But gradually the buzz of foreign languages soothed her, and, chewing, she rested her eyes on the donkeyman, huge and silent, mopping up his plate with a hunk of bread. The room with its clinking forks and buzz of voices slowly rose and fell, creaking. She sat back, full, and stretched. She had nothing to complain about—a sore back was nothing. And she had her cabin afterward, her blue spread and her sofa chair, and her four portholes around her.

Cleaning the crew's quarters later, she felt a small stolid triumph as the soreness faded. Or if it had faded, or if she had just gotten used to it, so that she couldn't tell it apart from what she was doing, she didn't know, nor did she care. It was late afternoon when she was finished, and she went out on deck before serving dinner, and leaned against the rail. A light rain was falling, but in the distance a stripe of crimson lay across the water like a sword slash.

Down in the galley the bits of food lay smeary on the steel floor, as if on a hot griddle. The porthole was white with steam. The cook's mate had his arm plunged to its hairy pit in a vat of chocolate pudding, agitating lumps, while the cook with his tomato face stood splashing soup into tureens. "Keep the goddamn mouths full! Keep the bloody wheels turning!" He ought to try for something different, but he liked the sound of this, it did something for him. Lifting the tray of soup tureens, she balanced it overhead and made her way smoothly up the ladder.

With everything on the tables, she smoothed her apron and sat down with the men. Gandhi grinned and called to her, waving his fork. You pushed his face and he didn't notice. She gave him a nod anyway, poor clod, and turned to her food. It always tasted good to her, she couldn't understand the little idiot picking at it. She had a second helping, and when that was done she rested her head in her hand and looked over at the donkeyman, who was gripping a soupbone in both hands and gnawing off the meat. "I say, Donkeyman," yelled Gandhi, "ever been to the Savoy Bar and Grill in London?" The donkeyman kept gnawing. Then he splintered the bone with his great teeth and sucked out the marrow. He set the bone down with a thud. Evening lay dark and round in the portholes.

Washing up the dishes in the pantry, Ingeborg hummed loudly offkey, her face damp and flushed in the steam. Then, having set out the mugs for the night crew, she took her after-dinner cigar from her pocket and went back into the messroom. Gandhi was fiddling with the radio in the corner, snapping his fingers, his hips swinging, but only static filled the room. He switched it off and hopped over to her.

"Well, how goes it, ma'am?"

She blew smoke breezily past his face, watching the donkeyman carve.

"You know what he's carving? Ask him, ma'am. He don't know either. He don't even know how to talk. Bloody imbecile never opens his mouth."

"Good. You should do the same."

"I hate to see a man waste his time. He don't have it in him, he don't have the talent. It's sad."

She watched a long, perfect peeling curl away, and smiled.

Gandhi clapped her shoulder. "You ought to smile more, ma'am."

Brushing her shoulder off, she settled herself in a different direction at the table, watching the cardplayers. The table rocked slowly, the men slapping cards down, picking others up, murmuring, complaining, breaking into laughter. She had never learned how to play cards, could never figure them out, but she didn't mind sitting here watching. One of the men offered her a beer, and she took it, drinking and smoking her cigar as she looked on.

"What did I tell you?" the Dutchman asked her, looking over his cards.

"Tell me what," she said.

"What did I tell you? Listen."

She listened. It came floating down through the noise of rain and waves, the sound of accordion music, a polka.

Getting up, cards still in hand, the Dutchman stepped out into the passageway and pushed open the door to the deck. He came back a moment later. "The old man's laughing like a hyena."

"Ah, hell," sighed Gandhi.

"What's one more or less to you?" asked the Dutchman, sitting down again and turning to Ingeborg. "You hear the wind out there, ma'am? That's the whole female population of Pedro standing on the dock panting for him."

Gandhi snorted with laughter, but Ingeborg heard only the accordion, which filled her with a fierce need to cry. She tapped her cigar stiffly over the ashtray, trying not to blink, for her eyes stung, and continued watching as the game resumed. Gandhi was quiet for once, rolling cigarettes. The music had ended, and now it began again, something sweet and slow. The big grimy clock on the wall ticked. She should go now and start packing.

But to sign off a ship because of some music—you could get used to it, you could get used to anything. Already it was becoming part of the other sounds around her, part of the wind and the creaking and the cards slapping down. And it wouldn't make any dent in the mattress if she signed off, she wouldn't even notice.

No, you couldn't just rush off a ship like that, you had to think it out, figure it through. She didn't like to figure things out, though, it didn't come easy to her. But there were times when you had to. She sat gazing down at the tabletop, at the frayed oilcloth, not seeing it, trying to start thinking. Her cigar had gone out, and rested cold between her fingers. After a while a line of concentration grew between her eyes.

What it was, if you were honest—the captain was right—it was jealousy. It was painful to admit, but here you stood ready to sign off a ship for that worthless reason. Couldn't stand the thought of their having a good time up there, going off to bed together afterward. And the music was finished now, silent, and they were going out of the saloon, and in a few minutes they would be lying naked in each other's arms. And you, you old thing, don't you miss that part of your life? If you were honest? Don't you miss it so badly it's like a pain, wanting it back? Remember how it was, lying naked, and that sudden deep feeling, like a melting, as the man's face pressed hot and like sandpaper on your neck. . . .

She could still remember a face or two, though most had faded away. Not that there had been a lot, just a handful. On board, in some bunk or other, and a couple of times in some harbor hotel room, and once on a beach in summer, and that was very nice. It was always very nice, and she had liked it very much, but those times had trailed off to a natural end, and she couldn't remember once feeling a pain of wanting them back.

She brought her hand down irritably and stubbed out her dead cigar in the ashtray. Thinking was no better than talking. You already knew whatever you knew. And what she knew was that the two of them could roll around on the saloon table for all she cared, if things weren't what they were.

The donkeyman gave a cavernous yawn as he worked, showing his great teeth. She looked over at the clock. Past nine. She ought to get started with her packing now, it was late. Still she sat, and the line of concentration returned, deepened. No, it wasn't jealousy, it was something much worse. You ought to take stock of yourself, Ingeborg, your hardness, your meanness. Look how you treated that poor idiot over there, pushing his face. Look how you shoo out the missionaries with your broom, those pale mousy pairs in their dark suits creeping aboard in every port with their little booklets. Shooing them out with your broom, no patience, no mercy. For her upstairs, black with hatred. And you'd known her when she was a young girl, think of it, Ingeborg, living down the street from you when the war began and you got landlocked, seventeen, schoolbooks and brown bangs, and she always said hello, and once in a rainstorm when your umbrella whipped inside out she grabbed it to help you and you both cried out and laughed. She had the same boneless face then, in a way pretty, or maybe just young, and if she started using too much makeup and staying out all night, so that people talked, that was her own business, that's how some girls went, but then she took up with the Gestapo. That was one of the things you didn't see but you heard about, and Ingeborg never saw her again until the liberation, and then she saw her standing inside a crowd in the town square with her hair shaved off. She was with a couple others, and people were spitting on them, in their faces, and that same day they were hounded down the main street out of town.

Wasn't it enough? And to float around ever since with her yellowing teeth and tight sweaters, humping that accordion on her back looking for a corner, looking for a pair of fat cheeks to glow, Lord to have to smile that much, laugh that much, wasn't it enough?

Still gazing down at the oilcloth, Ingeborg sat rubbing and squeezing her forehead. Then, taking her hand away, she felt a deep shame, a deep offense with herself. There was nothing about it to figure out, nothing to keep sitting here for. It was a simple thing.

Getting heavily to her feet, she gave a nod of goodnight, and went up to her cabin to pack.

Gorm

Their mother being dead and their father out drinking, Helga had to look out for her younger brother, Gorm. His was an old Viking name, a king's to boot, their father's doing—like a lot of drunkards, he had a grandiose streak. But Gorm was only a raw-nosed sniffler, even at the best of times; reedy, prone to bronchitis, and to white hysteria when his father rampaged; the boy was a seeker of dark and quiet corners. There was a certain sweetness in him, but he was too long-faced; he got on your nerves. Helga did what she could. She asked him along when she went for walks in the beech wood—she was afraid to go alone anyway; she let him touch her puzzle-piece set as soon as she outgrew it; and she cooked for him, throwing together his meal in the dark little kitchen; but then she was out the door, already a grown girl after all, and madly enamored of a young cabinetmaker down the street.

They lived in the Danish harbor town of Esbjerg, and when Gorm turned fourteen his father got him aboard a freighter as a messboy. Helga stood by the herring crates on the dock and shouted, *"Held og lykke!* Good luck!"* until her throat ached and the gangway was up. Then she turned around and strolled home. She was glad to be free, and the ship would make a man of him.

While Gorm was on this yearlong voyage their father's liver did everyone a great favor and killed him. Helga married Georg, her young cabinetmaker, and moved to the United States with him, settling in Oregon. In a way it was a pity, Helga felt, because Gorm would have no one to come home to; but she had no choice in the matter. This was in 1928.

Gorm's letters came regularly over the years, cramped, carefully written accounts of foreign places, mostly in the South Pacific. At first Helga read them dutifully, murmuring "hum" at the bottom of every page; then she fell into the habit of skipping paragraphs at a time and putting the letters away with the intention of rereading them some other time.

In 1935 she and her family—for she now had a young child—were having a hard time keeping their heads above water, but Gorm's letters had grown animated. He had settled in Manila with a job as apprentice ship's chandler and a Filipino bride. The wedding picture he sent showed him to be much the same as she remembered: thin-faced, narrow-shouldered, a little bent; but his hand rested happily in his bride's. The girl, whose name was Elena, had a flat, swarthy, but rather attractive face, notable mainly for a lot of dark lipstick.

From then on it was Elena this and Elena that in every letter. A child was born to them, whom they named Juana Helga. Helga was touched, though it had a clumsy ring. "There's no doubt she'll be a beauty when she grows up," Gorm wrote. He sent photographs. The baby was, in fact, beautiful, luckily having inherited from her father only his blue eyes.

Then for a year there was no word. The times were bad, he wrote at last from New Zealand, where they had decided to homestead. After that, trying to keep his family afloat, he corresponded only at Christmas. Eventually he gave up New Zealand, and they left for India, where he had been offered a job on a rubber plantation. Here, at last, he did very well, and in 1947 he wrote to say that he was going to show his homeland to Elena and Juana. He would travel on ahead to Copenhagen and arrange for an apartment—they would stay a year—and he would route his trip so that he could visit Helga in Oregon.

Two months later, Helga drove from her small town to the Portland train depot to meet him, feeling quite ordinary. But when she saw him she held him tightly; she found herself squeezing from his narrow, familiar shoulders all those distant afternoons in the flickering beech woods, in the little kitchen with its blue coffeepot, herself humming the latest songs and looking out the window at the sea. She could smell the salt water, and the coffee simmering on the stove. They were smells that had meant nothing to her at the time, but now they caused a deep, broken sigh to fall from her lips. Then, spent and gratified, she blew her nose.

He was crying without a sound.

"Gorm," she scolded, laughing, and lifted his chin.

He was a little old man of thirty-two. His bronzed face was cross-hatched with wrinkles, his yellow hair had thinned and faded, and his eyes had sunk into his head from squinting at the sun. But he was smartly dressed in a white linen suit with a red carnation in the lapel, and on his feet were pointed, white, perforated shoes. At last he too blew his nose, and linking her arm in his she led him to the car.

The town she lived in wasn't much, nor was the little bungalow, but Gorm walked around the small rooms admiring them. When he was introduced to Barbara, his thirteen-year-old niece, his whole face lit up and he planted a radiant kiss on her cheek. Among the gifts he had brought from India was a pair of silver toe bells, and these he gave to the child. She pulled off her shoes and socks, slipped on the rings, and sped around the room, jingling. Then she dragged him off, chattering in his ear.

Helga took great pains to make the first evening a memorable one. In Portland she had bought all the imported Danish delicacies most likely to please her brother, plus good cigars and akvavit. Now she set a fine table with her best china and silver. She was happy to see that Georg and Barbara liked Gorm, but then there had always been something approachable about him, a desire to please. It was a lovely evening, even if she had spent too much money on it.

But the next morning when she came into the kitchen to her dirty dishes, she said to herself with an accepting shrug, "We finished the food, the akvavit, and all that we had to say to each other." And it was true.

He was to stay two weeks, but already by the third day she was tired of him. In the first place, the house was too small. He offered to stay at a hotel, but Georg put his foot down, though Helga herself didn't think it such a bad idea. As the days wore on, she had whispered arguments with Georg about this, but he was adamant; she couldn't imagine why. Then she understood. He thought Gorm's suggestion was a slam at their hospitality; Gorm must feel they were too poor to put him up. Her husband had come to this country to make good, and he had not done so, and it was a sore spot with him. It was a sore spot with her, too; he had disappointed her. And here was Gorm, marked at the start as a failure, wearing white perforated shoes, and dribbling dollars like a leaky faucet, treating them to big dinners at the only restaurant in town, and buying expensive gifts for Barbara—even a coat. It was going a little far, she had to admit.

At the beginning Barbara was mad about Gorm because he was mad about her. Except that Juana was dark, and a couple of years younger, she and her cousin could have been twins, he said; and they had the same sweetness of character.

"Yes, I suppose Barbara's got her sweet side," Helga agreed with a sigh, trying to get on with her housework as Gorm hung at her side, talking, talking. By now she knew all that there was to know about his family. Juana attended a Catholic school run by the nuns, and was good at languages. Elena had taken to the Indian ways and wore a sari—much more beautiful than Western dress. He sent his two girls to the north of India during the hot season and joined them there on his holiday. They swam together in a little lake.

"And we can't even offer you a municipal pool," Helga said with a sarcastic edge. "Excuse me, Gorm, I have to sweep."

But Barbara loved his tales. He told her all that he did on the plantation and she hung on every word.

"Let her teacher try to explain a rubber plantation and she'd be bored stiff," Helga said. Barbara had her sweet side, no doubt, but she was like any other child; she had her faults, she was troublesome and forgetful. It was not wise to idolize a child; children themselves realized this; and finally she saw the girl grow tired of her uncle's attentiveness.

Or, Helga wondered for a moment, was it because he no longer bought her presents, having finally noticed Georg's coolness toward his lavishness? Was the child really as false as that? Was there something missing in her? And she thought further. Maybe there was something missing in all three of them—where was the affection that burned like a red coal in Gorm's family? Yes, but Gorm was a freak of nature, his gratitude for his family went beyond all bounds, his sentimentality was cloying, unbearable. If she had to hear once more how he missed them she would tell him to be quiet. Still, she found herself realizing that it had been many years since Georg had looked at her with tenderness. But that was how life went.

She tried to make herself scarce, rewriting old recipes and ironing in her bedroom, anything to keep Gorm at bay. But sometimes her conscience got the best of her and she sought him out. One afternoon she joined him in the backyard. She was ashamed of the yard, dinky, crisscrossed with clotheslines, kitchen chairs and a card table doing for the garden furniture she would have liked. As they sat together in the crisp winter sunlight, Gorm noticed something glinting on the ground. He picked it up and, holding it in his fingers, gave an embarrassed smile. It was one of the silver toe rings, bent and encrusted with dirt.

"She is so careless," Helga apologized. But children always broke everything you gave them; it shouldn't be taken personally.

Soon after, he made plans to leave. He should be in Copenhagen the beginning of March, as his family would be arriving in April. They had already sailed from Bombay two weeks ago.

"We couldn't all of us have gone by way of the States," he said. "It would have been too expensive."

"Well, you don't say," Helga heard her husband mutter under his breath.

Now the festivity of Gorm's arrival was repeated in the advent of his departure. She cooked his favorite dishes, he went over train routes and schedules, they stayed up late talking, and, nine days after his arrival Helga drove him back to the train depot. Standing on the platform, he broke down as he had the first time.

"Come, come, Gorm," she admonished gently.

Squeezing her hand, he turned abruptly and boarded the train. She drove home feeling relieved.

A few weeks later he wrote from Copenhagen, thanking them for their hospitality. He said he had rented a nice apartment, probably with a good view if ever it stopped snowing. It was late in the year for a heavy snowfall, he was not used to such bitter cold and suffered from it, but in a way he hoped it would last till Elena and Juana came. The white city would dazzle them. He expected them soon.

Then there was a second letter from Copenhagen, this time from Elena, written in a childish, illiterate scrawl.

"I can't even read it," Helga complained.

"She's just a Filipino, what d'you expect?" Georg said, squinting over her shoulder at the sheet of paper. Helga studied it three times before she could translate it into sense: the terrible weather, it was pneumonia, her ship docked in the morning, he died already that night, her Gorm that she loved, maybe too much, how to live on? and this big apartment with him nowhere in it, her grief half crazed her—

Helga put the letter down slowly and looked at her husband.

"Gorm is dead," she said, and went into the bedroom to be alone.

The next day she sat down and wrote Elena a letter of condolence, but she never heard from her again. In her heart she wondered if Gorm, in his last hours, had told his wife he had not felt welcome during his visit. It hardly seemed plausible. More likely, after the shock wore off and she had time to think, the woman was ashamed of her English.

By 1962 things had looked up for Georg. He had gone into the contracting business and it was flourishing. He and Helga had moved into a large split-level ranch house in the Portland suburbs; they had beds of flowers in the back, a big patio, and garden furniture of wrought iron. Barbara had surprised them by not marrying, but as a single girl she was doing well, with a high-paying advertising job in Portland. Though she lived only a few miles away from them, they never saw her, and Helga accepted it, knowing that that was what happened when children grew up.

She and Georg had a decision to make this summer. Should they buy a boat or take a trip back to Denmark? They were not quite at the point where they could do both. Denmark won. In June they flew to London, traveled up to Harwich, and from there took the boat to Esbjerg, where they stayed a week, visiting old friends and looking over the little streets where they had grown up. When they had purged themselves of a homesickness they had been largely unaware of, they continued without regret to Copenhagen, where they checked into a moderately expensive hotel. They shopped along Strøget, they went to Tivoli, they took tours on excursion boats and went to nightclubs where they even danced together. Then one day, while her husband visited an old uncle—Helga refused to go; old people always wound up making her impatient—she set off for Gorm and Elena's apartment of fifteen years ago, transferring from tram to bus with a map in her hand.

Most likely Elena and the girl had gone back to India or the Philippines, but it was possible that they had stayed on in Denmark, and if so, she would be curious to meet them. If they still lived at the apartment (of course the girl would be in her middle twenties now, married or on her own) that would be fine, she would have a visit with them. If they were not there, that would be fine too. She would not trouble further.

It was a dirty run-down place, which surprised her; of course it might have changed in fifteen years. The landlady was a Fru Snostrup, a thin-haired old woman whose pendulous lips shot Copenhagen argot left and right. She asked Helga in.

"Fru Petersen you want? Devil take me if I can keep track of all the Hansens, Jensens, and Petersens in this place . . ."

"Fru Gorm Petersen?"

"Gorm? What kind of crazy name is that? No, nobody here with a name like that."

"She came in 1947, if you could try to remember back . . ."

"Forty-seven? How the hell d'you expect me to—"

"A Latin woman with a little girl? Her first name was Elena?"

The old woman's face filled with light. "Latin? Oh, her? Right enough! We had our fill of her I can tell you. Nothing but a street-walker. She was from one of those Latin places all right, Milan, Italy; used to give my nephew the stamps from her letters—but don't let that fool you, she was rotten."

"No, no," Helga shook her head. "Do you remember a *Herr* Petersen? Gorm Petersen. He came in '47 too, just before she did. A sickly-looking young man, over from India?"

Again light filled the old woman's face. "Him? Sure, sure, I remember *him* right enough. Looked like a sausage that's lain too long. I had his number right away, don't know why I took him in except I'm such an easy mark. Sat like a lump for days on end, finally landed up in the nuthouse with three hundred kroner owing me."

"This Herr Petersen died. His wife and child were with him."

"There wasn't nobody with that man."

"Well, it was someone else."

"I'm pleased to hope so. That man wasn't good for nothing. Went out and bought himself a whole outfit all in black and just sat in his room. Think he figured on doing himself in but couldn't get up the energy. I kept going up to ask for my rent but he just looked through me, or else he was writing like a maniac. Never no attention to the money he owed me. Got to where I poked around myself, but all he had was some papers and some fancy white clothes that wouldn't have kept the weakest wind out, and crazy white shoes with little holes drilled in them like a sieve. Finally I called the police and they carted him off to the nuthouse, and three hundred kroner owing me."

Helga felt behind her for a chair.

"You getting sick?"

After sitting for a while, she said, "Where was he taken?"

"Damned if I know. The Bronsehoj, I suppose." And with that she screamed at her cat, who was sharpening its claws on her leg.

He sat in a ward with some twenty others of his kind, staring straight ahead. In order to make him notice her, Helga placed herself in the line of his vision. He stared through her.

"He doesn't see you," said the technician at her side. "You can stand there all day."

She was silent. She gazed at the immobile figure. After a while she said, "Do you know how old he is? He is only forty-seven."

The blue eyes seemed webbed over by some senile mucus. The skin, once bronzed by the Eastern sun, was dead white. The last of his hair had gone, disclosing a bony skull as fragile as an eggshell. She put her hand, trembling, on his, and felt a dryness, a coldness. She turned and left him.

"I don't understand. I don't understand," she said.

She was told to make an appointment with the doctor. She did so, and returned two days later, again alone. She had told Georg, but she did not want him with her.

The doctor was a young man—too young, she thought angrily, her hands in her lap spread out in order not to clench. She had felt very angry the last two days, almost furious, and Georg had commented, "Well, that's par for the course, whenever you get depressed it comes out in your being mad." That angered her further—that he had never mentioned this before, and they had known each other thirty-five years.

"You are his sister?" the doctor said.

She told him that she had seen her brother only once in the last thirty-five years, in 1947, and she was angered by the cool, clinical way his eyes went over the file spread out before him on the desk. "The year he came here," he said, arranging the papers. As though that aged, subhuman creature down the hall did not exist, only papers existed.

"What is the matter with my brother?" she demanded.

She was informed that he was a catatonic schizophrenic. The term meant nothing to her. She wanted to know what was wrong with him, how he got that way, what could be done.

"What is the *reason?*" she snapped, her head trembling.

The young doctor looked at her for a moment, then said, "Apparently Herr Petersen never recovered from the blow of losing his wife and child. But let's start at the beginning. If you'll tell me—"

"Lost *them?* They lost *him!*" She pressed her hand to her forehead.

"I'm sorry, I didn't mean to shout. But it's such a shock to have found him here, I'm completely confused . . . if you could be as clear as you can . . ."

"If you'll give me the opportunity," he said, courteously. "You do understand that his wife left him, taking the child? Our records show that she . . ."

"But she was with him when he died! I mean when he—I don't know—but she wrote me! From right here in Copenhagen, from his apartment! She came to join him—that's why he took the apartment!"

"No, you misunderstand. It was in 1936 that she left him. We have here . . ."

But Helga was not listening. She could not grasp what he had said. She stared at a corner of the desk, and presently a sound of wind went through her head: the Catholic school, the lake, the sari that was more beautiful than Western dress . . .

The doctor was still talking.

"No," she broke in harshly. "It is you who misunderstand! What you say is impossible!"

"If you'll allow me to continue, please. Believe me, I understand that you're upset—" He laid his finger on a worn, yellowed envelope stapled to a sheet of typewritten paper. "There was only one letter found among his effects. It was dated 1936, addressed to him in Manila, and sent from some other part of the Philippines. It was obviously from his wife—common-law, perhaps—telling him that she had taken their child and left him for another man. It was written in Spanish, and signed Elena. Was that the wife's name?"

Helga gave a slight, automatic nod.

"You see, it will be of great assistance to us if you, as his sister, can fill us in. We have almost nothing to go by—"

She took a deep, impatient breath. "This letter—"

"Well, by itself the letter wasn't particularly illuminating, but in view of what was discovered when he came here—" He picked up another typed sheet. "Incidentally, it says here, 'dressed entirely in black'—they were able to put some of the pieces together. They found in his pockets some dozen or so notes signed with his wife's name, each one saying 'Gorm has died, I grieve for him,' or some variation—" He read from the sheet: " 'I am mad with grief,' 'I long for Gorm, but he is dead.' The notes themselves are almost indecipherable." He nudged a small packet, bound with rubber bands, across the desk. "Degeneration is commonly manifested in the handwriting."

She looked at the packet. She recognized the scrawl. Her anger had left her; in its place was a sharp, rising nausea.

"Well, there it is. We know very little. There was nothing to go by in his effects except for the letter. And his passport, of course, and a pile of old clothes—that was all there was in his room, it says here." He tapped the sheet of paper. "He must have gotten rid of everything else—a man preparing for death."

"But he didn't die, he didn't kill himself."

"What would you call it?"

He began putting the papers back in the folder.

She sat forward in her chair. "There must be something else. Isn't there something else?"

"Not really. Through his passport they checked his birthplace, of course." He opened the folder and shuffled through the papers. He read: " 'Born December 20, 1914, in Aalborg, to Poul and Anna Petersen. No further information.' "

"No, we left there when he was an infant. He grew up in Esbjerg."

"Well, you see, his early years are a total blank to us. That's where you—"

"And that was as far as you looked?"

"Not at all," he said, glancing back at the sheet. "His place of residence in India was of course on his passport; they were able to get in touch with his employer there. A sketchy report, though. 'Minor plantation official . . . began employment in 1939 . . . married, family to join him . . . this status maintained . . . an indifferent worker, but not incompetent . . . kept to himself . . . took year's leave of absence January of this year . . .' Dated May of 1947. And there you are. We're really very much in the dark, still. He has never spoken a word. As I said before, it would be helpful to us if you would tell us whatever you know—his early years—his condition when he visited you—"

"There is hope then?" she asked quickly.

"One can never say for sure that there is no hope. In this case— I must be candid; fifteen years is a very long time. But we wouldn't be doing our job if we didn't make as thorough a—"

"Of course." She nodded, getting heavily to her feet. "But I'm not up to it now. I'll have to come back. A day or two."

"Of course," he said, "I understand."

Outside, she stood waiting for the bus. Then she turned and started walking. It was a long distance back to the hotel. The sky was clear and the sun shone hot on her face. She had not walked so far since she was a girl in Esbjerg, wandering through the beech woods, which frightened her if she was alone, and humming snatches of the latest songs and thinking of Georg and how she could get a dress that would dazzle his eyes, and calling over her shoulder, "Gorm, stay close. No, don't talk. Be quiet. Don't interrupt my thoughts."